KISSED AT MIDNIGHT

THE LOST ROYALS: BOOK ONE

AINSLEY WYNTER

Ainsley
Wynter
Press

DEDICATION

For my husband.

Thank you for your general awesomeness and for believing in me.

CHAPTER ONE

Tulip Ball, Chateau Peletierre
Kingdom of L'Ortagia
April 1784

*A*fter a smattering of applause, the musicians lowered their instruments. Princess Sidony's partner bowed and left her on the parquet dance floor. She plucked at her gold skirts, swaying slightly, loathe to end the evening.

Perhaps Sidony should have searched for the time-bending nocturne who'd attended last year. He could have added a few extra hours to the night.

Finding and persuading that particular nocturne to use his powers was a trifling. The real challenge would have been keeping the queen from finding out. Though Chateau Peletierre was far from the royal seat of Mondelac Castle, news would have gotten back to her mother. A nocturne's display of magic at a near-public event would have enraged the queen.

She was a nocturne too, a human born with a set of abilities most deemed magical. Her unique power wasn't helping her tonight, either. The music and dancing was already, naturally, quite lovely and wouldn't benefit from her enhancement. All she wanted was for time to hold still a little longer, for Zara to be able to choose a man to take as a husband.

Sidony dabbed a lace handkerchief to her forehead. At her sister Zara's urging, she'd thrown herself into the ball, adoring the attention. Dancing into the wee hours of the night, wearing theatrical costumes for the masquerade, and being away from the watchful eye of the queen—she'd exalted in it. It couldn't be over.

All that spinning, all those steps, wouldn't stop the inevitable. On her mother's command, her sister would wed the heir to the neighboring kingdom in two months. Zara had been quietly distraught at the news. Sidony was devastated for her. While Zara lived with her new husband in Embury for the next several years, Sidony would take on her sister's role at her mother's side.

Sidony tugged on the jewels at her throat, grateful the queen had decided to forgo the ball, despite their impending visitors. Sidony had so few nights to do as she pleased. Spying a tray of champagne near a set of open doors, she raised her chin and grabbed a glass on her way out of the ballroom.

On the terrace, she sipped her drink before pirouetting across the paved stones. She adjusted her gold lace mask, tucking it against the chain of coins woven through her coiffure.

Her step faltered. What if this was the last year she could attend the Tulip Ball? It was a tradition she loved. Zara, who had gone to bed nearly an hour ago, merely tolerated it. But they'd co-hosted the masquerade ball for the past few years. She wouldn't want to hold it without her sister.

Sidony glanced back at the manor house, the ballroom's sparkling chandeliers like beacons. Voices rose in peals of laughter. The main entertainment of the evening was nearly over. Tomorrow would bring emissaries who would finalize

Zara's betrothal. The desperation Sidony had tried to hide bubbled up inside her, mimicking the effervescence in her glass.

Eyes burning, she stumbled down the steps, seeking her favorite terrace. The private spot afforded a view of the lush gardens at the back and was partially hidden from watchful eyes in the chateau.

Sidony reached the landing overlooking a reflecting pool. Tiny lights decorated the trees along the promenade below and candles floated in the water. Her feet ached, so she leaned against a large urn. It was filled with one of the tropical trees her mother had been given. She took another sip of her champagne, grateful it was cold.

Out here, tomorrow would wait. She could escape fate and linger under the stars. She just needed to catch her breath.

One step onto the private terrace, and she saw she wasn't alone. A masked man sat on *her* bench, staring out at the water.

"Damn," she muttered. Her toes were numb, and the flight of stairs was dishearteningly long.

I won't go back yet.

Given his costume of unrelieved black, the man resembled Hades. Actually, he could be any number of shadowy characters—a highwayman, even. She hadn't seen him earlier. It would be impossible to forget such a striking figure.

The masked man lounged along the far side of the bench, a booted foot resting on his knee, his right arm along the back. His clothing had a military cut, though it lacked the ornamentation most costumes would add. No medals, lengths of braid, or bold sashes. A soldier, possibly. He wore his dark hair pulled back in a queue. A black domino mask covered his eyes. Below was a pair of pensive lips.

Pensive lips? That last glass of champagne must have hit her.

He was so still. Though she'd huffed when she'd spotted him, he hadn't turned at her approach, his gaze fixed firmly ahead. She couldn't imagine being by herself that long. Sitting out here, impervious to the world around him, he carried an air of loneliness.

Since she'd turn maudlin if she stayed in the wings any longer, she walked onto the balcony.

The sweet scent of wisteria drifted from a nearby trellis. The space was charming. She and Zara had enjoyed tea out here just this morning. She could regain her equilibrium before returning to the ballroom. Since she'd interrupted his deep contemplation, she thought it polite to start a conversation.

"Missing your Persephone?" she asked.

The man startled, blinking in confusion at her. She was several feet away, but took a cautious step back.

"No, wait." He stood, a hand rubbing at his forehead. Perhaps it was a trick of the light, but his eyes had a faraway look. If the practice of magic weren't forbidden in L'Ortagia, she'd have guessed he was enchanted. Maybe under the spell of another hidden nocturne?

Dark eyes locked on her. "Do you hear that? What have you...?" He shook his head.

"Hear what? Are you all right?" Sidony asked.

"I...nothing. Just a long day of traveling." He ran a hand over his mouth. "My lady, did you say 'Persephone'?" His softly accented voice made him sound as if he was from the Kingdom of Embury...and somewhere else. She'd danced with a few members of the Emburian court this evening, but no one quite like him.

Several more dignitaries were due to arrive in the morning, but she didn't want to think of protocol or ceremony tonight. The appeal of the masquerade was the absence of such roles.

Once he seemed to have gotten his bearings, she walked toward the man, waving a hand. "You look like Hades, god of the underworld, with all that black you're wearing." It was silly, but the champagne had emboldened her, so she continued. "Are you waiting for someone?"

"I was taking in the view." He glanced down, as if he was just noticing his garments. "Hmm. Hades."

His low voice rolled over her, stirring up a shiver along her shoulders. Those lips, that voice. All evening she'd danced with dozens of men, but none had attracted her. It wouldn't help matters if any had. But this man was different, alluring in a way that pulled her in.

Zara would advise her to be practical, a realist to her core. She'd tell Sidony to leave this man alone and get some rest for the long day ahead.

Instead, Sidony tucked a curl behind her ear. "Who are you supposed to be?"

He shrugged. "I don't know. I added the mask but hadn't decided the rest."

Oh dear. Her breaths quickened. He actually walked around like that. Like a finely dressed brigand.

"It suits you." She meandered closer.

"Persephone, wasn't it?" He cocked his head. "Since it's springtime, she'd be gone. I would indeed be missing her."

He spoke with the charm of a courtier, playing along with her. She gave him a half smile for that.

"I...surely she's a fool to have left you." Where had he been all evening? "I must have missed you in the ballroom."

He was tall, the cut of his clothes emphasizing a muscular physique. His neatly tailored cuffs were too austere to be fashionable. But his plain breeches emphasized a fine pair of legs. While the look suited him, it distracted her. She wanted to ask him to turn, certain his tailor would ensure the backside was displayed similarly.

He shook his head slowly. "No dancing for me tonight." He gestured to the bench, offering her his seat.

"No, thank you. It's lovely out here. Please. You don't have to stand." Though she longed to rest, she couldn't sit next to him, much as she wanted to. The bench was made for lovers. Two people could hardly share it with any distance between them.

If her mother had been in her place, she would have demanded the bench. Sidony was tired of imperial orders—so she went over to the railing.

"My mother taught me not to sit while a lady stands." His gaze flicked over her. "How many dances have you had?"

"Dozens. I could dance until sunrise." She reached down and slipped off her shoes, flexing her toes.

"Madam, please take this bench so you can rest."

A considerate, mannerly brigand.

She eyed the brickwork. "Thank you, but I don't want to ruin my new stockings." Her own indelicate statement made her blush.

He strode toward her. "Let me offer my assistance. I promise not to ruin them."

Heat curled through her. She wiped her hands on her gold skirts, liking his straightforwardness.

"Very well."

The handsome stranger bent and scooped her up into his arms.

As he lifted her high against his chest, her pulse sped up. She looped an arm around his neck to hold on. This close, she got a view behind the mask. Spiky, dark lashes framed eyes the color of old bronze. Before she lost her nerve, her fingers trailed over his coat, the wool soft and finely made. His face was clean shaven, with high cheekbones, and full, bow-shaped lips. This man smelled more decadent than any of the desserts she'd tasted earlier. Her eyelids felt heavy. She couldn't decide if her evening was getting better or worse.

"There." He set her down gently, then took a spot at the railing.

"Thank you." She curled up on the bench and arranged her skirts over her aching feet. "I admit, I came down to the terrace for this bench."

"Well, now it's yours." His tone was warm.

"Now it's mine." When she glanced at him, she almost wished she hadn't. He leaned back on his elbows. The simple pose was one she'd seen scores of men strike. For him, it was masculine and relaxed. He charmed her, in a sinking, hopeless way.

He seemed close to her age, handsome, courteous, and with a body like a dancer. All traits she likely wouldn't have in a husband. She wasn't promised to anyone yet, but she knew her mother would choose her husband based on whomever would be the best for L'Ortagia.

Sidony sighed in frustrated appreciation of the man before her. If he heard her, he again didn't react. A sword hung at his belt, likely part of a regular uniform. Even in costume he kept a piece of himself. That much, she understood. She had dressed with care for the evening. Only Zara had understood the lavish gold skirts and adornment weren't an expression of affluence. They were a bittersweet expression of her value to the crown.

Strains of music carried from the ballroom. Someone must have persuaded the musicians to play again. The man straightened as if called to attention.

"Pardon, my lady. Let me introduce myself."

"Please don't." Sidony held up a hand and tapped her lace mask. "It's a masquerade for a few hours more."

His eyes narrowed. Laughter rang out from a terrace above. The brigand swept his arms wide and bowed.

"As you wish."

~

PRINCE ADRIAN ROSE and rested his hands along the railing,

assessing the woman before him. Her mask hid little. He didn't need to use his powers to see her face behind it. She was bewitching. She had masses of long blond hair, most of it caught up at the back of her head. A few tendrils had slipped out and curled along her neck.

The coins in her hair jingled and the sound amplified in his ears for a few seconds. Strange. Ever since she'd stepped onto the terrace with him, his powers had been...off.

"Why stay out here with me like this?" he asked.

"I don't want the party to end." Her voice was melodic, cultured. She shifted along the bench, arching her back. Her breasts strained against her bodice, and he swallowed. She was graceful and curvy, the style of her dress accentuating her hips. As he'd carried her to the bench, he'd seen her eyes were green and wide. Her skin had a honeyed tint, adding to the golden air about her.

This must be how a pirate beholds treasure.

"It's more than that. Give me another reason," Adrian said.

She brought a hand to her chin, brushing a finger against her cheek and pursing her lips. The gesture was flirtatious, playful. It was a combination he rarely had the chance to experience. In Embury, the ladies of court were sophisticated and guarded. They had to be. King Gracchus's court was known for being cold-blooded. When Adrian had first arrived from Daeso, he'd had liaisons with a few. Those ended abruptly, with his uncle Gracchus sending the women away for distracting him or trying to use him to influence the king. After that, Adrian avoided entanglements. His uncle had enough of a hold on him.

This woman with gold strewn from her head to her embroidered stockings talked to him of parties that lasted into the wee hours. Such frivolity. He couldn't help pushing her for more, content to play her game but wanting to know why she wanted to play.

Tonight was a luxury, being out on the grounds unaccompanied by royal guards, much less talking with a charming woman. His tasks as his uncle's emissary could resume on the morrow.

"Fine. The first reason is true, though. I like parties, and I especially love masquerade balls." She shrugged. "The second is I enjoy being out here with you." Her gaze met his, holding it for a long moment.

Adrian's mouth went dry.

"We've hardly gone about other proprieties." She nodded at her shoes, which laid on the ground inches from where he stood. "Why start now?"

Why not, indeed. "How daring."

"For the masquerade, I get to be whomever I wish for a few hours." She shrugged as if pretending were an easy thing for her. "Haven't you ever wanted to be someone else?"

Adrian pushed up on his hands, stomach tight, as if bracing for a blow. He was sick of serving a dishonorable king. It was why he'd stayed out in the garden after talking with Marlowe tonight. His duties would begin again as soon as the sun came up. Tonight he could be himself.

"I wouldn't put it that way," Adrian said slowly.

"How would you say it?" she asked.

"Sometimes I'd rather be somewhere else, present company excluded." He paused, reflecting that he'd perhaps said too much. She had him out of sorts.

She nodded. "Some place where obligations and duties can't follow. A bother, and for what?" There was an edge to her voice that hadn't been there before.

He felt a kinship with her in that moment, unable to remember a time when he wasn't laden with responsibility. "For family."

"For family." A shadow passed over her face. "If only we could be left to choose those paths ourselves."

"Some you can't choose. They are promises kept." Bitterness seeped into his voice, but he couldn't stop the words.

"Promises broken," she said in a soft voice. She folded her hands in her lap.

Adrian used his powers to get a closer view, seeing one hand clenched around the other.

She'd come out here for a reprieve. The same reason he'd stayed in the garden and not retreated to his room.

"So you'd rather stay here and play pretend."

With a small sigh, she flexed her hand, staring at the tangle of her fingers.

"Yes." She lifted her chin. "Maybe I'm better at acting."

"Maybe you are." The moment stretched between them. Adrian wished he'd seen her dance tonight. He imagined she'd been dazzling. Out here, she thrummed with energy. There'd been a charge in the air the moment she'd walked onto the terrace.

Around her, his powers acted oddly, his senses amplified. He could discern the different instruments playing in the ballroom, all while mostly keeping his attention on her. He tracked two separate conversations—some with fewer words than others—between couples scattered throughout the gardens. He'd never been able to do that before. It was why he normally traveled with a guard, because he couldn't use his powers without having to stand still to do so. His powers usually left him drained, but tonight he felt...invigorated.

It could be the fresh air, or it could be her. Did her mask hide a nocturne?

She shook her head. "I should get back."

"Could you stay a little longer?" he asked before he could stop himself.

Her breath hitched and she gave a slow smile.

CHAPTER TWO

*W*hile Sidony couldn't change the course set for her family, and likely herself, she could enjoy the temptation standing a few feet away. "I could."

She strolled over to him. Stockings be damned.

Sidony rested her hip on the balustrade and smoothed her skirts. "Are you married?"

He crossed his arms. "No."

"I imagine we're not too different from other couples in the gardens." Bitterness crept into her voice.

"Unlike other couples who arranged to meet, we stumbled upon the same spot."

"Then why all the questions?" Sidony asked.

"Force of habit." His gaze dropped to her feet. "Seems a shame to ruin your pretty stockings."

She flushed with pleasure. "I'll risk it."

"You are entirely unlike any woman I've ever known." He glanced away, facing the reflecting pool.

She slid closer to his side. "Why don't I know who you are?" Being with him was a unique experience as well. He didn't know her position and rank. Whatever the reason, his manner and attention made her feel wanted, though he was shy of truly flirting with her.

"What if we've already met and you've forgotten?" And there it was. His tone was teasing, emboldening her. Perhaps standing this close to him made her brazen.

She needed to forget about tomorrow, forget about being more than a pretty pawn.

"Pity I've forgotten meeting you." She peered at the water, angling her head to the side.

He swung his head around. She met his stare, getting a little lost in his dark eyes glittering behind the mask.

"Ah, how cruel. How could you?" He put a hand to his chest.

She fiddled with one of her escaped curls. "Perhaps you could remind me?"

He froze, as if she'd caught him by surprise. Not possible. He likely hid out here to avoid women throwing themselves at him all night. Well, she was no different.

"Since you've forgotten me, I need to make more of an impression." His gaze dropped to her lips. Now he was definitely flirting with her.

Tingles rushed along her skin like bubbles trailing up the side of a glass. It was just the thing she'd been hoping he'd say. Provocative. She uncovered another rebellious soul out here on the balcony. The hour was late. She would need to return to the ballroom soon.

Tilting her face up, she leaned in, summoning all her daring. "Impress me."

His eyes widened almost imperceptibly. He edged closer, enough for his boots to brush against her skirts.

"Are you going to kiss me?" she teased.

He chuckled. "Would you like me to?"

"Yes." She stared at his lips, wondering what they'd feel like against her own.

"Close your eyes."

Sidony closed them, which lasted all of two seconds. His fingers skimmed her jaw, barely touching her. She peeked up at him. He tugged his mask back over his head, revealing the rest of his startlingly handsome face. She nearly melted on the spot.

"Oh," she breathed.

He pressed a kiss against her lips. *Oh.*

Those pensive lips of his were softer than they looked. She shivered. She wanted to get closer, to press along his length, but she held still. If she moved, would he stop? He'd been guarded; she didn't want to scare him off.

His fingers trailed from her jaw to the curls at the back of her head. He kissed her gently, his lips coasting across hers, filled with a restraint that maddened her.

She placed a hand on his chest for balance and tipped her head, leaning in to the kiss. His mouth slanted over hers, making her chest ache. With a moan, she kissed him back like she wanted to, arching up from her toes.

The nature of the kiss changed. It went from tender and sweet under the moonlight, to what most couples who escaped outside during a ball hoped to do.

As his arm came around her, any doubt fled. She knew this territory with men. He'd been difficult to read, courteous and remote, but he wanted her too.

Her mysterious brigand put a hand on her waist, pulling her close, and she loved it. She sensed his strength in the hard muscles of his chest. His breathing grew faster, but little else about his movements changed. It was as if he kept a tight leash on his passion, holding himself slightly out of reach. She was used to throwing herself into situations, sometimes stumbling through them with forced grace. There was no protocol for this.

His threads of restraint kept the kiss frustrating. Their time was short. *Kiss me now.*

Sidony wasn't a woman who sat idle, waiting for things to

happen. Her mother and sister both cautioned her to be less impulsive. But she had run out of time. Tonight, in this moment, she was going after what she wanted. She pulled back and from his heated gaze, maybe he wanted to get lost with her too.

Instead of teasing or goading him, she offered her sincerity this time. "I won't forget you."

His indrawn breath proved she'd pleased him.

"You should."

She frowned at him, impatient. "Give me a memory to think on in the nights to come."

His hands tightened at her waist. His eyes narrowed.

She wanted to yank his face down to hers, but she didn't dare. All she allowed herself was to curl her thumb around his lapel.

"For us both, then."

With a heart-stopping half smile, he angled his head and kissed her.

Yes. Sidony tugged at his coat, sliding her other hand up the wide plain of his chest. He crushed their lips together. She opened her mouth under the pressure of his, gasping when he sucked her lower lip into his mouth. He nibbled on it, his tongue tracing along the edge. Desire coursed through her. Sharp. Sweet. She moaned, kissing him back.

He groaned when her tongue slid along his. Sidony pressed her body against him for more feeling, more sensation, more of everything he was offering her. His kiss was delicious. Indulgent. She could keep kissing him until the sun rose.

Her head swam. She had no idea who he was, aside from being a handsome stranger.

She broke away and put a finger to his lips, ready to ask his name.

"Sidony, are you out here?" Lucia, her lady-in-waiting,

called. Her voice seemed to be coming from the stairs, so they were still hidden from view.

"I have to go." She ran a hand down his chest.

"Who is she?" He ducked his head and pulled on his mask.

They stood close enough that his breath tickled the tip of her ear.

"Who are you?" Sidony countered.

A hint of disappointment, perhaps, lit his eyes. "Adrian of Embury."

Prince Adrian of Embury? Prince Adrian, the man who served at the king's behest. A royal spy, charged with doing the king's bidding. Even his own people were afraid of the prince.

No, no, no.

Adrian was the man King Gracchus had sent to finalize the betrothal agreement between her sister and his cousin. He wasn't due to arrive until tomorrow.

Adrian straightened his coat and gave her a considering look. "And you are Sidony d'Arles."

"Yes." Sidony adjusted her mask to hide how her hands shook. "This has been...you are...I have to go."

"I recognized you from a portrait." Apparently, he'd shown up early, and he knew all about her.

This couldn't be happening. A kiss was one thing. But to possibly damage her country's negotiations with Embury by her actions was quite another. A brigand indeed.

"Wonderful," she replied weakly.

He chuckled, and she straightened her spine.

She scooped up her shoes and gathered her skirts to leave. When she reached the giant urn, she turned for one last glimpse. Her mother would berate her, and her sister would shake her head, but Sidony had meant every word tonight.

Adrian stared at her, his lips curled in a half grin. If he had stayed the mystery she'd thought him to be, she would have blown him a kiss. He was the wrong man, but utterly unfor-gettable.

~

IF THE WORLD exploded around him, Adrian wouldn't have noticed a thing. His lips burned, his chest squeezed tight, and his cock was hard as the bricks under his feet, all for an enchantress he'd just met.

A breeze swept across the terrace, bringing her sweet scent back to him. Her voice carried over the steps as she made reas-surances to the woman who'd come looking for her.

Princess Sidony's look of shock when he'd told her his name had seemed sincere. He was so used to manipulations, he wouldn't put it past his uncle to scheme for yet another hold on him.

What had come over him to kiss her like that? For a few moments, he'd tried to keep it chaste. Then she'd reached for him, and he'd given in, so drawn to her.

He let her show him what he'd been missing: passion, gentleness, and the soft feel of a woman looking at him with desire in her eyes.

He gripped the railing where she'd leaned. His powers were on overdrive, along with the rest of his body. Each sense was louder, brighter, stronger. His heightened senses picked up everything around him. Her honeysuckle scent drifted around him. Another wave of lust rolled through him, and he squeezed his eyes shut.

Coveting her, he narrowed his senses to listen for her voice again. Sidony was almost out of range, but she said, "Lucia, I'm exhausted. I was getting some air." The sound of their footsteps faded as they walked down the halls of the estate.

Adrian pressed harder, the stone nearly cutting his palms. This was the safest and closest she should ever be to his world.

Her sister would join the Embury court once she wed his cousin Torwyn. Adrian understood the queen's motivation to keep a wily king at bay. Most days, Adrian felt like he'd been swallowed whole and waited to die. A spirited creature like Sidony would never survive it. He winced. If Princess Zara were anything like the woman he'd met tonight, she too would long to return home.

But until he freed his family, he was under Gracchus's command, another nocturne pressed into the king's service. The king needed the alliance a royal marriage would provide. It would strengthen his sovereignty over Embury. Adrian had no means to oppose him, so he went along arranging a marriage with the L'Ortagian heir.

Adrian was glad he'd taken Marlowe's suggestion to explore the grounds of the estate. The reflecting pool had caught his attention, and he'd stayed for long moments on the balcony, watching the water ripple in the breeze. Music and laughter from the party added to the dreamlike atmosphere. He wished he could've sat and stared at it until the sun rose, anonymous behind his mask.

Now his mask was back in place. It had been freeing to take it off for her. He rubbed a finger across his upper lip, recalling Sidony's reactions to him. Their kiss was unexpected, but he couldn't bring himself to regret it. They would have to forget it ever happened.

The music was loud, the smells of wine and bodies becoming noxious. His clothes chafed his skin, and even the glow of the candles seemed too bright for the night sky, all save for the taste of her. His powers truly had changed tonight, strengthening after they'd kissed. Sidony was somehow the catalyst. She must be a nocturne too.

The king's, and therefore Adrian's, knowledge of nocturnes in L'Ortagia was scant. Most hid their powers, using them in secret or not at all. The true number of nocturnes in the country was impossible to know. Adrian didn't know what Gracchus would do with the fact that one of the princesses possessed powers. He would likely seek to use her in some way.

Adrian was certain of one thing: Gracchus must never know about tonight.

CHAPTER THREE

"Outside isn't so bad." Sidony took a seat next to Zara at a luncheon along the back of the estate. Her fingertips were icy despite the day's warmth. "I'm sorry I missed this morning."

"It was optional for you, and early, so I wasn't expecting you to attend." Zara gave her a tight smile.

Rows of tables dotted the lawn. Children played a game of hoops, rolling them across the lush grass. Several guests played whist at a grouping of tables. Others strolled in the gardens. A competitive cricket match engaged a fair-sized crowd farther down on the lawn.

"The ball went late," Sidony said. She considered telling Zara what happened with Adrian. She wasn't in the habit of keeping secrets from her sister.

"Did you enjoy yourself?" Zara asked. "I realized this morning that was my last Tulip Ball as an unmarried woman. Perhaps yours as well."

"Yes. That…occurred to me last night."

Zara gave her a sympathetic look. "Then I hope it didn't ruin your evening."

Sidony's temples pounded with strain. "I tried to enjoy myself."

If he had been anyone else, she would have told her sister about the mysterious man on the terrace, about how she'd never been so attracted to someone. She might have even told her about how she'd begged him to kiss her. Sidony was appalled at herself. She might have damaged her country's standings in this upcoming deal. She dreaded being on her mother's bad side. Ruining Zara's betrothal would ensure it.

Hopefully, once she saw Adrian in the daytime, she could put the incident behind her. She needed to forget him. She should have turned and walked the other way when she realized he was from Embury. Shame soured her throat. She was a fool.

"The prince is playing cricket," Zara continued. "But our introductions were so fast this morning, I hardly got a good look at him."

Handsome fellow, Sidony wanted to say.

"Does his cousin resemble him physically?" Sidony spotted Adrian on the pitch. The sun shone on his dark hair.

It was his team's turn to go out to field. She dragged her gaze back to Zara.

"Somewhat. Not that it matters. Here." Zara slid a miniature of Prince Torwyn over to Sidony. "They are close in age."

"He's settled into his seat beside the king, it seems." Sidony studied the small portrait. Torwyn was pleasant looking, with similar dark eyes and hair to his cousin. He had the hint of a petulant mouth, though.

The circumstances of his birth were contentious, as the prince was born on the wrong side of the blanket. The king had rectified that, retroactively legitimizing him. For the Emburians, marrying their prince off to an established house was a coup.

"It doesn't sound too difficult." Zara took the picture and snapped the frame shut.

Sidony knew her sister dreaded this weekend's meetings, having begged their mother not to make her marry. "Were any terms discussed this morning?"

"Nothing I didn't already know." Zara's lips thinned. "The deal is set. I'm sure the prince is here as a formality."

"So at this point, nothing could change?" Sidony asked.

Zara paused. Her eyes were hard when she said, "Despite my reservations, despite any news from our neighbors, the arrangements have been made."

"Oh." Sidony swallowed. Now was the time to tell her. She pinched the tablecloth, focused on making neat, even pleats. "Zara, there's something you should know."

"Can you make it quick? The Duke and Duchess of Corentin are leading the prince to us."

The Duke and Duchess of Corentin were cohosting the week's events with the princesses. Zara rose and walked to the edge of the row of tables. Sidony followed, her mind blanking at the thought of how she'd likely disappoint her sister. Zara could lose political ground in Embury if word got out about what Sidony had done. Adrian was the last man she should have kissed on the terrace. Zara wouldn't begrudge her the kissing, so much as not having the presence of mind to know whom she kissed.

"Trust mother to turn one of our favorite spring social events into matrimonial hell," Sidony said. "How are you managing this?"

"It's all I can do not to scream." Zara snapped open her fan. "Here they come. What did you want to tell me?"

Adrian, along with the duke and duchess, walked across the lawn. As he neared, her lips parted. The Prince of Embury was gorgeous in the midday sun.

Sidony took in Adrian's long stride, the set of his shoulders, and the way he held his chest high. The graceful precision of his movements hinted at military training.

Adrian's coat was a deep shade of green, austere aside from a row of silver buttons down the front. The cut showed off his linen shirt and buff-colored breeches. He was finely made and dressed with class, if not in a courtly fashion.

Sidony's hands trembled, and she surreptitiously wiped her damp palms on a handkerchief.

It didn't matter. Not even how good he looked in breeches. What mattered was whether her sister was happy. This man, with the blessing of two monarchs, was here to finalize a complicated betrothal—and her sister's matrimonial misery.

The possibility of making it worse for her sister was not an option. "It's nothing. I'll follow your lead with our guest. That was all I wanted to say."

Zara frowned with confusion but nodded. "Soon, you'll be doing more of this on your own."

"I will," she said in a soft voice.

Sidony tucked her chilled hands into the folds of her skirts as Adrian and Zara greeted each other. She had to find a way to get through this.

"And this is Princess Sidony, Her Royal Highness's sister," the duchess said.

Adrian's gaze was assessing, but his expression was nothing but polite. She took a moment longer than she should have to offer her hand. He kissed the back of it. It was perfunctory, dignified, and bland—in contrast to their meeting last night.

As if sensing the tension, the duke gestured to his wife, and they left the trio to get better acquainted.

"Prince Adrian, would you like a tour of the grounds?" her sister asked.

"I would." He offered his arm to Zara, and Sidony fell into step beside them.

"We've been enjoying watching the children play for much of the morning. When did you arrive?"

"Too late for the ball last night." Adrian paused, turning to view the children tossing around a ball in a patch of grass. "Though my rooms had a nice view of the garden, the reflecting pond caught my attention."

"Did you venture into the garden last night?" Zara asked Sidony.

"No, not at all." Sidony's voice rose, sweat beading between her breasts. "I wasn't in the garden. I wasn't even near any plants."

Zara blinked at her but turned back to the prince. "We've hosted the Tulip Ball for a few years now. Sidony usually has to be peeled off the ballroom floor. I'm sorry you missed it."

"I wager she made a lovely dancer last night," Adrian said.

"Thank you." Sidony's cheeks heated at his compliment. Then she remembered how she'd fallen for his charm last night, and she clenched her toes hard in her shoes.

Zara and Adrian chatted, their solemn natures eerily similar. The prince kept his attention mostly on Zara and smiled cordially. He had better manners than most royals and actually asked her sister about herself. Occasionally, he tried to include Sidony in the conversation too. She answered but turned it back to a topic for them.

The prince was different today.

She tapped her fingers against her skirt. If Adrian's cousin was like him, Zara and Torwyn might make a good match. They were both engrossed in the relations between Embury and L'Ortagia. Goodness, they discussed trade routes between the countries for nearly ten minutes.

Remembering how he'd played along with her silly ruse before ensuring she wouldn't forget him had her cheeks heating with embarrassment. Next to her sister, she knew she came across as both flighty and fanciful. How had this serious man kept from rolling his eyes at her?

Even worse, she allowed herself to remember being in his arms. His reserve had been intriguing. Her lips burned at the recollection of kissing him and how good it felt.

Had he gone along with her games because he knew who she was? Had he kissed her for the same reason? Had the royal spy of Embury simply humored her with his attention?

In those first few moments with him, he'd been detached, formal, and dutiful. She came to a realization. This man, who conversed amiably with her sister, had many faces. She had no idea how they all fit together.

She didn't know what that would mean for Zara's marriage, but it did not bring her comfort. It didn't matter how well Adrian got on with her and her sister. His cousin was the man Zara would wed.

"Sidony?" Zara tapped her wrist. "Sidony?"

"Yes?" Apparently her sister had been trying to get her attention. They'd strolled around the reflecting pond just below the terrace where she'd kissed Adrian.

"Please keep Prince Adrian company for a moment," Zara whispered in her ear. "I had too much tea while we waited. Be a dear and entertain him."

Understanding hit. "Certainly."

Sidony strode over to where Adrian stood waiting. Around them, guests ventured along the back steps of the estate, conversations muted so as to eavesdrop on every word between the two of them.

"Since you missed the gardens last night, would you like to walk with me?" Adrian asked.

She met his gaze, searching his face to see if she could detect a hidden agenda. She saw nothing but a polite, interested expression.

"I do enjoy the garden maze at Peletierre. Let me show you."

He held out his arm, and she took it, fingers pressing into the fine wool. They walked in silence across the grass to the start of the maze. Sidony's heart thundered in her ears.

"I hadn't planned on telling her about last night," Adrian said, his tone crisp. "It was an aberration. It won't happen again."

"Of course not."

A lock of hair escaped his queue and blew across Adrian's forehead. He tucked it behind his ear with a grumble. That small sound did things to her, reminding her how she'd felt when he'd kissed her back. She pressed her lips together as if that could stem such feelings.

"You don't need to charm me," she said. "I don't like keeping things from my sister."

He tilted his head. "I understand if you want to tell her what happened."

"The arrangement is hard enough on her. I won't complicate the situation with my actions."

They reached an ivy-covered archway. True to the reason the ball had its name, tulips bloomed at the base of several topiaries interspersed in the maze's walls. They walked along the path, and the sounds of the garden party hushed, leaving only the crunch of their shoes along the gravel.

"Gracchus will likely finalize the betrothal once I return. This meeting was a last step of good faith." Tugging on a coat sleeve, he stopped. Perhaps he'd said more than he'd intended.

"And has it been? Did you kiss me in good faith?"

"Madam," he said, and she caught a hint of his Daeson accent again. "You joined *me* on that terrace."

"I didn't know who you were."

"But for some reason, you trusted me not to hurt you."

"After a while, yes," she said. She knew how her mother worked. Zara and Torwyn's wedding would be held soon. Then

Zara would leave, and Sidony didn't know how she would bear it. "You have no idea what I'm facing."

He blinked at her before leaning in. "I understand loyalty to family. I understand sacrifice. I understand more than you think."

She wanted to scoff at his words but held back.

They continued along the path, winding in a slow circle until they reached the center of the maze. More tulips bloomed at the base of a narrow fountain.

Sidony bent down and ran a finger over the petals that curved and formed a cup. She twisted the round stem, snapping it. Then she twisted another. Four more and she clutched her impromptu bouquet to her waist, arranging them in her hand.

"Do you?" she asked. "In a matter of weeks, my sister, my best friend in the world, will be married off to a stranger in order to keep peace between our countries. I'll stand in for her at court."

Adrian reached out and adjusted one of the blooms, tugging it free. "Then we have that in common." He held the flower, spinning it slowly.

Sidony lifted her hand, unsure if she wanted to reach out or ward him off. The practice of magic was forbidden in L'Ortagia. But when they were alone, it was like her body was drawn to his, despite her resolve. She fairly hummed with longing. "I think the garden is bespelled," she said, half joking.

Adrian's features froze. "I was under the impression the queen outlawed magic."

"Not quite." Sidony gave him a half smile. "Nocturnes live more openly in Embury, but they are here too. They use their powers surreptitiously."

"Was last night the effect of a spell, then?" he asked.

Boldly, she met his gaze, spying a fissure in his reserve, one she knew how to press to get what she wanted. "Most likely."

He opened his mouth to reply when she spotted her sister joining them in the maze. She waved. "Zara."

"You two finally made it out here. That's wonderful." Zara linked her arm in Sidony's.

"Princess Sidony helped me navigate. She's quite handy. Your mother will be in her capable hands while you are in Embury."

Zara gave him a tight smile. "I think you are right about that. Sidony's skills are underrated."

"Zara knows every nook and cranny of our estates and grounds, and the fastest way to get from one place to the next."

"I do," Zara said in a wistful tone.

The three walked in silence toward the exit of the maze.

Zara inclined her head toward Adrian. "Pleased to have made your acquaintance before the negotiations are complete."

CHAPTER FOUR

*A*drian followed Sidony and Zara out of the maze and watched them ascend the back stairs of the estate. They barely looked related, much less like sisters.

He'd done his duty to meet with Zara at Peletierre. He would do it again and accompany his cousin to their wedding in the coming weeks. He had to. He needed to buy more time.

Kissing Sidony was a mistake. Could it have been caused by a nocturne nearby? Or had she bespelled him herself?

Lord Marlowe Sullivan, one of Gracchus's trusted advisors, approached Adrian on the path. "How's the future bride? Will she and Torwyn suit?"

"Zara will make a great queen some day." Adrian's chest ached, but he ignored it. Sympathy wasn't wasted on the princess, but he couldn't help her either. "Torwyn is a fortunate man."

"What about her sister?"

"Princess Sidony." In her haste to leave, she'd dropped a tulip. He hesitated, fingers twitching.

Marlowe scooped up the red flower, twirling it in his hand. "Quite the dancer at the ball last night."

Adrian frowned. "You went inside?"

"I watched." Marlowe's eyes flashed. "Gold dress, coins tucked into all that blond hair? Stunning."

Marlowe *knew*. Adrian had been so distracted by her, and his amplified powers, that he'd missed being spied on. "I'm assuming you watched her leave."

"I did." They continued in silence for several steps. "It's too bad the king didn't make a match for you with her."

Adrian considered how she'd gathered a bouquet of tulips, as if she couldn't help herself. She'd ruined a pair of stockings just to flirt with him. She wouldn't last long in Embury.

"She's a whimsical woman."

"And you are altogether too serious," Marlowe said, echoing his words from last night.

A couple strolled nearby, their heads angled toward each other. Such a simple intimacy, to stroll along a path with one's beloved.

Adrian turned from them. "Embury requires a watchfulness."

"True," Marlowe said. "But you can't spend all your days in service, putting off your life." The courtier waved, indicating the terraces along the back of the estate. "You could ask the king to petition the queen for her hand."

Adrian considered his words. "He covets the heir to the throne to the point of fixation."

"What if you insisted, said you met the younger and had to have her?"

Cold permeated Adrian's chest, spreading outward to his shoulders. The need to protect her overwhelmed him. "Gracchus detained my family. I can't bring Sidony into that."

"You're here, making sure her sister will marry into the family soon enough." Marlowe shrugged and nodded at another group of guests. "Sidony may be more adaptable than you think."

Being close to Sidony again had strengthened Adrian's powers. It wasn't clear how she'd managed that. She was either an incredibly self-contained nocturne, or she might not be aware she was amplifying them. He'd heard of some isolated nocturnes who did not realize they had abilities until they were older. Since her abilities seemed to affect others and not herself —that he could tell—she might not fully realize what she could do.

One thing was certain: If Gracchus discovered her ability, he'd use her up and never let her go. Adrian wouldn't sentence even an enemy to share his fate. He turned back to Marlowe. "*Not her.* The king has already shown the lengths to which he'll go to keep me by his side."

"What would he want with her?" Marlowe asked.

Not ready to trust anyone with his thoughts on Sidony, Adrian reached for the first answer he could think of. "She's comely. My uncle covets beauty, wants to be surrounded by it. Like Zara's."

"The younger sister is just as lovely." Marlowe tilted his head. "Though spending, ah, heated moments with her last night may be coloring your opinion."

Adrian slashed his hand through the air. Sidony could not be his. "Zara has her own throne to return to. I would not trap another, no matter how much I may wish to, with me in Embury."

"Fair enough."

The ice that had seized Adrian's chest dissipated at Marlowe's acquiescence. They turned their attention to the far field, where shouts and cheers carried. For a brief moment, he recalled watching smaller matches when his father took him into the city of Sinchon. Different games, but the same sounds from the crowd.

"Let's catch the end of the cricket match," Marlow said.

Adrian nodded, grateful the noise from the crowd would cover their conversation.

Once the pitch was in view, Marlowe delivered news Adrian had been waiting on. "I can help you find your mother and sister."

The news made him dizzy. "I'm not certain of what you're speaking."

"I know you are," Marlowe said. "You don't need to prevaricate with me."

"How do I know you aren't working for the king?"

"I do work for him. I also have my own agenda." Marlowe's long face with its sharp cheekbones remained impassive.

"We all do." Adrian clenched his hands, grappling to keep an outward sense of calm. "I need to know why I should involve you in this."

"You can trust me not to betray you." Marlowe paced at Adrian's side.

"Why is that?" Adrian had too much at stake to put his trust in someone too easily, but he was also growing desperate. He had to find his family.

"I have a particular aversion to what he's done to them. Using them to leverage your…skills was unnecessary."

Adrian rubbed a hand across the back of his neck. His uncle didn't let obstacles stand in his way for very long. That Marlowe had a different set of ethics was a boon. "Fine."

"You aren't the only one disillusioned with the king."

He had always known Marlowe held a great many secrets. Adrian would have to be careful not to underestimate him. "This agenda of yours? Elaborate."

"Another time. All you need to know is that I want to help you and keep you alive."

The crowd cheered. Adrian stopped two paces away from the baron. "I need more than that."

"My loyalties do not lie with the king." Marlowe's voice was barely audible.

His admission was treason; the exact thing the king had tasked Adrian with uncovering for all these years. Once he'd known his nephew possessed this specific set of nocturne abilities, to project his senses outside of his corporeal body, he'd used him to ferret out traitors in the kingdom.

Now Adrian was standing next to one from the king's inner circle.

It had been nine years since he'd seen his family when he left Sinchon. They were his focus. He had to trust someone in order to find them.

Marlowe tapped the flower against his thigh. "I don't like it when women are threatened or held as prisoners."

"You've seen them?" A spark of hope lit inside him. Gracchus had held them for three years. Maybe they were in Embury. Maybe one of Gracchus's allies housed them. "They're alive?"

"I haven't seen them, but I believe I will. I can help you get them free. Do you want my help or not?"

Out of options, as well as friends who would oppose his uncle, Adrian had no choice. "I do."

"Excellent. Wait for me to contact you. I'll head back first. Here." Marlowe handed him the tulip.

He took it, nearly snapping the stem.

CHAPTER FIVE

"*M*other's in a temper this morning." Zara breezed past Sidony in the hallway outside the queen's small throne room.

"That bad?" Sidony had known it was coming soon after their return. From Zara's stricken expression, it hadn't gone well.

Zara nodded, her hands shaking. "It's not that it was unexpected." Tears welled in her eyes. Zara stood up to their mother regularly, but facing her down came at a cost.

Sidony handed her a handkerchief. "She wants you to marry the prince."

"She reminded me it's for L'Ortagia." Zara waved her hand. "I don't know if I mind him so much as I don't like being ordered. I also mind him though."

Sidony nodded, familiar with her sister's independent streak.

"And the wedding is in five weeks."

Sidony's mouth fell open. "Why that soon?"

"Gracchus and Mother want the alliance done." Zara

frowned, gaze turning inward. "I begged her for more time. He's a dangerous man."

Sidony nodded, familiar with Zara's wariness of their neighbor. "Has he threatened us?" she asked in a low voice.

"No." Zara's gaze shot to her. "But he threatens his own people. I've begged her to meet with members of a group who've challenged his sovereignty, but she refuses. It isn't really between Torwyn and me anyway."

"No, I guess not." Sidony tried to swallow, her throat dry. It was all too much.

Zara clasped one of Sidony's hands. "Have you talked to her about your concerns about the small council?"

Sidony glanced at her sister. Now that Zara's wedding was inevitable, she might not ever tell their mother. What would be the point?

"Not yet. It's just better when I go along with what she wants." When Zara looked like she would start in on how Sidony should speak up about things that were important to her, Sidony held up a hand. "I am only looking out for you."

They walked along companionably for a few moments before Zara stuck her nose in again. She inclined her head toward the script Sidony had tucked under her arm. "Sneaking in time to read those? Enjoy them. You love that."

Sidony ran her fingers over the fine leather, grateful her sister understood her.

"So, when is the wedding?"

"The middle of June." Zara swallowed.

"IT WOULD BE LOVELY to see more exports going to Marenburg, you are quite right."

Sidony sat in a chair by the window, attending her mother's morning toilette. Waiting out the other courtiers' requests had taken close to an hour, but she reminded herself what was at stake. Her sister's happiness, and possibly her own.

Her mother conducting affairs of the kingdom while she readied for the day was not unusual. Sidony was impressed, actually. It was quite efficient. She imagined conducting a meeting from her own chamber, but dismissed the thought as quickly as it came. The last thing she wanted was another meeting.

She giggled, drawing an amused look from her mother.

"Sidony, how unlike you to spend the morning with me." The queen stood in front of a long table where Lady Emmanuelle, Chief Diplomat of Foreign Affairs, had laid out several maps. "Usually you are attending to some upcoming performance or exhibit."

"I wondered if you needed me today." That was something Zara would say. It was doubtful whether her mother would believe her capable of such a thought. "And I wished to speak with you," she hastened to add.

Isabeau pursed her lips but appeared satisfied. Her mother angled her face in the mirror, back and forth.

"Could we have a moment alone please?" Sidony asked.

Isabeau met her eyes and, with a wave of her hand, cleared the room.

"Preparations for Zara's wedding have me thinking of what it will be like when she's gone." Sidony was proud her tone stayed even.

Her mother's smile was patronizing. "Do you know why an alliance with Embury is paramount?"

Sidony reluctantly nodded.

"Zara's marriage was always going to be a more complex arrangement. Gracchus's ambitions sped up our timetable. He was insistent on the arrangement with my heir."

Sidony had little taste for politics, although ignoring them completely wasn't an option. "What would happen if she didn't wed Torwyn?"

"War. Famine. More debt than we can take on. L'Ortagia has to be protected." Isabeau's eyes flashed. "I know you haven't agreed with my choices, but your sister's match is for her own good, and yours will be someday too."

"But what if I never married? Or Zara married for love?"

Sidony braced for her mother's skepticism. Isabeau was the ultimate pragmatist: Love was a strategy, not a goal or happenstance.

"Neither of you has the luxury of a love match. Most royals don't."

"That is starting to change. You've never given us the chance." The tiniest spark hit her: perhaps she and Adrian could bridge L'Ortagia and Embury.

"Darling, we've run out of time." Her mother raised an elegant brow. "Zara's marriage to Torwyn makes us allies of countries with whom we've had tenuous ties. Our legitimacy of his rule brings peace to Embury and us. You owe much to your sister."

Shame struck Sidony's chest and she dropped her gaze to the floor. So much was riding on Zara. Sidony had no idea how she'd live up to her sister's sacrifice, or whether she was even capable.

CHAPTER SIX

Blackthorne Palace
Kingdom of Embury
May 1784

*A*drian stood in the king's personal library with his back against the wall, as if repelled to the outer edge of the room. Once he had what he needed, he could leave.

Gracchus was at his usual spot in front of the fire, seated in a massive silk-covered armchair. Two of his advisors sat on the settee to his left, and his secretary carefully scribbled notes from a nearby escritoire. Adrian used his enhanced hearing to listen in on their discussion, but it was of no interest to him.

From where he stood, the room looked cozy and inviting, the kind of room where one could read a favorite book and sip tea. For his uncle, however, the room was but one of many places on the estate's grounds where he conducted affairs of state. The room housed a particular collection of books, including catalogues of nocturnes and demonic encyclopedias, along with a locked cabinet of artifacts, many of which Gracchus used for his dark rituals. He wore an amulet around his neck that Adrian suspected was an occult artifact too.

Though he was a "mere human," that fact didn't stop the king from trying to acquire, through any means, abilities various nocturnes possessed. His obsession with the occult had become almost a religion.

Gracchus's rise to power was secured after the previous royal family had been killed. He was a second cousin to King Angus, his predecessor. After the assassinations, Gracchus had been next in line. Rebellion against his rule marked the eight years of his reign. While Angus had been merciful, Gracchus was calculating and secretive, hardly qualities that inspired loyalty in a people who mourned the previous monarch and his lost family.

Adrian hadn't given matrimony more than a passing thought. It didn't matter. His duty was to his uncle. And yet, he was drawn to Sidony. She was unlike anyone he knew. Bold and sweet and...*fun*.

"That will be all," the king said.

A chorus of "yes, Your Highness" sounded as the advisors stood and left the library, leaving Adrian alone with Gracchus. Once the door closed behind them, Gracchus got up and stood by the hearth.

"Come closer to the fire, Adrian. Tell me about your trip."

Adrian took a few steps into the room. He stood behind a settee that faced the fireplace and rested his hands along the back. Gracchus's conversational tone kept him on alert. He rarely used it when they were alone.

"The deal was successful, Uncle," Adrian said.

"How did you find Princess Zara?" Gracchus gazed into the fire as he spoke.

"Exactly what one would want in a future wife and queen," he answered honestly and kept his expression neutral. Zara was more opinionated than he knew his uncle would have wanted, but Gracchus admired intelligence.

"Did she accept the match?"

Adrian nodded. "I don't believe she had a choice. She didn't mention any misgivings to me."

"The young get notions in their heads." Gracchus grunted. "Torwyn needs a strong woman. I don't want him paired with some silly chit."

Adrian frowned at the memory of Sidony's insistence on pretending the night of the ball. Silliness had its place. He kept his opinion of what his cousin needed to himself. "There's no danger of that."

"Good." Gracchus faced him and gripped the mantel. The effect made him resemble a bird of prey stretching out a wing. "The rebels will fear our new resolve."

Adrian had no doubt they would.

Gracchus rested a hand on his waistcoat, fingering the watch he always kept on his person. It was his father's, having been passed down in his family, after skipping over Adrian's father. "It has been foretold that Zara will make a great queen of Embury. And Sidony, the lovely girl, will be the sacrifice we have been waiting for."

Adrian's heart thudded in his chest. Blood drained from his face.

"What do you mean?" His voice broke. "You're going to sacrifice Sidony?"

"The future queen will be spared." Gracchus held out his left hand, patting the air as if he were petting a hound. "The younger is needed."

"A human sacrifice for your rituals? You would kill a princess?" Tingles of fear shot down Adrian's legs, making him feel weak. Velvet split under his fingers as his grip tightened on the settee. If only he could jump over it and strangle his uncle.

"Yes, of course. She's beloved by her people. She would be

41

the perfect sacrifice." His tone was reverent, his excitement plain.

It was futile to argue, but he tried anyway. "You risk war with L'Ortagia, which you worked hard to make into a stronger ally. You cannot sacrifice a princess of the neighboring realm, or anyone else, for that matter."

"It's not up to me. The sacrifice must be someone of royal blood. The magic needs to be strong."

Adrian was given little leeway to challenge Gracchus's beliefs, but whenever he spoke of a sacrifice, Adrian tried to dissuade the king from choosing a human. Until now, as far as he knew, he had succeeded. This was unacceptable, torturous for him to hear. He had to find a way to keep her safe.

"Has it been foretold or do you need her blood for a spell? You're mixing your magics, Uncle."

Gracchus squinted, grabbing a figurine off the mantel. "It's both. She serves dual purposes, perhaps more because we'll blame her death on the rebels, thus cementing L'Ortagia's loyalty to me."

"Whatever your magic requires cannot be at the sake of your army, your alliances, and your efforts to secure those," Adrian reasoned. It was pointless to argue for his uncle's conscience, as he'd long since lost it. "Sidony is too young. Whatever your reasons for choosing her, you must find another way." Though it went against his beliefs, he said, "The woods are teeming with animals. Pick one for your slaughter."

"We need a human sacrifice, nephew. The rebels grow bold and strong. They must be punished. A sacrifice will allow me to become more powerful and mete justice upon the rebels." Gracchus glared.

"How many of your foretellings have come true without you making them so?" Adrian asked.

"I have to make them so. The foretelling is only informa-tion. Action must follow." For years, Gracchus had tried to get

Adrian to join his practices, but Adrian had refused, accusing his uncle of being manipulated by the lure of dark magics.

"Everything you do helps you defeat them. Why would you risk that?"

The king's gaze swept the room, his anger palpable. A ceramic figurine snapped between his fingers. He tossed the fragments into the fire.

Adrian racked his mind for a way to spare Sidony. If he told Gracchus he suspected she was a nocturne who could make others stronger, it would save her life but at an enormous cost. Gracchus would bleed her dry to take her nocturne powers. And once Adrian told Gracchus, he wouldn't be able to take back the words. He needed to keep her safe.

"This marriage legitimizes your claim to the monarchy, thus quashing the rebel's attempts to dethrone you. L'Ortagia is one of the oldest kingdoms, yet you would risk your alliance with them? You would make an enemy of one of your greatest allies by sacrificing her. And Princess Zara cares deeply for her sister. You would begin her life in Embury in mourning?"

Gracchus scoffed. "The magics demand this. They need to be fed. L'Ortagia's ties to Embury will cut off any remaining support for the rebels. *They'll* be blamed for the young princess's death. Zara will want her sister's life avenged, never knowing the true honor her sister will have wrought for Embury."

"True honor?" Adrian choked out.

"Our alliances will grow stronger once the rebels are blamed. They will lose support from our enemies, and we will crush them."

Adrian inhaled slowly, trying not to retch. He'd had many such reactions to Gracchus in the past. The king's ruthlessness knew no limits, but Adrian thought he'd seen them all by now.

"This is wrong, and there's too much risk. Find another way to gain a tactical advantage."

"Why do you carry on so on her behalf?" Gracchus took a sip of his wine, contemplating his nephew over the edge of his drink.

Adrian loosened his grip and backed away. He rubbed a hand across his eyes while he considered what to say. "You know why. I've disagreed with you about this since I found out what you were doing."

"No, no." Another swallow. "It's more than that. Perhaps a weakness for the fairer sex?"

"Your sacrifices are wrong, Uncle." Desperation pounded in his chest. "Your magic asks too high a price for something we will win anyway, given time. What if the nocturnes in L'Ortagia would rise against you in retaliation? Maybe Zara's their queen."

"Then they have good taste. Such powerful magic always has a high price. Lest you forget," Gracchus said.

It was how he explained his reasons for what he did to Adrian's family. *The price you pay.* Adrian wished he could take back the hand he had extended to his uncle those many years ago. He'd been desperate for family after his father died. He'd wanted to fulfill his father's desire to return to his homeland, so he'd embraced the uncle who had appeared with an incredible offer. His naiveté had cost them all their freedom.

"I speak from experience," Adrian said, a challenge in his eyes.

"You speak because I allow it. You speak because I needed an heir." Gracchus adjusted his neckcloth and set his jaw. "Even though Torwyn took your place, I still need you in this fight, nephew."

Adrian would be punished.

Fighting for Sidony's life is worth my uncle's retaliation.

The glass case that housed Gracchus's artifacts and implements was against the far wall. Adrian knew most of the items and what they did, but his uncle loved keeping him on his toes.

Gracchus's course was set; Adrian couldn't make it much worse. "You risk everything you worked for. Magic is no way to hold a kingdom."

"Magic brings me that much closer to transformation." Gracchus bared his teeth. "You seem anxious for your punishment tonight. Perhaps you have missed it?"

Adrian forced his body to still and retreated into his mind. He needed to get through whatever punishment his uncle would mete out, then he could find a way to prevent Sidony from being harmed. He was nearly numb by the time his uncle spoke at his ear.

"Adrian, come back. Let me show you something. Come over by the fire, dear nephew." Gracchus twisted the ring on his finger, his expression neutral.

Grounding his feet, Adrian took his place on the other side of the mantel. He kept his hands at his sides, his gaze unfocused. The threat of punishment was long past frightening to him. He had survived what Gracchus did, and would continue to do, for three reasons: one, Adrian needed to protect his family; two, he had vowed revenge; three, that he was the second in line after his cousin mattered, but not by much.

Tonight, he added a fourth reason to maintain his survival: Sidony.

Gracchus snapped his fingers in his Adrian's face. He focused on his uncle, his breaths ragged. Gracchus held out a glass ball the size of a large apple. Its surface was smooth, and it looked to be filled with smoke.

"It's an orb, powered by a nocturne who was an old friend. I use it to monitor activities in the kingdom. This time you will be the witness." Smoke in the crystal began to clear. A scene appeared.

Minah, Adrian's younger sister, wearing a simple dress and no shoes, was led from a doorway of a one-story building into a courtyard. She was taller and thinner than when he had last seen her. Her long, black hair was braided loosely, as several strands fell into her face. She stopped before a post in the yard, holding out her wrists to the guard. A thin chain bound her hands. The guard looped the chain over a peg set into the pole. Minah grabbed the pole and lowered her head between her arms.

Adrian's hands shook. Any remaining numbness washed away.

"No. Don't do this. Not her," Adrian begged, unable to take his eyes off his sister.

"We all make choices, nephew. See what yours have done?"

Desperate and raw, Adrian stared at the scene of his sister strung up on a pole in the middle of a dusty courtyard. His thoughts scattered. Pain rattled around his chest like a trapped bear. "How do I know this is happening now, and you haven't already done something to her?"

"You don't. Our agreement was your obedience for their safety. You broke it, now I will break her."

"She's been imprisoned by you for years. Isn't that enough?" Words rushed out, thoughts he'd only spoken to his uncle once before. "I've been obedient. Done everything you've asked."

He had been ready to take some punishment and wouldn't have argued, but now Gracchus was going to harm his sister.

"Show me you can stop her beating now or this is done. They were not to be hurt in any way," Adrian demanded. He had to get them free.

Gracchus took the orb and the view fogged over. He cupped the amulet he carried on a chain around his neck and traced it with his thumb, murmuring an incantation.

"The magics must be fed. That is how we rule Embury, and that is the price we pay." He handed the orb back to Adrian and walked over to his favorite chair. "Observe that she is unharmed, mostly. She will stay that way as long as you show me obedience toward our cause."

Adrian stared at the image of his sister, the orb once again cleared of smoke. She crouched at the base of the pole, sweat dotting her forehead, her hands shaking. He squinted at the picture, gritting his teeth in resignation. Minah raised her head, tears streaming down her cheeks, and struggled to stand. She held her head high, and Adrian took it as a sign that she was not beaten down. Not yet.

He peered into the windows of the building that circled the courtyard, desperate for a glimpse of his mother. There. Off to the side, seated at the edge of the porch, was a woman with silvered hair who sat in a rocking chair. When his sister walked past her, she didn't acknowledge her. She kept rocking, her eyes vacant.

"You have my obedience, Uncle." He forced himself to say the words slowly. "Do not harm them again."

"That is entirely up to you, Adrian."

CHAPTER SEVEN

Mondelac Castle
Kingdom of L'Ortagia
June 1784

*S*idony's heart sank for her sister.

Prince Torwyn and Prince Adrian had arrived this morning, accompanied by several courtiers, guards, and servants. After a chance to refresh themselves, they'd been ushered into the scarlet room for a reception.

The receiving line was long, based on L'Ortagian protocol as well as negotiated dealings with the Emburian court. Sidony stood next to Zara, who was next to their mother, the queen. Such lines were generally uneventful.

Zara's betrothed was a self-obsessed boor. Within minutes of making Torwyn's acquaintance, he'd listed for Sidony an exhaustive number of accomplishments, many of which were the defeat of some of his countrymen.

"The rebels need a firm hand," Torwyn said. His wig was brilliantly white, in stark contrast to his thick, black brows. He'd be considered handsome, if not for the ease with which his mouth pulled into a slight sneer. His clothing was more fashionable than Adrian's, his frock coat embroidered with glossy thread, and he wore a jeweled neck pin larger than an egg.

Sidony had half a mind to root for the rabble-rousers in Embury. She wondered how Adrian stood being in his presence.

The prince appeared to have little in common with his cousin, save for his decisive glare and coloring.

Torwyn's interest in Sidony consisted of verifying her age. Sidony was nearly desperate enough to feign a headache to avoid another moment in Prince Torwyn's presence.

She was about to do so when Marlowe, Lord Sullivan, who had been waiting at the prince's elbow, stepped forward to whisper in Torwyn's ear. The prince smiled and quickly excused himself, walking off with the tall, auburn-haired baron.

"Lucia, I think I'll check on the plans for tonight's entertainment," Sidony said to her lady-in-waiting. She turned, Lucia at her side, and spotted Adrian among a group of courtiers.

He kept to the edge of the circle, a neutral expression on his face. When he caught her watching him, he bowed slightly and caught up to her.

"I need to talk to you," he said in a low tone.

"I have a few minutes," she replied coolly, as if she'd forgotten what it was like to be around him, or, rather, alone with him.

It was terrible and wonderful, all at the same time. It would have been simpler had he been an attractive courtier. They could have danced a bit, flirted a lot, and then it would end when he departed for Embury. Instead, she was left with a sense of *what if* every time she was around him.

What if they hadn't met outside the ball? What if she'd

figured out who he was before she'd kissed him? What if he wasn't the king's spy?

A younger man stood two feet to Adrian's side, similar to how Lord Sullivan had stayed close to Torwyn. Catching her gaze, Adrian indicated the man. "That's Lieutenant Wills."

"Yes, I seem to remember him from the receiving line," she said, wondering where this was going.

"You're a lovely dancer, Sidony," Adrian said.

Her smile was so tight, her face powder could settle into it. "Ah, there's the charming brigand." Damn him.

What if they'd met in a different way and he could actually court her? What if the rumors about him being the king's spy weren't true? Was he any different than Prince Torwyn and King Gracchus? Underneath his charm and good looks, was he just as shallow and unconscionable as they were?

He cursed under his breath. "I'll find you tomorrow. Meet me before the ceremony?"

She wanted to refuse him. Manners and protocol prevented her from doing so, but she resolved to find a way.

"Of course."

His eyes narrowed in a look he shared with his odious cousin. "I assure you, it's important."

"I'm sure it is." Sidony stiffened her spine. "Now, if you'll excuse me, I have to help prepare for tonight's entertainment."

CHAPTER EIGHT

*T*he rest of the evening consisted of a formal dinner, followed by dancing. Sidony had arranged for the musicians to perform traditional Emburian songs. After their awkward conversation at the reception, she hadn't anticipated talking much with Adrian again. They'd been paired for a contredanse, but aside from him complimenting her song choices, he spoke little to her.

Zara had retired to her room after dancing with Prince Torwyn twice. Sidony had stayed, even suffering through a dance with the prince.

Lucia stood next to Sidony when she knocked on the door to Zara's suite later that evening. Lucia gave her a kind smile, her wide, brown eyes tired, and lifted a plate-sized tin.

"Thank you," Sidony said. "You always know just the thing."

"She mentioned wanting to see you if you weren't too tired tonight," Lucia said. Her delicate brows raised slightly, as if Sidony would ever ignore one of Zara's requests.

Zara answered the door, already in her nightclothes, relief plain on her face.

"Come in." She reached for the tin. "Ah, Lucia. You think of everything."

Lucia paused in the hall, her sharp gaze missing nothing in Zara's tear-streaked face. "Best to get it all out tonight. Face tomorrow with resolve."

Zara's fingers twitched as she straightened her neckline. "You are right," she said.

Lucia padded off, and Zara shut the door, pulling Sidony in for a quick hug once they were alone.

"I already miss you," Sidony said.

"Don't start. I just got myself pulled together. Come on."

They crossed to the canopied bed and crawled up. Zara leaned back against her headboard and smoothed the sheet across her chest. Sidony reclined against the footboard, slippers tossed behind her.

Sidony opened the package of sweets, offering them to her sister.

"Lucia is most indispensable." Zara leaned forward and took one of the treats.

"Second only to my sister." Sidony tucked her feet under her, sucking on her own treat. "How are you?"

Zara hesitated, frustration and something else etched in her features. "I've come to a decision. I won't do it."

"Won't get married? Will you refuse him at the altar?" Sidony asked, wincing.

"I'd like to," Zara said. "I'd love to refuse him right to his smug face. But, no. I have a different plan. You have to promise me you won't tell anyone anything about what I'm going to say."

Sidony nodded, used to keeping secrets over the years, though they tended to be her own.

"Promise me. Say it."

Usually Sidony was the one known to bring dramatics to a

situation. Despite weeks of preparing for the inevitable, Zara had apparently reached her breaking point.

Sidony took her sister's hands in hers, squeezing gently. "I swear not to repeat anything you tell me tonight."

Zara squeezed back and pulled her hands free.

"Very well. I have been in correspondence with a leader of the rebellion in Embury, and I'll be leaving with him tomorrow. We are staging it to look like a kidnapping. I wanted you to know that I'll be safe."

Sidony choked on the sweet in her mouth. Eyes wide, Zara shook her until she spat out the sugary morsel.

When she could draw an even breath, she stared at her sister. "No, Zara. You can't do this. You can't just run off."

"I've already agreed to it. Everything is set." Zara's fingers twitched again, but she gripped them with her other hand.

"Zara, this is madness. You have to reconsider. Don't leave with them. You don't even know them. Just tonight Torwyn told me about how much strife they cause in Embury."

Her sister lifted her chin. "I'm well aware. We've heard only a fraction of the truth of what has been happening. Besides, why would it make sense to take Torwyn's side?"

Sidony nodded. Zara had a point. "It doesn't matter. You can't put yourself in danger like that. They're just using you to get to him."

Zara crossed her arms. "I'm aware of that. That's part of the appeal."

Heat crawled up Sidony's neck. "Are you doing this to thumb your nose at Mother? You realize you'll put us all in jeopardy with your actions."

"It's not about getting back at her, though I thought you'd take my side—"

"—I do!"

Zara's hand slashed, cutting her off. "This is much bigger

than my squabbles with her. This is for our country's future. We cannot ally with Embury like this."

Sidony sat back and reached for another sweet. Thoughts swirled but she was overwhelmed by her sister's plan.

"Have you truly thought through all of this?" she asked Zara.

"Yes! I've thought of little else. I have to do something."

Sidony threw her hands up. "Are you coming back? Are you just going to join a band of merry men in the forest? Zara, there has to be another way."

Tears welled in Zara's eyes, and Sidony was done for. She'd only seen her sister cry twice: when their father died and after their mother told Zara she was to wed. Since that day, Zara had seemed like a hollowed-out version of herself.

Zara shook her head. "I've gone over every angle. Maybe if I had more time, more resources, I could find another way, but there isn't any. I have to do this. And I need your help. I need you to keep my secret while I'm gone."

"How long will you be gone? Can you get a message to me? Will this be days? Weeks?"

Zara brushed a tear off her cheek. "It could be months. I won't return until I have a different solution."

Sidony made a decision in that moment. Her mother and sister may say they found her impulsive, but she knew she was making the only choice she had.

"Promise me you'll be safe. Come back as soon as you can."

Zara hugged her close, squeezing her hard. "Thank you, Sidony. I knew you would understand why I have to do this."

"I don't understand any of it, but I trust that you do."

Zara gave a watery laugh, and finally Sidony's own tears broke free.

CHAPTER NINE

*A*drian doubted Sidony would show, but there she stood in the courtyard, sunlight catching her hair so the strands shone like gold. Her demeanor was dimmed, her mouth slightly downturned, the dimple in her cheek absent. The only times he'd seen it was when he'd arrived and when they'd danced together last night. That seemed fitting, unfortunately.

He rubbed a finger across his lips. His presence in her life would only bring her pain.

Today, he had to help her.

Adrian turned back to Torwyn, who had arrived earlier this morning. He wore a decorative breastplate of black armor, emblazoned with Gracchus's crest. His cousin was not quite his height but weighed a good stone or two more. On the occasions they were sparring partners, Adrian's arms and shoulders would ache for days.

"You seem pleased," Adrian said. They were paired together on certain missions for the king. Adrian had had to temper Torwyn's aggression more than once.

"I'm meeting with the queen later for a prenuptial tea."

Torwyn flicked a speck of dust from his armor. "I find I'm enjoying this without my father's presence. He should turn more of the running of the kingdom over to me."

Gracchus had a vitality that belied his age. Barring accidents, Torwyn would be waiting several years before assuming the throne.

"I'm sure you will enjoy it. The L'Ortagians are planning a grand event."

"I should hope so." Torwyn glared at the crowd milling about the middle of the courtyard, his dark scowl causing a few guests to give him a wide berth. "Any surprises out here?"

They walked to the side of the entrance of the main bailey. As he watched, guards stopped each wagon or carriage to inspect it, greet the inhabitants, or both.

Adrian had been assigned to use his powers to detect rebel plots that sought to ruin the wedding. He doubted they'd make such a play, given how few resources they had in Embury. To be able to travel outside the kingdom and disrupt the ceremony would be nigh impossible. He wished they'd try, though.

He scanned out with his senses, catching snippets of conversation, but finding no overt hostility. It drained him to use his powers widely and across the sheer number of people on the castle grounds. But dancing with Sidony had expanded his powers last night. He didn't have to concentrate to the exclusion of anything else. He could release them like he was exhaling. All five out, then in.

He was nearly convinced she was unaware of it; Sidony's expansive power seemed to flow out of her effortlessly too. Yesterday it had happened when she'd smiled at him in the receiving line. She'd shown no reaction, but he'd gotten a surge. Maybe she was just that good.

Using his powers, he spotted a group of hunters gathered at the edge of the woods surrounding the castle. From this distance, their faces were too vague to identify. They were

nearly silent, which made identification that much more difficult. Perhaps they wanted to sell their game to the castle
kitchens. He counted several hares and a couple larger fowls.
They could surely use the extra food. He'd track them again
after talking with Sidony about hunters in the area to be sure.

"None," he told Torwyn.

The prince grunted in acknowledgment.

"Update me if anything changes." He left Torwyn to
his post.

Adrian crossed the path of wagons and carriages and met
Marlowe by a small well in the courtyard.

"Don't do it." Marlowe's flinty gaze pinned him.

"Look at her. I won't let him hurt her." Adrian kept his voice
low, his hands at his sides, striving to appear relaxed. The back
of his throat burned.

Both men turned to watch the princess, who was
surrounded by a group of young children. One handed her a
posy. She plucked the side of her skirt, and they mimicked her,
practicing their curtsies. Sidony laughed and directed one into
a turn. Her lady-in-waiting stood behind her and pressed her
lips together, clearly amused but trying not to laugh.

Sidony's enchanting nature would be powerful fuel for the
king's dark magics.

Her ability to amplify powers would make her irresistible.
And in a kingdom open to supernatural beings, she'd be treated
with reverence, until he sacrificed her.

"Does Gracchus know she's a nocturne?" he asked Marlowe.
It was a risky question, but she was already in grave danger.
Marlowe was perhaps better than Adrian at weighing the odds.

"He isn't certain of it." Marlowe peered into the well, his
back to the princess once again. "You risk your family."

Marlowe was probably right. Warning Sidony might not
work and could endanger his plans to save his sister and
mother, if the king found out what he'd done.

Sidony bent down, and the children tucked flowers into her hair. She, in turn, pulled flowers from the posy to set into their braids. It was bucolic enough for a painting. He remembered his sister running around the house with flowers tucked into her braids after playing outside.

He set his jaw. "Minah and my mother wouldn't want me to let the king sacrifice her."

"Live long enough and you won't let a pretty face stand in your way." Marlowe brushed a speck of dust off his coat.

"Be careful or your bitterness will swallow you whole, Marlowe."

"It hasn't yet."

Adrian moved toward Sidony, but Marlowe stopped him with a hand on his arm. "Don't stay too long."

Adrian nodded. As he approached, Sidony shooed the children away. Her smile faded.

"Prince Adrian, have all the guests from Embury arrived?"

"Not quite." He needed to get her alone. In the courtyard, they made a spectacle amid the teeming carriages. "The queen said you gave the most entertaining tours of the castle. Would you grant me one?"

She paused, and he thought she might refuse him despite agreeing to meet last night. "Haven't you seen it already?"

Her lady-in-waiting gasped at Sidony's bluntness. Adrian pushed ahead. "I've yet to see the royal apartments. I was saving them for you."

Sidony blinked up at him. "By all means, let me show you." She tugged him toward the open doorway. Before they went inside, she called over her shoulder, "Lucia, I need you to check that everything is in readiness for tomorrow's performance."

Now he'd have an opportunity to convince her to leave.

～

"AND THIS IS MY SUITE." Sidony stopped in front of her door. Two maids carrying linens passed them in the hallway.

"May we have a moment of privacy?" Adrian asked. "I need to talk with you."

She frowned at him. He'd been cordial, asking questions about this wing of the castle. Though he'd been polite, he practically thrummed with nervous energy.

"Very well." Sidony opened her door and beckoned for Adrian to follow. Once he was inside, she closed it and crossed her arms.

"What do you want?" Her nerves were already strained being around him and trying to act normal, whatever that meant.

"Sidony, I..." He walked the perimeter of the space, steering clear of the bed, and returned to her. They stood in the sitting area of her chamber. A pair of pink-and-cream striped chairs faced a velvet divan. Her desk was tucked under one of the narrow windows, scripts piled up across the left side.

"We're alone," she prompted.

He nodded and crossed to her, holding out his hands, palms up. She put her hands in his. Her cold fingers tingled against his warmth. They'd held hands briefly the night before, light touches while they danced. This was entirely different. She slid her hands along his, grateful and not a little bit greedy to be able to touch him.

"Sidony, you have to leave Mondelac after the wedding, preferably leave L'Ortagia. Take a trip somewhere, anywhere. But you can't stay here."

"What are you talking about? This is my home. My sister is leaving. I can't leave too."

He pressed his lips together. "I need you to believe me that the threat against you is real. You won't be safe here."

Sidony squeezed his hands almost reflexively. Cold snaked

across her shoulders, making her shiver. "What is going on?" Her mind raced. Why would anyone wish to harm her?

"Sidony, your nocturne gifts make you a target for powerful people. I can't protect you."

She flushed with embarrassment. "I'm not a nocturne. What are you talking about?"

Adrian's gaze searched her face, his expression imploring. She'd never seen him so open. Why did it have to be now? They had to get back to the rest of the guests and preparations. In a few days he'd be leaving again.

"Never mind about that," he said with a note of impatience. "You cannot go to Embury, not even to visit, and it would be best if you left right after the wedding."

She shook her head. There was too much going on. She didn't know how to take a possible threat on her life on top of what Zara had shared with her last night. How could she leave after a wedding if it wasn't going to happen?

"I've lived with the fear of kidnapping and assassination over my head my entire life. You have to give me more information."

He ran a hand over his hair. "I can't give you much more aside from assuring you the threat is quite real. The king... thirsts for power and has his eyes on you to help him acquire more of it. I can tell your mother when it is safe for you to return."

"I've never met him, nor would I help him. You are wasting my time. What do I do with a vague threat?"

"The threat is very real. Your sister's marriage helps the king very much. Stay away from Embury. Be on guard if you stay here."

She threw up her hands. "If you wanted me to stay away from you, you could just say it. I wasn't intending on visiting my sister. The queen won't allow it."

Adrian winced. "I had to warn you."

"Why?" she asked, sick of the whole set of circumstances between them.

His face shuttered, as if to ward off—or keep in—some emotion.

"Is this some attempt to assuage your guilt? Are you trying to protect me? Why? I'm just a silly girl, just a chess piece. But you've gone to a lot of trouble to warn me."

He shook his head, his stare hard.

"Whatever you feel for me, I don't need to hear it. But you could at least do me the courtesy of acknowledging it." Sidony clenched her fists, her lower lip trembling.

"Sidony." His lips parted and she stared at his mouth.

A flare of hope burned low in her belly. "Yes?"

Adrian stepped closer and kissed her. *Finally.*

Her hands crept to his chest, lips molding to his, kissing him back. Part of her wanted to push him away so he could know the torture she'd been feeling since that first night. But she couldn't. Relief and something more rushed through her, heating her limbs. She'd wanted to be back in his arms, held against him again for weeks. There couldn't be anything between them, but it didn't stop her from wanting it.

He broke away. One of his hands pressed hers against his heart. "You deserve better than this."

She nodded, but his words didn't stop her eyes from burning. She was a fool. "Was that a goodbye kiss?"

He didn't hesitate before responding. "It has to be." Adrian stepped away from her, dropping their hands. "Consider my request."

"How long?" She brushed at her cheek, catching a tear that had managed to fall.

"Maybe a year. Once Zara is settled at Blackthorne for several months, you should be safe."

When he left, she held still, her gaze lighting on the familiar objects in her quarters, a pair of silk gloves she'd worn this morning resting across the back of a chair, a miniature of her and Zara when they'd been younger, and a sash she'd been given by one of the theatre houses when she'd become a patroness. She collapsed into her favorite chair, her shoulders sagging as if pulled by one of her heavy court gowns.

All her pent-up emotion from the last few weeks rose inside her. She gasped as the tears fell, harsh sobs nearly cutting her from within.

Once the largest wave had passed, she worked to regain her composure. They had guests, a formal dinner, and she didn't want to worry Zara.

Sidony went to her vanity and poured water over one of the cloths at the wash basin. She pressed the cool fabric to her heated face and breathed, resolving not to spend another moment crying over a man who could never be hers.

CHAPTER TEN

Once Adrian left Sidony's suite, he continued down the rug-lined corridor. If he hadn't, he would have rested his head against her door. Anything to be near her.

Almost on instinct, his senses stretched out. The ragged sounds of her weeping, the thump of her heartbeat, and the image of her curled up in a chair would haunt him. His gut clenched. He could bring her no comfort. He focused on her promise to stay away from Embury, knowing that she'd taken his warning seriously.

The back of his neck tightened as he strode down the hallway, the sensation crawling across his head until it pounded. Total honesty with her wouldn't keep his family safe. He had to find the orb and use it to locate his family. For years Gracchus had hidden them, and if Adrian didn't hurry, he could lose them again.

His hands shook when he pulled back his powers. That had never happened before.

Adrian had been aware of his own attraction to her, but she surprised him with her declaration of...*feelings*. If he had any sense of what he felt anymore, of what a tender emotion was, he was sure he would feel it for her. The closest he'd come to feeling anything for anyone since he'd come to Embury were the times he'd spent with her.

And he'd kissed her because he'd had to. She'd melted against him, making him ache with want.

Have to get away from her.

He funneled his powers back to his reserves, as they weren't needed now. He similarly tamped down his emotions.

Continuing along the wing of Mondelac Castle, he ended up walking a full circle. His head pounded harder. Each time he walked away, he found himself coming back to her.

It can't happen.

As he went past Sidony's rooms, he sensed she was no longer there. Lucia had likely dragged her to the wedding preparations. He needed to report to Torwyn anyway, before his absence was noted. He had formal attire to change into before the evening's meal.

Just as he turned another corridor, he heard several footfalls and the rattle of a key.

He paused at one of the windows and sent out his senses. The setting sun shone through the stained glass, casting muted colors across the carpet at his feet. Mondelac was old but had extravagant touches. His uncle had taken extravagance to an extreme in Embury, but Mondelac had a history that had been preserved and was connected to the people living here.

Several doors down, he heard a familiar voice. He pushed harder and caught a glimpse of a group of soldiers clustered in a small room with Zara.

Adrian drew his sword and approached the door of the small room. He cast his senses inside, spotting Zara's wedding gown in one corner on a dressing form. A group of Emburian rebel soldiers held Zara. She stood with her back to one of the men and faced who Adrian presumed was the leader.

The tall man spoke again, in a language he didn't know. But

Adrian recognized the brown-haired man as Callum, one of the rebel leaders and rumored to be one of the Lost Princes of Embury.

Strangely, he couldn't see Zara's lower half, or those of the group of rebels behind her. There was a sparking oval in front of them, somehow obscuring part of their bodies. Adrian had heard of nocturnes who were able to cast mystical portals. Adrian tightened his grip on his sword.

The rebels *had* been plotting something for the royal wedding. They were about to steal the princess away.

Adrian strode into the room, sword ready. Quickly banking their surprised looks, the group of rebels backed farther into the portal. He couldn't read the expression on Zara's face. Callum put her behind him and spoke to the group.

The rebels must be desperate, to resort to kidnapping. Though they lacked resources, they made up for them with courage and passion for their cause. Adrian faced a determined group of soldiers.

Prince Callum stepped over the edge of the sparking portal and into the room. Sword drawn, Adrian charged him. They parried thrusts, dodging articles of furniture and the dress model in the room. Adrian avoided stepping on the train that was spread out behind Zara's wedding gown. He kicked it aside.

Adrian had never faced Callum, but he had seen the leader fight and knew he was a formidable opponent. A female soldier in the group chanted, likely part of the spell. He struck at Callum repeatedly, trying to get to Zara, but Callum dodged and parried his blows. Adrian landed a cut on Callum's forearm and another into his left shoulder.

Callum staggered back and Adrian prepared to follow. Too late, he fell for a feint and Callum's sword sliced down Adrian's side. Blood flowed from both their wounds, but Callum didn't press his advantage.

Adrian held a hand to his bleeding side and peered at the portal. Though his heart wasn't in the words, he said, between panted breaths, "You cannot have her, rebel."

A crackling sound intensified and Callum froze.

The soldiers in the portal scuffled with Zara, one holding her tightly at his front.

"Unhand me! Put me down!" Zara shouted. The soldier clamped a hand across her mouth, and Adrian gritted his teeth.

He charged Callum, only half hearing the other man's order to stop the chant. Circling around slightly, he attacked, raining blows while Callum shouted strange words. Callum's face clouded with rage, but his sword fighting remained unmatched.

He lunged at Adrian, stabbing him along the top of his shoulder. He struck again and got in another hit along the top of Adrian's shoulder. The chanting and crackling noises crowded the space in the room. But then only the sound of their swords clanging remained. The portal had shut. Zara had gotten free of both the soldiers and the portal.

Callum grimaced at the spot where they portal had been, then pivoted and beckoned Adrian to follow. His eyes widened at the sound of rustling material. Callum shook his head just slightly. By standing on the dress, he'd effectively be telegraphing his moves, giving him another disadvantage.

"Princess Zara, stay there," Adrian said from his corner of the room.

Zara's gaze darted between the two men. With the princess between them, both men held their swords steady.

She turned and launched herself at Callum, landing on his back. Clutching his coat with one hand, she rained blows across his upper body. "Let him go! He's only trying to protect me! Stop!"

Adrian backed up, unwilling to risk harming the princess, although she did an admirable job attacking her would-be kidnapper. Her dark hair swung free as she grappled in her day gown, demonstrating a fierceness that seemed natural to her.

Callum grunted and charged Adrian, bringing his sword down again. Adrian side-stepped but was a hair slower than the rebel. Callum grabbed his arm, yanked him close, and slammed the hilt of his sword into the back of Adrian's head.

Adrian sank to the floor.

ADRIAN AWOKE TO find he was alone in the room. He lay on the floor, the wound on his head oozing blood at a slow trickle. His side burned, his shirt already wet with blood. His shoulder stung, but he didn't think the wound was very deep. Head throbbing with pain, he couldn't spare a thought for the rest of this body. He guessed he'd been unconscious for only a quarter hour. The blood on the carpet was still warm.

He sat up, pulling out a handkerchief to press to his bleeding head. He needed to alert the castle guards of Zara's kidnapping. *Right?* There was every chance her abductor had already been caught before leaving the castle with her. It would be nigh impossible to get a hostage out of a castle full of guests.

Adrian took a deep breath and pushed to a stand, steadying himself against the bed. Before reaching the door, he considered calling out to a passing servant, but he didn't hear any in the hall outside. Callum must have picked the timing of Zara's kidnapping deliberately. While the castle was abuzz with guests, most of the staff would be overloaded with work, preparing for the grand meal served in the next half hour. He looked over his shoulder to where he'd seen the portal. Maybe Callum had been able to reopen it and they'd left that way.

His dizziness returned, and Adrian sat on the edge of the bed. He worried about Zara, but something nagged at his memory. His bash on the head slowed his thoughts, but he tried to recall what he knew of the rebel leader. Callum was known for being fair and honorable. Adrian knew firsthand that those traits would make it more difficult for him to defeat Gracchus, but honorable men did not abandon their principles easily.

Callum had knocked him out and left him when he could have easily killed him. Also, when Adrian had spotted Zara in the portal, he'd been surprised that she was conscious and neither bound nor gagged. The rebel leader was pragmatic. If his goal was to steal the princess, the rebels could have trussed her up and left with her. Instead, Callum had let her walk on her own. If Adrian hadn't seen her attacking Callum, he might have thought she was participating in her own kidnapping.

His head swam as he considered the rebel's behavior.

None of Callum's actions were the behavior of a cold-blooded kidnapper or a royal assassin. What did the rebel leader want with her? Zara was clearly worth more to the rebels alive than dead, as Adrian sensed that Callum valued her. In fending off her attacks, he'd taken pains not to hurt her. He could have easily struck her to ensure submission, not that Adrian approved of striking women.

He shook his head, but there it was, a nagging sense of mercy and protection from a man he should consider his enemy.

But Callum wasn't. That saying about "the enemy of my enemy" applied. Adrian could use Zara's kidnapping to his advantage. Anything that thwarted his uncle's ambitions would help his own cause, wouldn't it? If Callum had been able to escape with Zara, that could distract Gracchus long enough so that Adrian could get the orb and find his family on his own. Was it worth the risks to Zara's safety?

That brought him up short. He grabbed his sword off the floor and stumbled to the door.

He opened it to find Molly, one of the maids, standing on

the other side with a satchel clutched in her arms. He spotted sewing supplies inside.

She gaped at him. "Your Highness, is Princess Zara here? I'm to help with another fitting."

Adrian stepped in front of the bloodstained carpet, keeping his left arm behind the door. A wave of dizziness hit him, and he leaned against the frame. "She's not here."

The back of his neck was wet with blood. Hopefully none of it showed on his face. The cut on his arm no longer stung, but blood had seeped through his coat and spattered across his dark breeches.

"I wonder where she could be then." Molly's eyes went wide. "The princess is always prompt. I'll put this away and fit her later."

She backed up and retreated down the hallway. Once she was gone, he dashed out of the room, stretching out his senses to see if he could locate Zara.

He caught a hint of Zara and Callum's scents in a nearby servant stairwell, and he ran toward it. Their scents lingered, and he chased after them, his head and side throbbing. At the bottom, the door swung open into the courtyard. He ran out a few steps, sweeping through each wagon that lined the edge of the wall. Three were in a row at the gates. A set of guards were doing inspections before each wagon could leave.

There. Zara sat in the second wagon.

Callum sat in the front, a hat pulled low over his brow, his back hunched. Zara was crouched inside the wagon in front of another woman who wore a rough, woolen coat. He recognized her from the group of hunters that he'd spotted outside the castle earlier in the day and then again in the portal.

He stepped toward them, his body still in the shadow the castle cast over the courtyard.

Inside the wagon, Zara wore a cloak across her head and shoulders and sat between the front of the wagon and a load of casks of wine. She stared at a ring, her lips moving soundlessly.

Their wagon had advanced to the front of the line. Callum climbed down and ambled around the side of the wagon, his voice pitched gravelly and in a north county accent of Embury. The guard paced around the wagon, not appearing to suspect that he stood two feet from the rebel leader.

Zara's hands and mouth were unbound. Her entire focus was on the ring. He strained harder to hear her speaking softly to the woman.

"It's him, isn't it? He's alive?" Zara ran her thumb over the ring. It was an intaglio; one Gracchus had sought across every county in Embury. Callum must have handed it to the woman when he'd disguised himself.

"Yes," the woman replied. She closed her hand over the ring, looking up at Zara, a grim set to her features. The princess held their safety in her hands. At that moment, she could call out and save herself.

Adrian halted his steps as he watched Callum open one of the back flaps of the wagon and offer a cask to Wills.

Of course, the lieutenant refused it. A half smile tilted Adrian's lips.

Zara turned her face away so Wills wouldn't see her. She pulled her cloak lower across her jaw, her other hand tucking in her loose strands of hair.

The flap lowered, and Zara said nothing.

Adrian again scanned the wagon, looking for a weapon that might be held against her. He came up short. Of her own free will, she stayed silent as the wagon rumbled across the bridge and under the gate.

The princess had apparently made her choice. She didn't want to be rescued.

CHAPTER ELEVEN

"*Your* Highness, let's get you dressed." Lucia stood outside Sidony's door, her maids Molly and Elise brushing past her to quickly begin readying the princess for the prenuptial dinner.

"Come in, come in," Sidony said. "I needed some time..." She didn't want to say much more in front of her maids.

Lucia stepped into the room, her knowing gaze taking in Sidony's face. "How did your tour go with the prince?"

"As well as I thought," Sidony said, unsure how to explain any of it.

"Hmm." Lucia's full lips set tightly together.

Sidony hadn't broached the subject of Adrian with her lady-in-waiting, but she knew her sensible friend would have told her to put her feelings aside.

"I've decided to take a trip after the wedding celebrations."

Molly began fastening the buttons along the back of Sidony's green silk dress.

"Will you need me to accompany you?" Lucia asked.

"Very much." Sidony held up her hair. She blew out a breath, preparing her story. "I'm taking my own Grand Tour."

She forced the next words out, wanting them to be true. "I plan to look for a husband during my travels. Obviously, this would all need the queen's approval."

"Of course." The maid smoothed her dress along the back. "Your sister's wedding must have put ideas in your head I never thought I'd hear."

Their gazes met in the mirror. "You're the first I've told. Better I find a husband myself." Sidony searched the floor for her slippers, needing to change the subject. "We can talk more about it after dinner."

"Certainly." Lucia gave her shoulder a light pat. "I'll put some ideas together. Elise, she's ready for you."

That was Sidony's cue to sit at her dressing table so Elise could do her hair. "Lucia, has Zara gone down to dinner yet?"

"Let me check on her progress."

Sidony waited while Elise quickly touched up the curls in her coiffure, persuading her to keep a few of the children's blossoms from earlier tucked in. Elise dusted her hair lightly with powder while Sidony held a small mask over her face and a sheet draped over her gown. Her mother had insisted the princesses wear their hair in the more formal style for the wedding festivities. For once, Sidony was grateful for face powder as it would disguise the redness around her eyes.

She was ready by the time Lucia returned, distress marking the girl's features. Lucia handed her a folded piece of paper:

Please excuse me for the next hour, as I will be resting before the evening meal. –Zara

"Elise and Molly, thank you. That will be all."

She's done it.

Sidony wished she'd been able to say goodbye to her sister. For the moment, she needed to buy her time to get away.

Once the maids left, Sidony held up the note and tried to ignore the pounding of her heart. "What does this mean?"

"I found Francis in the hall and she gave it to me. Said Her

Highness would get ready herself before coming down to dinner."

"Has anyone unlocked her door?" Sidony's brows raised so high, flecks of powder landed on her chest.

"I didn't bring my keys."

Sidony shrugged. "I'm sure she'll be down before too long."

"Should we be alarmed?" Lucia asked.

"Not yet. Perhaps she wanted time to herself."

CHAPTER TWELVE

*S*idony smiled tightly at the distantly related earl seated across from her. Her cheeks hurt, and she kept dropping her hand to her lap to keep from tapping her utensil against her plate. She waited for the prenuptial dinner to be interrupted with cries that the princess was missing. Zara could make progress on her escape during what was surely the longest meal ever served in the banquet hall. At least the earl did not require her to participate in their conversation. He handled it all by himself.

Sidony wanted Zara to have the time she needed to do whatever she planned about her wedding. She was glad her sister was finally taking a stand, but her timing was terrible.

As the minutes crawled and Zara did not appear, Sidony worried she had made the wrong decision and jeopardized her sister's safety. Would Zara be safe with a group of rebels? Should she have tried harder to stop her?

Her mother was likely furious. Sidony hadn't missed the queen's icy acknowledgment of her arrival when she'd taken her seat just before the first course.

Adrian had yet to show up at the banquet either. When

Sidony first sat down, guests had made jokes about the bride already avoiding the marriage bed. Polite, awkward laughter had followed.

She scanned the hall, waiting for Adrian to walk in or Lucia to signal her as to her sister's absence. At the head table, the conversations were boisterous. Her uncle Bear and his wife, Lady Bieranne, were seated close to her mother, Lady Bieranne, a never-ending font of chatter. From her mother's pinched expression, Bieranne was succeeding at talking. Prince Torwyn sat to her mother's left, socializing with the other guests. The spot on her mother's right, reserved for Zara, was empty.

Oddly, the L'Ortagians seated with Torwyn wore wary expressions, their smiles not quite reaching their eyes. The few Emburian courtiers at her table said little but seemed to absorb every word. They were an ambitious, assessing bunch.

When Adrian entered the banquet hall, Sidony excused herself and rose to greet him. He was to sit at the table the farthest away from her, next to other dignitaries. She took his arm and pulled him into the corridor near the end of the table, by the kitchens.

"Where have you been?" she asked.

"I can't explain right now." He frowned at the dining hall. "Do you know where Zara is?"

"Not here." Sidony repeated her story about Zara's intentions to rest after the day's long wedding preparations. She added, "You were both absent. It was hard to explain to everyone where you both disappeared to."

Their conversation had attracted the attention of nearby guests, some of whom watched them openly.

Sidony strove for a pleasant expression while speaking through gritted teeth. "Where have you been?"

Before he could answer, her mother's voice rose above the din.

"My heir must be busy with preparations." Isabeau effectively reset their guests' attention back to herself.

"I did a round of the castle grounds before coming to dinner." Adrian straightened. "And I had to change before dinner."

"Why?"

The muscles in his arm tensed. Sidony snatched her hand away, unaware she had been touching him. He checked her movement.

Adrian wouldn't meet her gaze. He also seemed to be favoring his left side. What was going on? Sidony glanced at the tables, her heart in her throat as the servants brought out another round of dishes. Did Adrian know anything about Zara's whereabouts?

"Come, we can't miss another course." She needed him distracted by the dinner.

Adrian let her lead him to his seat. He bowed to the queen, who inclined her head. Before he took his chair, he turned to Sidony and kissed the back of her hand.

His eyes were fathomless pools. "I'm sorry, Sidony." His words were pitched for her ears alone. That, along with his courtly gesture, nearly undid her.

She pulled away and walked back to her table, emotion welling up. Her eyes stung. She pictured the children she'd played with in the courtyard earlier so as not to cry. She couldn't let it show, but maintaining her composure drained her. Lucia appeared at her side at the end of the course.

"The maids can't find her," Lucia whispered in her ear. "None of them have seen her for hours. Sidony, I'm worried."

"I'm sure it's nothing." As she turned to speak to Lucia, her gaze was drawn to Adrian again. He was watching her too. Now was not the time to focus on him. "Let's wait until after the meal. Then we can alert my mother."

"Yes, Your Highness." Lucia retreated to her seat at the far table. Sidony imagined Lucia had arranged for the maids to give her regular updates. It really was too bad Sidony couldn't tell her lady-in-waiting what was going on. Lucia was quite shrewd. She'd have had a dozen ideas about how to help Zara succeed in her plan.

Sidony turned to her left, hoping to catch her mother's eye at the head table. The queen raised her glass, her gaze sweeping the room. Sidony tried to signal her, but her mother ignored her. "To the bride and groom!"

The guests in the banquet hall raised their cups, echoing the queen's cheer.

A crash sounded behind her, at the table where Zara was supposed to be sitting. Adrian leaped over his table and was running toward Sidony.

"Get down!"

An explosion rocked the castle, breaking the row of stained glass windows that lined the top of the hall. Glass shattered across the room.

CHAPTER THIRTEEN

*S*creams filled the banquet hall, the initial chaos overloading Adrian's senses. As he had been seated at the table closest to the windows, his supernatural senses had picked up on the smell of burning fuses in the courtyard outside.

He had a few cuts on the back of his neck and hands from the falling shards. He'd bandaged his previous wounds before coming down to dinner but barely felt his injuries. He had to get to Sidony. Though smoke poured in through the broken windows, the fire was from a building outside.

He hadn't been able to get to her in time. Sidony crouched on the floor by an elderly noblewoman. Her lady-in-waiting assisted guests away from the smoke-filled room. He stumbled over to Sidony, searching her with his senses, and found several scratches. One high on her forehead was bleeding.

Larger pieces of glass had fallen on guests seated at the middle table. The sharp tang of blood filled the air. Adrian shook his head to clear it. Servants filled the room, attending to the injured. Guards sounded from outside the broken windows. The outer bailey was in chaos with what looked to be an entire building engulfed in flames. With her arm wrapped in a cloth, Isabeau stood at the end of the room and directed the servants to set up another room for the injured.

He grabbed a napkin, shook it to remove any glass, and pressed it to Sidony's head.

She glared at him, wincing in pain.

"Are you all right?" he asked.

She scuttled back, holding the cloth to her head. "Don't touch me. Why were you running toward me? I should have you arrested." She pulled herself up and searched the crowd.

"You think I had something to do with this?" He reached out to check the cut on her head, but she flinched. He dropped his hand, searching beyond the banquet hall for a safe place to take her.

He spotted his cousin, who was at the middle table, though he'd moved to the other side. A noblewoman leaned against him, her pale face dotted with blood. The prince pressed a napkin to a cut along the side of her neck. Torwyn stared back at him grimly. Adrian searched him quickly, noting the prince had also escaped injury aside from some minor cuts. He cast his voice into his cousin's ear. "Rebels?" he asked.

Torwyn shrugged, mouthing, "We shall see." A courtier handed a fresh cloth to him. Torwyn took it, dabbing at the blood that oozed from the wound when the lady regained consciousness. He murmured something to her, and she relaxed back against his side.

Adrian tried to contain his shock at Torwyn's tenderness towards the woman.

He turned back to Sidony, noting the scratch on her head had stopped bleeding. "I smelled smoke. Are you hurt anywhere else?" He was frantic to help her, his guilt at seeing her hurt eroding his composure.

"Your Highness, we need to get you out of here." Lucia was at her side, offering a hand.

Adrian couldn't take his eyes off Sidony, but she ignored him, standing and holding the cloth to her head. "Lucia, are you hurt? We have to make sure the injured get help. We have to find her." She moved closer to her lady-in-waiting.

"Sidony, wait."

Sidony stalked back to him, the side of her face streaked with blood. "Find my sister." She left before he could reply.

Adrian stood motionless, his thoughts racing. Zara was gone. Callum had managed to escape with her, without anyone sounding an alarm. He'd gone back up to the room where he'd fought Callum. Apparently the servants hadn't checked it again aside from when Molly had met him at the door. He'd moved the rug to hide the bloodstain, turning it so the bed sat atop it. He also righted the fallen dress form.

He'd watched Zara make her choice, but that didn't stop guilt from eating at him.

He approached Torwyn, coughing at the smoke pouring into the hall. Wills and Marlowe were a few feet away, conferring with a group of guards.

"Cousin, we need to get you out of here."

"I was enjoying a good meal." Torwyn nodded at a cut along his wrist. "Dirty rebels."

Adrian pinched his brow. Whether rebels had caused the explosion was debatable, but it certainly distracted from the missing princess. "Once you're safe, I'm going outside to see what I can find out about the fire."

Torwyn gestured to the woman leaning on him. "This is Lady Bieranne. She was entertaining us with stories of her children at dinner."

Adrian nodded to the woman, who offered a weak smile.

His cousin continued, "You'll find their rebel stink all over that fire."

Adrian doubted that, but didn't say so. "Yes, Cousin." He raised his voice to be heard above the din. "Lieutenant Wills, leave two men to guard the prince and one to help get Lady Bieranne to a bed. Send the rest with me outside."

~

IN THE BAILEY, Adrian used his powers to search the burning building again. Wills and another knight waited beside him. No one was inside what looked to be storage for the castle kitchens. Crates and sacks were stacked to the ceiling, providing the perfect kindling for the blaze. An old still sat near the door, closest to the keep. That was what had likely caused the explosion, although it was hard to be certain. He'd smelled burning fuses, not flames from a smaller fire.

"Your Highness, were there any bodies?" Wills asked.

Adrian ran a hand over his face. "I didn't see anyone in there."

"They wouldn't have made it out alive after that. I'll organize the men to secure the rest of the castle." Wills and the knight left him to wait for Yves to finish organizing a bucket brigade.

If they weren't searching for Zara already, he needed to alert Yves, the captain of the L'Ortagian guard, to the princess's absence.

After two rounds of buckets, the brigade was in motion. Adrian went over to the older guard and pulled him aside.

"Your Highness." Yves spared Adrian a glance, his lined face etched with worry.

"My men would like to help by securing the outer bailey," Adrian said.

"Fine. Now, if you'll excuse me." Adrian held the man's shoulder, pulling him back.

"Sir Yves, has Princess Zara been found?"

"She's missing? I heard she was late to dinner, but not that she hadn't shown up." Yves's brows furrowed.

"She is. I'm not certain whether the explosion was a distraction to cover for her going missing, or from something else. We need to find the princess." There. Pertinent facts, though possibly unrelated.

Yves's face screwed up, soot and sweat deepening the creases on his forehead. "I'll notify my men. Begin the search. We'll widen it once the fire is out. I'll not risk the rest of the residents of Mondelac."

Adrian crossed the bridge and searched the grounds, and then the forest beyond, outside the castle. The distance his powers could cover had increased in the last few weeks. He guessed that Callum already had Zara miles away from Mondelac Castle.

A guard named Hollis delivered a message from Torwyn:
Find my bride.

"I'm trying. Unless she's nearby, I won't be able to locate her," he told Hollis. He felt a buzz of joy that the rebel leader had stolen her away at such an important time for Gracchus.

"The prince is furious," Hollis said.

The bucket brigade brought the last of the flames to a smoking sizzle. The fire had not spread beyond the first building. Although there were a dozen injured, no one had died. The outside wall of the main hall was damaged in some places, windows would need to be repaired, and the old kitchen was a pile of wet stones.

Amidst the bedraggled servants and soldiers, Adrian searched for Sidony. Her light hair, though streaked with ash, made her easier to find. She stood next to the well, her gown damp and flecked with soot, looking like she'd been taking turns with Lucia to bring up water. Her jade-green gown glowed in the torchlight. He had taken a stutter step in the banquet hall when he'd seen her earlier in the evening. She might not know the meaning of the color she wore, but it was bittersweet to him. Jade was a precious stone held sacred to his mother's people and to him. He had jade stones embedded in the guard of his sword. Occasionally, he wore a jade ring his mother had given his father, though he knew Gracchus disapproved.

Sidony crossed to where Yves stood. She peered into the wet ruins of the now three-walled building. He watched Yves and one of her many ladies' maids try to get her to leave, but she seemed to have reached a breaking point as she stared into the smoky ruins, refusing to move. Someone threw a blanket over her shoulders and finally, Adrian had had enough.

He joined her by the former entrance. "I'll help her now, Sir Yves."

The exhausted captain nodded. "Any news?"

He hated to disappoint them. "No sign of her."

"Could she have been hurt in the fire?" Sidony asked.

"Your Highness, there was no one in the building," Yves assured her. "There's nothing more you can do for your sister tonight."

"She's been missing for hours." Sidony's shoulders slumped.

"We're sending out search parties across the countryside. We'll find her." Yves turned to address his second-in-command.

"Sidony, would you let me escort you to your rooms?"

Adrian offered his arm, but she didn't take it. He wanted to block her view of the burned building. Sidony closed her eyes, swaying slightly. He stepped around in front of her and steadied her with a gentle grip on her shoulders.

"The fire's out." He wiped a smudge of soot from her cheek. "Zara wasn't in there."

"I know." Her hands trembled, and she shivered.

"Let me get you out of here."

She staggered on the first couple of steps, so he swung her up in his arms.

Sidony tucked her head under his chin. Adrian pulled her

closer, the feel of her easing some of the ache in his chest. Hours ago, he'd been convinced he'd never touch her again; now here he was holding her like he had the night they met.

He stepped across the yard carefully, passing exhausted retainers. A few cast worried looks to their princess, but none impeded his progress.

The commotion in the castle had died down, the main hall and stairs quiet. Once he reached Sidony's door, she pulled a key from a hidden pocket in her gown. He set her down and backed up.

"Zara has a way with locks, but I keep a key."

Adrian frowned at her words, something niggling at him about Zara. Sidony clutched his sleeve. "Please stay. Just for a moment."

"Just for a moment." He followed her into the room.

"I should have told Yves or gotten a note to mother earlier." Inside the door, she bent to take off her muddy shoes.

"None of this is your fault." He hesitated. Should he tell her what he knew about Zara and Callum? He could allay her fears but something held him back. Zara leaving on the eve of her wedding was a huge thorn in his uncle's side. With so few cards to play, he wanted to let this one play out for a while longer. "We'll find her."

"Someone would have seen her if she'd been on the grounds somewhere." She ran a hand over her face, then took the handkerchief he held out. Her fingers were icy. "She could have been kidnapped."

"Then we'll get her back. If it's ransom they want, they won't hurt her." He moved behind her and loosened the buttons along the back of her gown. Guilt tore through his gut. He couldn't change the past few hours. Maybe he should have stopped the wagon Zara rode in despite her choice to stay hidden inside. Seeing how much Sidony hurt gave him pause.

"I know." She held her gown to her chest. "I'm scared for her."

There was a soft knock at the door, likely one of her maids. At her nod, he answered it. The maid who had been looking for Zara earlier startled at the sight of him.

"Come in, Molly," Sidony said.

Molly slid past him and began fussing over Sidony. His hands hovered in the air before settling at his sides.

CHAPTER FOURTEEN

*A*drian strode through the mirrored hall the next day to meet with his cousin, the reflection of the morning sunlight hurting his eyes. The hall bridged an older section of the castle with a much newer one. With its arched ceiling and rows of gilt mirrors lining the walls, it reminded him of the remodeled sections of Blackthorne Castle, which his uncle had renamed Blackthorne Palace. Gracchus had spared no expense, and the construction had stretched on for years. It wasn't a way to earn the citizens' admiration, but the king had been determined to remake the former seat of power into his own dwelling.

The black-and-white harlequin pattern on the floor was striking. For all Adrian's supernatural senses, the room affected his equilibrium. Or, perhaps, that was due to not sleeping last night.

Just past the middle of the hall, Torwyn stood, surrounded by his courtiers, including a few L'Ortagian nobles. The cluster of bodies was focused on the prince.

"You wanted to see me?" Adrian asked.

The crowd parted at his words. Torwyn rested a hand on his waist.

"I'm leaving Mondelac today. You are staying in my stead."

"Of course." Adrian bowed. "In what capacity would I be serving here?"

"I need you to be our eyes and ears at Mondelac."

There were a few mumblings amongst the L'Ortagians. Torwyn added, "And serve the queen in her search for the princess."

His job was the same here as it was in Embury. And with the prince leaving, his chance to search for the orb was further delayed. Some reaction must have shown on his face because the courtiers praised Torwyn's request.

"A splendid idea to leave Prince Adrian here."

"Absolutely!"

"Let him stay."

"Brilliant, as usual, Your Highness." The last reply was from Marlowe.

Adrian glowered at the group, his patience thin.

"You may all go, save my dear cousin. Be ready to depart in an hour." The swarming mass dispersed, save Marlowe, who often shadowed the royal family for their protection, and in other capacities.

"Torwyn, let me leave with you. I can help search for Zara along the road to Embury."

"No. She's too far out of range for you now. And we'll need you here to keep our ties with L'Ortagia. Be ready to send for me as soon as my bride returns," Torwyn said.

Arguing further would only anger Torwyn and cause him to complain to the king. Adrian needed no reminders of what his uncle could do to his family. He would have to search for his mother and sister some other way. Maybe Marlowe would have other leads on their location.

He inclined his head. "Yes, cousin. Is there anything I need to know about your meeting with the queen this morning?"

Torwyn chuckled. "She believes it to be a kidnapping. Said her daughter knew what duty meant. If we'd known when she went missing, we could have found her. Last night she must have been out of range for you." Torwyn stared hard at him, as if looking for a lie on his face.

"Did she say whether she wanted to recruit other nocturnes for the search?" Adrian knew the queen's stance but that didn't mean she wouldn't turn to such when her heir went missing.

"She refused." Torwyn rolled his eyes. "One might think her refusal of nocturnes was a personal matter."

"It's possible." Adrian wasn't sure what to think when every day he grew more convinced her daughter was a nocturne. "Without nocturnes' help, she only delays Zara's rescue."

"Eventually we all accept the inevitable." Torwyn shrugged. "And after Marlowe reported to me what was found in the forest early this morning, I have no doubt that the little shit used a nocturne's magic to abduct the princess."

Marlowe nodded once. He added, "One of the search parties found a spot in the forest outside the castle that had been used as a campsite. It could have been a hunting party or a band of Romany."

"How did you know magic had been used there?" Adrian asked.

"I'm familiar with the remnants of portal magic," Marlowe replied.

"Always so useful, aren't you, Marlowe?" Torwyn leveled his gaze at the courtier. He turned to Adrian. "Your powers were lacking yesterday, cousin, when we needed you."

Adrian didn't react.

The hunting grounds must have been where Callum's soldiers had disappeared to when the portal closed. Adrian had sensed them when he'd searched outside the castle's walls yesterday, but their disguises had clearly fooled him.

"Do you think Ash would hurt her?" He was careful not to use Callum's name directly to his cousin. The king also refused to acknowledge the rebel leader as one of the Lost Royals and only referred to him as Ash, the name he went by. To Gracchus, "lost" meant they were supposed to be dead.

"Cousin, you are entirely too soft. But, no. Ash wouldn't dare. This wedding was to solidify our ties to L'Ortagia and further legitimize my father's claim to Embury. The bastard only delays the inevitable."

Torwyn walked to the connecting corridor, crooking a finger for Adrian to follow. Marlowe stayed a step behind the prince on his other side.

"He could send Zara back," Adrian said.

"If she's not back in one piece, I'll finally put an end to him." Torwyn smiled with all his teeth. "That sounds like a good plan. Marlowe, what say you?"

"An excellent plan, Your Highness, particularly for a man rumored to have escaped death at the tender age of fifteen."

Torwyn looked back at Marlowe. "Are you mocking me?"

"Not at all," Marlowe said smoothly. "I'm commending your bravery."

"Good." Torwyn frowned and continued on. "Because I can never tell. Your humor is quite strange."

"My apologies," Marlowe said.

Adrian stayed silent. His family's bloodlust wouldn't abate regardless of his commentary.

Down the hall and into another corridor, they reached the door to Torwyn's suite of rooms. "Stay here and keep our ties strong. This delay means nothing. The true power of Embury lies in who holds the crown."

"Gracchus has it. Embury is his." Adrian recited the words as he had thousands of times before.

Torwyn punched his shoulder in satisfaction, striking inches from the spot Callum had injured yesterday. Adrian turned to hide his reaction, but not before Marlowe caught his eye.

"Safe travels, cousin."

CHAPTER FIFTEEN

*M*ondelac Castle resembled a warren made of stone. Adrian patted the note in his waistcoat that Sidony's maid Elise had delivered to him, asking him to meet outside her family's private chapel. He wound his way through the castle, stopping to greet Emburian nobles who had come for the wedding. After two tours, his own wanderings, and searching for Zara last night in case she and the rebels somehow hadn't left the castle grounds, he finally felt familiar with old Mondelac's winding halls.

After seeing Torwyn off, Yves had given Adrian an update about the search for Zara. Adrian had confessed that someone had hit him over the head and knocked him out. Hopefully his story of not remembering all the details before dinner would be believed. It would lead the search in the likely direction of the rebels, but they were already under suspicion. Yves had accepted his word without question. Adrian didn't like lying to him, but there was no other choice. And truly, Zara was likely much safer with the rebels than with Torwyn.

Adrian had to make a plan. He was stuck at Mondelac when he needed to return to Blackthorne to search for the orb. He considered sending a letter to the king in order to be relieved of his post. The longer he stayed away from Embury, the longer it would take to find his mother and sister.

The one consolation was that with the wedding delayed, Sidony was safe from Gracchus for the time being. He was also in a position to watch out for her since he was here.

She's worth staying for.

He shook his head at himself.

If Sidony knew he'd let her sister go, any feelings she might still have for him would be gone, as they likely deserved to be.

The chapel was in one of the oldest sections of Mondelac. The corridors were narrow, the ceiling low, and the stones well-worn. After rounding another corner, he found their meeting place. Sidony stood next to a plain wooden door, dabbing at her eyes with a handkerchief. A small bandage covered the cut on her head. Her back straightened when she noticed him. He checked the urge to sweep her up against his chest and comfort her like he had last night.

"Are you alone?" She edged around him, peering down the hall. She was close enough that Adrian could smell the soap she used in her hair. An ache swelled in his chest and he tried to ignore it.

"You said you wanted to talk in private."

She pulled out a key and unlocked the door.

"The rest of the castle is teeming with guests," she said. The door opened into the family chapel. The wood-paneled room resembled a small library. Cabinets lined one wall. Three rows of pews were along the opposite side. Sidony lit several candles, casting a soft glow over the room. She sat in the first pew and arranged her skirts.

"Is there a reason you didn't use the main door to the chapel?" Adrian walked down the narrow aisle. Stained-glass windows lined the wall at the end.

"Mother keeps it locked. There are family heirlooms in

here, and she didn't want any to be 'gifted' during the festivities."

"An excellent place to meet." He turned back to her, unsure where to begin.

Her eyes were puffy and the tip of her nose tinged with pink, but she was luminous even after she'd been crying.

There was an aloofness about her he hadn't experienced before.

He wished he could say for certain what the rebels' plans were for Zara and that he could guarantee her safety. He longed to relieve Sidony with the knowledge that Callum would never harm her sister. A thought occurred to him that Marlowe might know their plans, but he'd already left with Torwyn.

"Has Yves kept you updated about the search?" he asked.

"Yes. I saw him before they left for Cadeau." Yves had taken another group of soldiers into the capital city located at the base of the hill beyond the castle's exterior walls.

"Where were you when my sister disappeared?"

ADRIAN'S EXPRESSION didn't change. He leaned against the wall next to a stained-glass window. The right side of his face was cast in green and blue, giving him an eerie look.

"You left my room, my sister disappeared, and then you were late to arrive in the hall." She angled forward, gripping the edge of the pew.

Adrian crossed his arms. "You think I had something to do with her disappearance?"

"I think it strange that you didn't say a word about it to me last night." Why had he hidden that from her? What else did he know? If only she'd been able to see Zara off for herself, she could have judged, perhaps, whether she'd be safe.

"I was hit on the head and didn't remember what happened until later."

"Why didn't you tell me about your wounds?"

"There was no time. I patched myself up and went down to dinner."

She wasn't sure what reaction she wanted him to have. After the explosion, he'd rushed to help. Yves was all praise in his description of how Prince Adrian had searched for Zara and then come back to carry Sidony gallantly into the castle. It wasn't his actions after the fire that had her confused, though. It was before. Where had he been?

"Sidony, I'm sorry. We'll find her." He held out a hand to her, palm up.

She stared at it for a moment then turned in the pew.

"Tell me where you went after you left my room. Do you remember all of that now?" She had little reason to trust him, but somehow, over the course of their meetings, she had grown to. The fact that he'd kept the secret of their meeting the night of the ball was part of it. Finding out now that he'd kept a secret from her that involved her sister was alarming.

"I know you're worried about her," Adrian said.

"Don't comfort me. Tell me, Adrian. Where were you?" She didn't care that she was practically begging him. She needed to put the pieces together in case that meant Zara was in danger.

He rested his hand on the sill at his side, his gaze on the tiled floor between their feet. "After I left you, I was on my way to my room. There was a commotion in one of the rooms, and I walked in. I got hit on the head and a few other scrapes. When I woke up, I was confused, and there was blood on the floor. I cleaned up and went down to the banquet hall. I think that whoever hit me took your sister. Zara was with him."

"Oh." Sidony put her hands to her face. "Who was it?"

Adrian hesitated, brows drawn. "I saw her with a group of soldiers. I rushed in. We fought."

"Who was she with?" Not that she expected him to know, but as the king's spy, he might. "This is my sister. I need to know."

"Emburian rebels." He was silent for long moments, his jaw working. "I was injured during the fight. When I woke up, they were gone. I was already late. I heard Zara hadn't arrived at dinner, so I looked for her too."

"You heard? From who?"

"On my way down to dinner. There was gossip amongst your retainers that she was resting. I took the liberty to look for her."

He'd been hurt while trying to help. And here she was accusing him when she already knew her sister planned to leave.

"Adrian, I'm sorry. I didn't mean to accuse you." The burning tension in her chest eased at his explanation, leaving her tired. "I wish you'd told me last night."

"I couldn't tell you in the middle of all that. I thought you'd think badly of me."

Sounds from the castle filtered in. Children playing, chasing wooden hoops in the inner bailey. Dogs barking. The distant rumble of carriage wheels going across the bridge. Bells rang, reminding Sidony this was the time of day the players from the Gilded Rose Theatre would have been performing as part of the wedding celebration. With Zara gone, Sidony had sent them back to Cadeau this morning with full payment.

The silence between Sidony and Adrian was peaceful, and she appreciated the moment to compose her thoughts. She glanced at him.

"I arranged a play as part of the wedding festivities. They would have been performing now." She stared at her lap and swallowed heavily against the lump in her throat. "I'm good at that sort of thing. With Zara gone…there's just so much more I need to do."

"Sidony."

He stepped toward her, and she put him off, not wanting comfort yet. He'd been hurt trying to protect her sister.

"That must have been some blow to the head."

He took a deep breath. "I only remembered more details this morning."

"Well." She treaded carefully, fighting the urge to trust him with what Zara had done. "Why would the Emburian rebels kidnap my sister?"

"Yves told you this already."

"I want to hear it from you."

"The rebels will do anything to thwart the king. The royal wedding likely had great significance for them. When I walked in, there was an odd circle of light in the room. We think the rebels used a portal spell to get into the castle."

"Are they dangerous? Would they hurt her?"

"They don't keep prisoners." He held up a hand at her squeak of distress. "They don't take them after a skirmish. Mostly they disrupt trade routes, steal munitions, and spread the rumor that the Lost Royals will return."

"Will they?" Sidony willed her breathing to return to normal. Her sister believed at least one of the MacKinnons had returned.

"I'm told the people were happier under King Angus," Adrian said slowly. "Callum, or Ash, the rebel leader, was the one to take your sister."

There were layers upon layers to this. Her sister had always had a soft spot for the previous royal family. Zara grew up with a tendre for Callum, the middle prince, in particular. The rebels had brought a powerful ally into their midst. Sidony's fears for her sister abated.

"You're certain it was him?" she asked Adrian.

"Yes."

Adrian crossed to her, kneeling before her, and catching her hands in his. His hands were warm, his grip gentle, as if he could hold her steady.

"I've met many cruel people in my life," he said. His expression was earnest. "Callum, their leader, isn't like that."

She believed him. Adrian seemed convinced.

"Stealing Zara from her own castle was a bold move. Some men are cruel to any and all living things. A rare few are always kind. The rest can be pushed. From what I know, he's one of the rare ones."

"I doubt he truly understands who he is dealing with."

Adrian's gaze searched her face. "There's a chance she could take their side."

There it was, the hint that her sister would be willing to work with the rebels. She had to cover for her.

Sidony laughed, the sound brittle. "Then you don't know my sister." She needed to stick as close to the truth as possible. "Zara adores protocol. She lives for rules and structure. To help overthrow a sitting king? No. She'd never take their side."

"They probably won't even try," Adrian said. He slid her a glance. "Would your mother ever engage the services of nocturnes to help find Zara?"

"No. Never." Sidony felt a surge of irritation that the queen wouldn't get past her beliefs to help Zara. "She wouldn't want to give them any legitimacy."

"That's unfortunate then, and it will mean it takes longer to find her. They've likely taken her to one of their camps. Torwyn left with a search party a couple of hours ago. We don't know if the rebels have allies in L'Ortagia."

They'd taken a very important one.

"Are you leaving too?"

"The prince bade me to stay at Mondelac."

Her palms heated. He was staying. Sidony courted temptation, but she couldn't bring herself to pull away just yet.

"You were injured." She held his face in her hands, fingers

sliding along his jaw, bristles from his day-old beard scratching her palms. A flush rose slowly in her chest. She angled forward on her seat to search for his wound.

Will I use any excuse to touch him?

"Thank you for trying to save my sister. Let me see."

"I've tended it. I'm fine." But he held still for her.

"Show me where." She stroked her thumbs over his cheek-bones, worry and a curl of desire mixing together. She was wrecked for this man.

He stared into her eyes, the glow from the candles winking in those sable-brown depths.

"Very well. No one's fussed over me for a long time." He tipped his chin and she let go, her fingertips resting on his broad shoulders. He stiffened against her, sucking in a breath.

"Adrian, I…"

"It's just a scratch." He pressed on a spot under his coat and reached for one of her hands. "Go back to what you were doing."

She held his jaw with one hand, resting gently, wishing she could bring him a measure of comfort.

He pulled out the length of cord holding his hair back.

She stroked her fingers over his head, some of his hair spilling across the backs of her hands. "Someone should fuss over you," she murmured. His head was almost in her lap. The cool length tempted her to run her fingers through it and tug him closer.

Adrian parted the thick black strands. "Here it is."

She forced herself to concentrate on his injury. Her hands cupped his head, holding him lightly.

"There?" She squinted at the spot. For as hard as he must have been hit, the bump was smaller than she thought it would be. The skin was pink with no sign of blood.

"This was yesterday?" The cut had already closed.

"Yes." He swallowed. "I heal quickly."

"Or you have a hard head. Adrian, you must be mistaken about the blood. What if it's Zara's?"

He looked up and grasped her hands, placing them over his heart. "Sidony, I swear to you on my mother's life, the blood was from my injury and my opponent's, not Zara's."

Something about his words rang true. Maybe she wanted to believe him. It was an open secret the prince was a nocturne. Was this part of his powers? Had hers affected him in this way?

"Fine." She pressed her hands to his chest. "Will Torwyn be able to find Zara?"

"We sent word to the king, and Gracchus is...resourceful. The rebels should ransom her anyway. Once that is paid, she'll be returned."

His heart beat a rhythm against her palm, the faint thud steady. "And then you'll go back."

CHAPTER SIXTEEN

*H*ope for Zara's swift return faded. Search parties returned without her sister, only to go out again the next day, spreading farther into the kingdom. Days later they returned to report there was no sign of the princess in L'Ortagia. Sidony wanted her sister back, but also had faith Zara would return when she could.

The Emburian rebels didn't send any messengers, notes, or demands. The queen and her advisors believed they had taken Zara out of the country.

Sidony now went to all the small council meetings her sister used to attend. At the latest one, Sylvie, her mother's second-in-command of the Royal Guard, said she suspected Zara's kidnapping to be the result of nocturne witchcraft. The queen had quickly rejected that idea, sliding a look at Sidony.

There were old secrets her mother didn't want getting out.

Whether L'Ortagian nocturnes had played a part—which Sidony didn't know, but doubted—the fact remained that Zara was still gone. Sidony missed her terribly. One night, she went to Zara's room and lay on her bed, remembering the last time they'd sat together and talked. Hours passed before Lucia found her and dragged her from the room. She hadn't been back. There was too much to do.

Most of the visiting nobles had returned to their estates or their own countries, if they'd traveled that far. Adrian stayed at Mondelac along with a small group of his men. He'd also been allowed to sit in on the meetings regarding her sister. Like he had with her, he reassured the small council that as a political prisoner, it was "highly unlikely" the rebels would harm Zara.

Sidony wished Zara could find a way to get word to her. She trusted that her sister was trying.

Despite that, she slept fitfully, waking every couple of hours. The queen's physic had offered her a tonic for sleep, but she refused it. Keeping Zara's secret was as difficult as she'd thought it would be. All the worry and resources allocated to her sister when she'd left willingly sat heavy on Sidony's shoulders.

She trusted there were bigger things at stake for Zara. She wished she'd had more time to hear her sister's plan, to know how to proceed, and for how long.

She took to wandering the castle at all hours, treading the same paths on the stones. Sometimes her walks would tire her and she could return to bed. Other times she took a book or a bound script and read somewhere in the castle.

She often visited the wing of the castle that was under construction. In the mornings, before the workers arrived, she found a quiet place. She could read, review plans her mother made her learn, and worry and miss her sister.

Sidony sat against the wall on a low ottoman in the corner of what would be the new library. The grand room was complete enough that the windows had been installed. The walls would be covered with extensive woodwork. Carpenters had already completed one corner and would continue adding layers of intricate moldings around the room. Wood shavings lay scattered over the floor and sawhorses lined up along one side. For now, she was alone.

She'd read a few pages of her book, a collection of Beaumarchais's plays, when footsteps sounded from the hall. Adrian walked in carrying a lantern. He stopped in the doorway when he spotted her.

"Sidony."

There was a strain about his eyes and a length of dark hair had escaped his normally immaculate queue. Aside from updates on her sister, she'd barely seen him the last couple of weeks.

"Any news?" She clutched the book to her chest, trying to read his expression.

"We have confirmation she's with the rebels." He leaned against the doorjamb.

"Did they demand a ransom?"

"Not yet. I cannot fathom what they gain in keeping her." He walked into the room, setting the lantern he carried on the floor and sitting next to it. He stared out the long row of windows. The early morning sun was beginning to lighten the sky. The room was dark, save for the two lanterns. Flecks of sawdust swirled in the lantern light.

"What about rescuing her?" Sidony asked.

"Gracchus tried that. The rebels slipped away with her. Again."

"Oh." Sidony hid a smile at the rebels' skill.

His gaze met hers. "She was spotted in one of their camps. Guarded closely, but given freedom to walk around, at least."

"How did she look? Is she well?" Sidony asked.

"From the report I got, she is well, as far as they could tell."

"That's good news. It's like you said, they won't hurt her." Relief washed through her. "Any idea where they are taking her?"

"Marlowe told me they think it's farther into the north. The rebels have a larger base there." Adrian tapped his fingers on his knee. "I'll be off then."

"You just got here. Stay and watch the sunrise with me."

He peered out the window, his features relaxing infinitesimally, and she again felt prickles of guilt that he was stuck here because of Zara. Despite their talk in the chapel the day after Zara left, there'd been a distance between them. She didn't know how or whether to reach out to him. He could be here for weeks, but he'd be gone eventually.

"I need a place to train. The courtyard was too dark." He gestured to the book in her lap. "It's what I do when I can't sleep."

"Adrian, please." She brushed a curl off her forehead. "If it helps, pretend I'm not here. Train as you like. I was just about to leave."

ADRIAN ROLLED his shoulders as he walked across the room.

Pretend she isn't here? Ha.

He'd avoided her as much as he could, busying himself with searching for Zara, meeting with the L'Ortagians, and hoping to find another way to free his mother and sister.

He strode to the far side of the room and removed his coat, resting it on a sawhorse. The library contained a fireplace. He felt for a draft and set the lantern in the empty hearth. He walked around in a circle, drawing his sword, running through the training exercises he wanted to do.

Sidony's face was back in her book.

He needed to train. She wanted to read. They could exist separately. He lifted his sword, brushing sawdust off a seam in the floor with his boot. Stepping into position, he practiced advance and retreat patterns. He kept his feet along the seam, repeating each pattern multiple times before moving on to the next one.

Advance, advance, retreat.

He went the other direction, repeating the same footwork. Retreat, retreat, advance.

And again. Then he added more steps. Back and forth along the line, trying to keep his upper body still and his mind on the repetitive motions.

Each time he turned, his gaze snagged on her. The lamplight made her golden hair glow. She had a habit of tapping her finger as she read. His sense of smell picked up on her honeysuckle scent, making desire stir in his chest.

Sweat soaked his shirt. He'd hoped Sidony would leave before that happened. She must have found her book of plays particularly engrossing because she stayed.

He went back to his footwork drills, trying to outlast her, sweat dripping down his face.

Advance, advance, advance, retreat. Retreat, retreat, retreat, advance.

He wiped his arm across his forehead. He shook out his legs and walked in a circle, admiring the pinkened sky. Somewhere in the middle of his drills, Sidony had removed her pelisse. Her gown showed a hint of her décolletage, but it was enough that he knew he had to get back to his drills.

The room was getting warm. Her cheeks had a wash of pink to them too.

He yanked his shirt out of his breeches, fanning himself.

He raised his sword and bent his knees, ignoring the murmurs from her corner.

When he'd glanced up from another set, she was perched by the window, her book left on the ottoman.

"I don't mean to interrupt," she said. "Your training is quite *intense*." That she watched him overtly was a sweet torture.

Adrian swung his saber up, determined to ignore her pretty

flash of ankle peeking out below the hem of her skirt. He wiped a hand across his breeches. Shirt be damned.

Without looking at her, he loosened the ties at his neck and whipped it over his head, switching his sword to his nondominant hand. He strode over to her and put the shirt next to her on the bench.

Her eyes met his. The green shade darkened, nearly emerald. She tempted him in ways he didn't know how to handle.

Adrian couldn't help it. When he turned away, going back to his line on the floor, he stretched out his senses to watch her. Being close to her had amplified his powers again, a fact he'd never regretted until this moment. It was almost too much. He got in his stance and nearly dropped his sword. Not only had she ogled his backside as he'd walked away from her, she'd pulled his shirt into her lap. Using his sleeve, she dabbed at spots of moisture dotting the center of her cleavage.

Adrian stumbled off the line, cursing. Forget having a target, he worked on a pattern of lunges, his arms burning.

He should leave Sidony alone. They'd been apart for weeks, barely making eye contact during the small council meetings.

He slowed, breathing hard.

"Are girls in Embury allowed to train in fencing?" Sidony asked. She twirled a lock of hair. The rest was piled at the back of her head. Sunlight streaked through the sky behind her, a few rays catching her curls. So lovely.

What had she been saying?

"In Embury, no."

She rolled her eyes. "What about in your home country?"

Curious—and pleasing—that she'd differentiate the two. He certainly did. "Daeso? Not many."

"What about your sister?"

He smiled around a twist of pain in his heart. "Yes, Minah did. My mother insisted on it." He flexed his wrist, angling the saber in the air. "She was quite good, actually."

"Did she ever beat you in a match?"

"Regularly."

A corner of her mouth curled. It reminded him of the night they met, this teasing side of her. It could be so easy between them. He found himself opening up to her again, more than he had to anyone else in years. Marlowe, perhaps, being the exception. The courtier had his own agenda, though.

With Sidony, there were these moments when it was just the two of them, no agendas, no politics, no torn loyalties. He could be himself, or as close as he could get. He'd been keeping his distance, afraid of nurturing the attraction between them, afraid of what would happen if he stopped fighting it.

He slashed the sword, wanting to strike at an invisible enemy. Why was Sidony in his life now? He had no place where she could fit. But there she was, sitting in the morning light, hair tumbling over her shoulders. Her heart-shaped face and lush mouth so alluring it hurt to look at her.

The weeks apart left him feeling empty after times like this, of simply being in her company. Without realizing it, Adrian stood before her, breathing fast, his eyes searching her face.

Sidony tilted her head back, leaning toward him, and parted her lips.

"Your Highness," Lucia trilled from the hallway, her steps sounding on the unfinished wood. "Her Majesty has asked for you to join her in breaking her fast."

Adrian peered over his shoulder. Lucia came through the doorway, her eyes widening as she spotted them.

Sidony hopped down from the bench and walked around him. Was she shielding him? His shirt was clutched behind her back. "Has she? I was just leaving. I'll join you in a moment."

The *tap-tap* of Lucia's feet retreated into the hallway.

"Here." Sidony swung around and held out his shirt. "Thank you for keeping me company."

Instead of taking it, he moved closer, stepping toward her

until her knuckles brushed his chest. Her cool fingers slid down to his abdomen. He bit back a groan.

His fingers flexed at his side, his sword forgotten somewhere. He lifted a hand to her wrist, circling it gently. "Sidony."

"Adrian, I…" She sucked in a breath, blushing.

Lucia began humming a tune in the hallway, breaking the spell.

Sidony pressed harder on his chest and then let go of his shirt. He caught it before it hit the sawdust-covered floor.

"I'll be back tomorrow." She arched a brow. "Will you?"

Before he could answer, Sidony left. She hummed along with Lucia as she walked away.

He didn't trust himself. With the search narrowing to Embury, he'd be stuck at Mondelac Castle until Zara was found. Despite how much he wanted Sidony—craved her—he couldn't get this close to her again. The simple fact was that he lived in a world of machinations and divided loyalties. He wouldn't risk her by bringing her any further into it.

CHAPTER SEVENTEEN

Sidony knocked on Adrian's door before she lost her nerve. She twirled one of her rings. She jumped at a rumbling in the hallway, but it was only one of the castle's cats pausing on the rug to wash its face. Striving for a similar nonchalance, Sidony softly recited lines from the current play she was reading before knocking again. Still nothing. Surely at this late hour he was in his suite.

For the past few days, Adrian met her early each morning in the new library. He trained while she read her book of plays. Unlike the first morning, when she'd held his shirt and they'd flirted, he was back to being distant. Polite but close-lipped. The shirt stayed on, and he kept to the opposite side of the library. No touching. It was utterly maddening.

Briefly, she'd worried his attraction to her had waned, but then she'd catch him staring at her. Lucia teased her mercilessly, saying she'd had no idea he was such a fine specimen of a man.

But Adrian was in retreat. In meetings and at court, he was reserved. She wanted to find a way to break that shell around him. He wouldn't talk to her, never sought her out, aside from their early morning ritual.

Sidony hated it.

With her sister gone, she realized a few things. One, that life was changeable, often in unpredictable ways. And two, she now had time to get to know Adrian. Maybe she shouldn't nurture her attraction to him. But maybe they could discover whether there was something between them. More than an attraction. The longer Zara was away, the longer her wedding would be put off. What if, in that time, the betrothal to Torwyn was broken? What if Sidony could convince her mother to consider Adrian for her?

"Adrian, it's me. Open the door."

Here she was, done with loneliness and daydreaming about how he looked at her when he thought she couldn't see. She was ready to go after what she wanted. Only he must be sleeping like the dead.

Sidony raised her hand to knock again. The latch rattled and the door opened.

Adrian stood before her dressed in breeches. His shirt was loose and untucked, his feet bare. He crossed his arms.

"I hope Lucia is around the corner."

Her lady-in-waiting was thankfully asleep, but Sidony wasn't going to admit that. Adrian clearly wasn't going to make this easy.

"Hmm," she said in response.

The cat from the hallway walked over, and Adrian opened the door a crack, letting the feline in. A spark of envy streaked across her chest.

"Did you need something, Your Highness?" He reached down to rub between the cat's ears.

The cat purred loudly and strolled past him, curling a fluffy tail around his shin before disappearing into the room. Lucky puss.

"I'm breaking you out."

He straightened at her words. A heartbeat passed, and she was certain hers was loud enough for him to count each pounding beat.

"Out?"

"Out of your rut, out of your routine. It's called fun, Adrian. I'm going to show you some."

His jaw dropped. He took a step back, shaking his head slowly.

"I've had a full day. How about tomorrow for your grand plan?" A dark piece of hair brushed over his forehead, and she flicked her thumb across her fingers, checking the urge to smooth it back. Or maybe pull more forward and mess him up a bit.

"Oh, no. Right now." She looked down. Goodness, the man even had sexy toes. "Throw on some boots. We're getting out of here."

He fascinated her. The more she got to know him, the deeper that fascination grew. Given he parceled out his time with her, she determined to get him off balance and see what else she could find out about him. The added bonus was she enjoyed breaking the rules, something she was positive Adrian had never done.

"It's late."

"All the better. Let me show you something."

"What are you planning?" He looked out into the hallway, rubbing that finger over his lip.

"I had my personal guard clear the area where we are going. Yves knows I do this." At least she was pretty certain he knew about it. "We won't be gone long. It's safe."

"You don't know that." He narrowed his gaze.

"Ah, but I'll have you. Bring your sword if you wish."

"Flattery doesn't work with me." He pushed away from the frame and retreated to his room, leaving the door open wide enough for her watch him. Masculine grumbling carried out into the hallway.

"I speak the truth. I know I'm safe with you." Sidony stayed outside his room while he buttoned and tucked in his shirt. She tapped her toes on the runner, so pleased she could dance with joy.

He put on his boots, grabbed a coat, and sheathed his sword, joining her. Dashing, strapping, and now properly dressed. She wanted to reach out for his hand once they started down the quiet hallway.

She'd gotten him out of his room, but she had another huge hurdle to face.

ADRIAN FOLLOWED Sidony down the maze of hallways, each one narrower than the last. He stayed close, tantalized by the swish of her skirts. She stopped at a tapestry and pulled it aside, opening a hidden door.

Along the way, she acquired a short candelabra off a table. As he stepped through the door behind her, he took in the narrow passageway the light illuminated. They went down a long set of stairs. At the bottom was a heavy iron door. Flashing a chatelaine, she handed him the light and unlocked the door.

A warm summer breeze hit his face.

"What is this place?" he asked.

"It's one of the lakes that surrounds the castle."

"I didn't know this was here. I could have sworn Captain Yves showed me the entire grounds."

"The lake is mystically hidden." She laughed at his raised brows. "I know. The queen pretends it's just hard to find. Yves bequeaths a small stipend to a nocturne who lives on the other side of the forest. In exchange for her safety, she agrees to use her cloaking power to keep the lake hidden. He probably took you close enough that you could sense something strange. Unless you knew the spell to unveil it, you wouldn't be able tell what it truly is."

That was the vibration he had sensed weeks ago when he'd searched the west end of the castle grounds. Although his powers had gotten stronger, they had limitations.

"So magic can be used when the queen allows it?" he asked with a dose of mockery in his tone.

She kept walking and waved her hand casually. "If you only knew. You can see the lake if you enter from that door."

"It's beautiful." It was serene and calm, the antithesis of his feelings lately, and he was drawn to it. "Thank you for bringing me here."

He tore his gaze away from the water and glanced at Sidony.

"Glad you like it. There's more, though."

"Did you want to walk around?"

"I had something else in mind." Her lips curled, and she rocked forward on her toes. Adrian pressed his forefinger into his thigh to keep from tracing it along the perfect shell of her ear. He tempted fate being with her like this. She was enchanting in the moonlight.

"...so that's why I brought you out here."

He shook his head, realizing he'd missed the first half of what she'd said. They stood on the shoreline, silvery waves splashing mere feet from them. As she'd done the night they met, Sidony bent down and removed her shoes.

"We're walking along the beach?"

"We're getting in the water. Please tell me you know how to swim."

Adrian gaped at her, then sputtered, "Of course I can swim. I grew up in a fishing village."

"Great. We're getting in. Decide what clothing you are

leaving on. And turn around, please. I didn't bring a bathing costume."

Adrian spun on his heel before he could find a reason not to. His cheeks flushed, and he imagined her undressing. He took his coat off, distracting himself so he wouldn't use his powers to watch her.

She surprised him constantly. It intrigued and terrified him. A heavy fall of clothing hit the ground, followed by a series of soft splashes. He waited a few seconds, considering whether he should join her. Despite her assurances that Yves's men patrolled the area, he hadn't sensed any of the Royal Guard. He'd checked when they'd first stepped into the clearing. Wouldn't she be safer with him closer to her?

Besides, he wanted to be with her. This was the perfect opportunity, though it came with a heady dose of temptation. Fists clenched, he took a deep breath and made a decision. He had come this far tonight, and he didn't want to imagine what could have been.

Keeping his back to the water, he scanned the beach with his powers, encountering two frogs and a family of owls in the nearby trees. His senses tapered off at the castle walls, but he'd seen the sentries along the top when they'd exited. They'd be safe from outside threats.

Adrian took off his clothing with careful movements, leaving his smalls. Sidony was already up to her shoulders in the water.

When he stepped into the lake, she cheered. He grinned back. The water was warm. Surrounded by trees and a canopy of stars, it was idyllic.

"Are you having fun yet?" she called.

He stepped toward her, soft mud squishing under his feet. The gentle current in the water tickled his legs.

"I haven't gone for a midnight swim in ages." With a pang, he remembered it was the summer before his father died.

A half smile pulled at her lips. "Has the water made you maudlin?"

"Must have." He was almost deep enough to dive in.

Sidony floated on her back a few feet away. He caught a glimpse of her breasts, nearly visible beneath her sheer, wet chemise. She straightened and treaded water before he could look his fill.

"This is to get your mind off of everything. To entertain you while you're here." She pushed a strand of hair out of her eyes. "Who did you used to go swimming with?"

"My sister and father, back in Sinchon," he said.

"Ah," she said softly.

He dove in, wanting to change the subject. She was right. This was just what he needed.

He surfaced a few feet away from her. "The water's warm, even for summer."

Sidony trailed a hand in the water, making circles. "That's part of the spell. It's always warm."

"Impressive. This would require the skills of a powerful nocturne." Adrian swam closer to her. The water was shallow enough for him to stand, his shoulders clearing the surface. "Why am I feeling a current?"

"The other side connects to a river that runs through Cadeau."

He nodded. The river he was familiar with. He peered at her, stifling his powers. "Please tell me you're wearing something."

She laughed. "My chemise."

He rolled his eyes. "I should be grateful for that."

"You're quite welcome."

"I can handle a challenge." The words slipped out. He wasn't sure if he meant the challenge was coming out here or if the challenge was her scrap of clothing. "Thank you for this." He meant it. Sidony knew just what he needed.

Her hair floated on the water around her, like the beckoning hands of a mermaid. She couldn't be lovelier. Seeing her like this did something to him, to a place near the center of his chest, where he kept such sensibilities locked tight. He ducked his head into the lake as if he could wash off his reaction to her.

Straightening, he brushed water out of his eyes. She hadn't moved. It hadn't done him any good.

Whether it was the mystical lake, the moonlight, or the magic of at least two fellow nocturnes, he didn't stop himself from moving closer to her.

CHAPTER EIGHTEEN

*S*idony rolled her lips together as Adrian cut through the water toward her. She lifted her chin to meet his burning gaze. This was what she'd been hoping for. A chance to be alone with him, unguarded and intimate. Not sure how far she intended to go, she resolved to see what was between them. She was tired of waiting.

Nights had become unbearable. She spent her days worrying for her sister and adjusting to her new role in the kingdom. Against her will, her attraction to Adrian had only grown. Each day she watched him, the dutiful prince, and each night she dreamed of him coming to her, the ardent lover.

Like the lover in her dreams, his gaze warmed, his eyelids lowered, and tiny droplets clung to his lashes. His mouth appeared softer, more relaxed, as if they'd already been kissing.

She treaded water in front of him.

"What are we doing out here?" Adrian was close enough to touch.

"I wanted to help you escape for a while." Water trickled down the side of his neck. She stopped herself from stretching out a hand and tracing the same path. She'd gotten him this far.

He'd taken the last few steps to get close to her. One more impulsive, reckless move. She wasn't sure which one of them was going to make it.

She spotted a pulse beating swiftly at his throat. Maybe he wasn't completely unaffected.

"Zara and I used to do this all the time when we were growing up," she blurted.

He blinked. "I can't see your sister sneaking out."

"She used to. She's more responsible now." She was starting to reconsider what she'd thought of her sister.

Silence stretched between them.

"You have responsibilities," he said. "New ones, but you take them seriously."

"No one's ever put it like that." She was touched by his words.

He considered her across the water, his features more relaxed than she'd seen in weeks.

Sidony smoothed her hair back. *Here goes.* She splashed him. It was a good-sized splash, the water hitting the wall of his chest and up to his chin.

He sputtered. "What was that for?"

"You need some fun in your life." She splashed him again. "All you do is sword-training, meet with advisors, and ride out with Yves. You need a break."

"I don't get breaks." He stepped back, toward the shore. She followed him.

"Well, you should. You work too hard. Has Gracchus got you working off a debt?" She'd meant it as a joke, but he flinched.

"Something like that." He pushed water at her. It wasn't enough to call a splash, but it was something. "Gracchus treats everyone that way."

"Ah. I know how that feels." While it was a sensitive subject, she'd at least gotten him to play a bit. "So let's have some fun, get that look off your face."

"What look?" He tapped on the water, harder this time, and it sent a wave in her direction.

"Closed off."

His lips thinned. "The king doesn't tolerate anything else."

"He's not here. That's why I took pity on you and busted you out."

"This is a pity swim?"

"Yes." She splashed him again. "You need all the fun you can get."

He splashed her back, lunging for her. She squealed and swam backwards, trying to get out of range, but he was much faster. Catching her under the arms, he pulled her into his embrace.

"Sidony. I've got you now" His gaze dropped to her mouth, and she parted her lips.

Their breaths came faster. He was going to kiss her. She'd gotten him out here, but she needed him to kiss her first. *Now.*

Instead, he pulled her under the water with him.

She shrieked when she came up, then burst into laughter and chased him around the water. Unbelievable. Thankfully, she'd closed her mouth. Otherwise she would have gotten a mouthful of lake water.

She swam after him, splashing like mad when he surfaced. He splashed her back, enough that she had to turn away to breathe. Then he dove for her, pulling her under and letting her go only to chase her again. Once, she tried to hide underwater, but he found her, tossing her up in the air to land in a big splash.

And he laughed. Husky and deep at first. Then it rang out clearly across the water. Adrian wasn't much older than her. As they played in the water, this was the first time she thought he looked like the young man he was. Most of her reasons for bringing him out here were likely selfish. But this...this was also for him.

Their playful splashing continued but the tension between them grew. Each time she touched him, pulling an ankle, nudging his shoulder, or meeting his hands in the water, she lingered a bit. Her body was attuned to his. Every touch heating her from within, making her want more.

Adrian twirled her around as if to throw her farther out into the lake. When Sidony squirmed, he let go of her, dropping her legs. She turned to face him as she slid down the front of his body.

"Wait." She grabbed his shoulders.

He stared silently but locked an arm around her waist, holding her close. Gently, he lifted a fallen lock of hair out of her eyes, tucking it behind her ear.

It was sweet. It was killing her. Yet another of those small things he did, likely without realizing it. He was so tender with her. It tore her apart.

Before he could let go, she tipped up her face and kissed him. His lips were cool. One of her hands cupped his strong jaw. She loved that angle of his face. So proud and stubborn. Sidony soothed a finger across his cheek, beckoning him to return her kiss.

He held still for a tense moment, his dark eyes closed. Then he brushed his lips across hers. It was close to what she wanted.

"Kiss me like you did the night we met," she said.

His eyes snapped open. Adrian's hands spanned her ribs, his thumbs brushing under her breasts as he held her up. She thrilled at the feel of his muscles against her breasts, only her thin chemise between them.

After a few tentative brushes of his mouth against hers, he kissed her back. He sucked her tongue into his mouth, rubbing his against it.

There it was. Finally, she wasn't leading him, pushing him.

Their kiss was more than she'd hoped: steamy and intense in ways she had only dreamed. Her thighs rubbed together, trying to ease the ache between them. She felt her center growing hotter with every stroke of his tongue against her own. A moan escaped her, and she clutched him tighter.

Adrian kissed her as if he'd been dying to. Kissed her in acknowledgement of everything that had been simmering between them. Although he'd been cool to the touch at first, now the places her body met his were hot.

He pulled her higher against his chest, holding her up with one arm, and brought his other hand around her nape. He tilted her head back and kissed her neck, his lips burning, causing her to arch closer. He brought his face to hers again but didn't kiss her. Instead, his finger traced her lips.

Sidony opened for him. He rubbed along her sensitive lower lip, dipping to the inner edge. She closed her lips over him, sucking. It was wicked, but she couldn't resist. She'd held herself back for so long. She dove headlong into any sensation she could have with him, fearing at any moment he would pull away.

Sidony sucked harder, caressing his finger with the tip of her tongue. She stole a glance up at the sky, the twinkling lights mirroring her sparking nerves. She waited for what he would do next.

Adrian stared at her, his own lips parted, his gaze hot.

His finger edged deeper into her mouth then pulled back. He did it again, and she nibbled on the end. Adrian pulsed his finger against her. His breaths panted in the space between them. He dipped his head to press kisses up the side of her neck, each one more fervent than the last. She burned at the contact. When his lips reached her chin, she let him go and tipped down to meet his mouth. Adrian groaned against her lips, plundering with his tongue.

She hadn't known he could be so wild. He was a man who

moved with deliberation, as if he had an awareness of exactly where he had to be and how he would get there. His kisses were intense, showing her a hedonistic side she had only seen tiny glimpses of. She never wanted to leave the water. She'd bring him out here every night if it meant she could have his attentions like this.

She drew a hand across his neck, wrapping a finger around a strand of his hair. She'd rarely been this free to touch him. Her hands roamed his shoulders and neck, as she was torn between seeking a greater intimacy and letting him dictate what he wanted from her, just to see what he would do. Her body wasn't torn, though. Her peaked nipples rubbed against his chest, her thighs twisted against his.

Adrian walked with her toward the shore, one arm at her waist, and his hand clutching her bottom. Sidony held on, her fingers twined in his hair. With his first step out of the water, he set her on her feet, his gaze smoldering as he let go but didn't step away.

She tried to memorize his expression, certain hers looked the same. The insistent hardness of his sex pressed against her. She felt an answering ache.

He pressed a quick kiss against her mouth, then came back to trace a finger over her lips.

"Ah, Sidony."

SIDONY INCHED up on her toes and kissed him again, her hands gripping his shoulders.

"This was fun, but we should get back. I can't stay out here with you and not want to touch you."

"Tell me why we should stop." Sidony's hands moved to her hips. Her voice was husky, the sound making his toes curl into the sand.

When he didn't answer right away, she walked up to him and kissed him again, pulling his head down. He bent for her. Easily.

That's what he was afraid of. This was too easy. Too good. It was also incredibly complicated given his obligations and plans.

Despite his misgivings, and they clamored loudly in his head, he snatched her up against him and kissed her fiercely. He groaned at the press of her body angled along his.

Holding her, kissing her, eased an ache in his chest. She felt right in his arms. As if she were in his keeping and he in hers.

He broke their kiss and shook himself. "I can't do this. I want you, but I can't."

"Why?" she asked. "Why do you ignore what's between us?"

"Because there's no time for it," he bit out.

"What if this is all the time we have? Once Zara comes back, you'll be gone. I don't know what's between us, but I know I've never felt this way."

"Don't say that." His plea was half-hearted.

"It's true. Whatever's between us means something to me. You are...dear to me."

Adrian backed away from her.

Sidony continued, each word piercing into the shell he tried to keep clamped shut. "I've never had anyone treat me like you do. You don't want anything from me except me. Do you know what that's like? I suspect that you do. Well, some day soon you'll go back to Embury, I'll go on my Grand Tour or marry a royal my mother thinks she can control." She took a breath, her voice softening as she said, "The time for us is *now*, Adrian."

His eyes widened. "Your sister was betrothed to my cousin for mere weeks. Now look what's happened to her."

"That had nothing to do with you."

He ran a shaky hand through his hair. "You have no idea how much it does."

He would only bring her misery and pain. With Sidony, his heart made a plea. He just couldn't listen to it.

"Then explain it to me," she said. "Explain why you're pushing me away."

He debated it. He could tell her and watch her face change, betrayal flashing in her eyes.

As the days passed and Zara remained out of reach, Gracchus would end the betrothal. Her disappearance was a good enough reason for the king to do so, since he always had an exit strategy.

Adrian had learned to have several strategies going at once too. And the woman in front of him, no matter how much he longed to lay her back against the grass and finish what promised to be the most exciting sexual experience of his life, was not a part of his strategy. He was starting to feel deeply for her, which made her more vulnerable in his world. And his uncle already had plans to kill her. Adrian had to stay away from her.

But Sidony was right that they only had so much time.

He cleared the distance between them and cupped her face, leaning his forehead against hers. His hands moved lower, coasting along her chilled arms, unable to stop touching her.

"If it was just you and me, there would be no question," he said softly, wanting to give her that much.

"Why did you stop?" she whispered.

"I need you to understand that being close to me puts you in danger. The king has...ways to influence me, leverage over me, by threatening people I care about."

"Your family?"

He nodded. "He...has my mother and sister." He hadn't meant to tell her that part of it, but once the words tumbled out, relief eased the strain in his chest.

"Oh, Adrian, no." She petted his back, the warm strokes of her palms soothing.

"So we can't do this," he said. "Not here, not...now."

"I thought we were doing fine."

He kissed her pout then pulled away again.

"Yes, we were." Adrian ran a hand down her back, stopping before he reached the swell of her backside. He snatched his hand away before temptation had him cupping her sweet curves. He cleared his throat.

"Sidony, thank you for bringing me out here and showing me the lake. For showing me...ah, fun." He let go of her. She was so alluring; he knew she'd haunt his dreams. Nearly naked in her wet shift, her nipples puckered and pointing at him, the shadow between her legs was a temptation to behold. Sheer force of will and years of denying his own desires kept him from reaching for her again.

Sidony shook her head and gathered her damp hair, squeezing out the water. She surprised him by grabbing his hand with both of hers and tucking it under her chin. "I'm glad I brought you out here, even knowing it would end like this. You deserve a little fun, and I'm happy I could bring that to you."

Adrian was at a loss for words, grateful for her. Her sweetness called to him and terrified him. He brought her hands up to kiss her fingertips.

He kept the words he longed to speak to himself. He had already grown attached to her and, he feared, she to him. It went beyond mere desire. Sidony gave him a sense of belonging, a light in the darkness.

She let go and turned away to dress. They needed to return to the castle before he got so deep with her that he couldn't see and didn't want to find a way out.

CHAPTER NINETEEN

*A*fter escorting Sidony back to her room, Adrian returned to his own. The walk had cooled his ardor, but the complications remained. Tonight, they had gotten worse. One corner of his mouth tugged up as he recalled Sidony's shining face when he'd pulled her into the water. She brought him such...*joy*.

The longhaired, tortoiseshell castle cat greeted him at the door. He patted its head again and spotted Marlowe seated at the desk.

"Where were you?" Marlowe asked without turning around. His long form curled over the desk, the sharp scratches of the quill continuing while he spoke.

"When did you get back?" Adrian countered.

Marlowe peered over his shoulder to squint at him. "In the last hour. The king sent me ahead."

"Must be urgent then." Adrian crossed to his dressing table in search of a towel and fresh clothing. The dampness of his clothes gave him a chill. "It's been a long night."

"You hardly touch the stuff, but I poured you a drink

anyway." Marlowe waved to a set of glasses filled with amber liquid on a nearby table.

Adrian used his powers to glance over Marlowe's shoulder.

"You needn't bother. I'll be showing this to you first." Marlowe always seemed to know when Adrian was using his powers around him.

"Habit." Adrian washed his face in a nearby bowl, his head spinning. He found he wasn't ready to discuss Sidony with Marlowe. He hadn't figured out where he stood with her or what he was going to do. He doubted he'd ever share something that personal with the spy, who would likely seize on some way around his personal code of ethics. He didn't need further inducement. Adrian already wanted Sidony more than he could ever remember wanting another.

He settled on an easier topic: the city Marlowe was writing about. "Marenburg?"

"Aye," Marlowe answered, slipping into his native Emburian burr for a moment.

"What do I need to know?" Adrian walked over to the sitting area and grabbed one of the glasses.

Marlowe stopped writing and turned to face Adrian. "The dead don't always stay dead."

Adrian rubbed a hand along the back of his head. "I'm well aware of that. Who's in Marenburg?"

"I'm not certain of the veracity of the claim, but yet another member of the former royal family may have been located."

Adrian cradled the drink to his chest. "Besides Prince Callum? The king must think the claim is legitimate for him to send you." He nodded at the letter. "Is this what you do for Gracchus?"

"This is most definitely not for the king, though he may already know about it." Marlowe reached for his glass and took a healthy swallow.

Adrian had to work to keep focused on their conversation.

Sidony in the water, hair trailing over her shoulders. Kissing Sidony, her tongue in my mouth. Standing on the shore with her, moonlight outlining every sweet curve of her body. Kissing her again.

"Have you been listening?" Marlowe scowled at him.

Adrian pinched the bridge of his nose, mentally shaking off thoughts of Sidony.

"Yes, of course." He met Marlowe's gaze and tried to recall their conversation. "Marenburg, not-dead, royal family. Wait. What will Gracchus do about this? Will my family be safe?"

"As safe as they are now." He signed the letter and blew on it. "I left a copy for you. Destroy it once I leave."

"And if this claim is true? That another Lost Royal survived the massacre, what will that mean for the king?" Adrian sat, weariness making his limbs heavy.

"He would lose his hold on the throne if another was proven a true heir. Prince Callum's claim would be further along if the king hadn't tied up the courts."

"Unless the prince gets killed first," Adrian said. He sipped his drink. Though he couldn't imagine how they had handled it, it seemed that two of the princes had survived the family's massacre. It was impressive and inspiring. He had been traveling to Embury with his uncle when the assassinations had taken place, but the country had been in mourning for years. Adrian had had a cold reception as the royal heir, so he'd worked hard to gain the loyalty of his father's people. Gracchus had reunited with Torwyn two years later. The pressure was off Adrian, but by that time, his loyalty to his father's dying wish was developing some cracks.

At least the timing of this latest rumor worked to his benefit as well. With the king distracted, Adrian might be able to get to his mother and sister sooner. Shards of hope warmed his chest.

Marlowe, of course, had his own agenda, which appeared to be working for the rebellion. "You understand the danger they face," he said, meaning the two princes.

Adrian grimaced. "I'm assuming you are handling that, or you would be giving me more specifics."

Marlowe gave a short nod.

"Then this could be what I've been waiting for."

Marlowe's lips curled. He raised his glass to Adrian.

"When does Gracchus leave?"

"First, the king has new orders for you. Torwyn will deliver them tomorrow."

Adrian shrugged and closed his eyes. As long as the king wouldn't require his company, he didn't care what the man wanted him to do. Adrian was close now. This was why he'd had to push Sidony away. His world was full of schemes and countermeasures. She'd never survive it, and he already had enough people to worry about.

The scent of smoke and whisky drifted up, reminding him of his adopted homeland. This extended time away had made him realize he missed Embury. Once he freed his mother and Minah, the likelihood of his being able to live there was low. It didn't matter. He'd have to leave Embury to its own problems, but even the thought of doing that nagged at him.

"Does Gracchus have the princess?"

Marlowe chuckled. "No."

THE NEXT DAY, Prince Torwyn returned to L'Ortagia to meet with the queen at Mondelac Castle. When he arrived, he requested Adrian accompany him on a ride outside the castle walls. Torwyn's guards, along with Lord Sullivan, formed a perimeter around them several feet away.

They dismounted and Adrian walked a couple paces behind his cousin across the land surrounding the castle. They walked in silence until they reached the crest of a low hill. Torwyn,

Marlowe, and Adrian would meet with the queen and her small council later that day.

"The king wanted you to have this." Torwyn handed him a letter.

The seal had already been broken, but Adrian did not comment on it. The note read:

DEAR ADRIAN,

We have a means for returning a bride to Embury. Our efforts to rescue Her Royal Highness Princess Zara D'Arles from the rebellious lot have not yet proved successful. Marlowe will share with you our plans for routing a settlement of rebels we believe housed the princess. You, my dear nephew, will remain in L'Ortagia and marry the younger heir, Princess Sidony. You will need to prove your suit to her mother, but I have every confidence that after our efforts to secure an arrangement between our countries, and your outstanding work as liaison to Embury during this trying time, that Her Royal Highness Queen Isabeau will accept your suit. Remain in L'Ortagia until you bring home your bride.

Your most beloved sovereign, King Gracchus

ADRIAN FROZE.

Marry Sidony? No, no, no. He needed to get back. He could not marry her. But, oh, how he wanted to.

"I was shocked when Father told me. I appreciate you taking the pressure off," Torwyn said with a grimace. "Although I must say that I've enjoyed the chase when it comes to Zara."

Adrian wasn't surprised. He was impressed that the wily rebels had been able to keep Zara out of his uncle's reach.

Torwyn stared along the horizon. Adrian studied the view, wondering what it was that drew his cousin.

"Word is spreading through Embury that another of the

princes has returned. Nothing like sentiment to pluck the heart strings."

"Gracchus has an army, cousin."

"We do. But we don't have their loyalty. Not in a true sense." It was back to his uncle's paranoia. This would never end.

Adrian needed to find the orb. Torwyn had to know where it was. Maybe he could bring it up in their conversation, get some clue as to its location.

"Did the king consult his magics in making this decision? Hold one of his ceremonies?"

"Regretting your lack of attendance the last couple of years?"

Adrian stayed silent. Sometimes Gracchus made him go, but when it was his choice, he avoided the mystical ceremonies. Aside from having objects imbued with nocturnes' power, he didn't think nocturnes could be made.

"I'm curious as to how he came to the decision...and what he used."

"Nothing you haven't seen before."

This was going nowhere. He had to assume that the orb was in Embury, along with the rest of Gracchus's collection.

"Tell me how you convinced him to let you out of the betrothal," Adrian said.

He might as well figure out whether to accept the carrot or wait to see the trap.

Torwyn shrugged. "Zara has lost value. She is *tainted*, or likely will be by the time she returns home. She could be carrying that bastard's child." Bastard referring to Callum, as his uncle was wont to do too.

Adrian stalled, his thoughts in chaos. "Marlowe told me you were bringing Zara back."

"We've sent out search parties." His cousin shrugged. "Either way, if she returns or if she doesn't, the time for her to marry me is over. We need a wedding and I'm not an available groom while my bride is still missing. But *you* could have a bride. We need alliances."

Adrian made himself nod. He tapped his fingers against his thigh, willing that sense of calmness he worked to cultivate to take over. His breathing shallowed.

"No one will have her after all this. Isabeau would disagree, but the girl's been gone too long. Time for the other one."

Adrian faced north, in the general direction of Embury, his plans and hopes fading. His uncle must have confidence in what strings to pull to get Isabeau to change the future she had mapped out for her daughters. He'd marry Sidony. It was terrifying, a nightmare. Another person stuck in Gracchus's web.

There was always another agenda. Gracchus had planned to assassinate Sidony following Torwyn's wedding to Zara. Would she be safe from that as Adrian's wife?

"It will take some persuading." Torwyn straightened his waistcoat, giving Adrian a sharp look. "You will marry the blond one, get a babe on her, and then we'll see."

"How would a child change anything?" Adrian asked.

The back of his neck tensed, the sensation crawling up to the top of his skull. What Gracchus would do to a child of his was unthinkable.

"It means that, like you, your lovely bride would need to be mindful of her place, her role. We are building a dynasty in Embury. Perhaps your child will be a nocturne too."

A legacy of supernatural beings for his uncle to use. Nausea cramped Adrian's gut.

"Is he planning to sacrifice her?" On a morning when he could barely focus, couldn't see Gracchus's angle, he needed to know whether the threat to Sidony was over.

"Not anymore. Cheer up, cousin. You've had a tendre for this one all along." Torwyn whistled and began walking down the hill, his guard flanking him.

CHAPTER TWENTY

*O*nce her carriage rolled under the raised portcullis, Sidony peeked out, searching for carriages bearing the Embury royal coat of arms. She'd missed Prince Torwyn's arrival that morning when she left for the city. She hadn't been ready to face Adrian after last night. She didn't regret her actions, especially after he'd kissed her. But he'd find a way to pull away from her again.

Objectively, they didn't have a future together. But today she was more alive, more *more* as the hours passed. Perhaps she was greedy. She knew if there was a chance for such stolen moments, she'd take them.

This morning she'd wanted to cancel her trip to Cadeau in case there was any information about Zara, but Lucia had encouraged her to leave.

"You don't know that there'll be news about your sister. Lord Sullivan specifically said she was not with the prince." Lucia added one more pin to secure Sidony's wide hat. "There. I like this style on you."

Sidony didn't bother to check in the mirror. She hurried to the door. "Send a rider to fetch me in case there's any word."

"Go. I'll send someone. You'll be back this afternoon."

She returned to Mondelac as quickly as she could. Lucia never sent a rider, which was ultimately not good news.

The front drive was empty. It was possible Torwyn's row of carriages had been taken to the stables. The last time Prince Torwyn had been at Mondelac Castle, he'd traveled with several.

"Is Prince Torwyn still here?" Sidony asked a footman as he helped her down.

"He left almost an hour ago, Your Highness." The footman bobbed his head.

Had he returned only to take Adrian back to Embury?

"Is Adrian with him?"

"The prince is training with his men, along the south lawn."

Sidony hurried down the path to the stables. As she rounded the old and new kitchens, the south courtyard came into view. She sat at a bench near the apple orchard and observed his training. Adrian hacked away at a series of straw men. By now, she was familiar with his routine, but she couldn't help wincing at the amount of loose straw scattered on the training field.

Lucia greeted her from the back steps. "The queen wants to see you. I believe the matter is urgent."

Sidony's shoulders tightened. Yves wouldn't have told her mother she'd gone swimming last night, would he?

"Very well."

She glanced at Adrian again. He must have finished tearing apart the straw forms. He stood by the fence with Lord Sullivan, or Marlowe as Adrian referred to him. Marlowe gave her a small bow. Adrian's expression was unreadable. She sighed inwardly. She'd tried last night. Today, she wasn't sure if she'd made any progress.

Sidony clasped her hands together. "Any news about my sister?"

"They haven't found her yet."

"Then, let's go."

As they turned, Adrian called her name. She waited for him on the steps. "Where's my mother?" she asked Lucia.

"The small council chamber. With Yves."

"Lucia, I need to speak with the princess," Adrian said once he caught up with them.

Sidony stopped. "The prince will escort me the rest of the way."

Lucia curtsied and left. Adrian fell into step beside her and they strode a few paces in silence.

"Can you tell me any news about my sister?"

"She's alive and unharmed." He offered his arm, and she reluctantly took it, careful not to curl into his side as they walked together. "They've taken her somewhere else, though."

"Are we planning a rescue?"

"Yes, Gracchus has sent out additional men. They think she's somewhere in the northeastern edge of the kingdom, assuming she's still in Embury."

They arrived at the door to the Small Council room. Adrian stared hard at it for a long moment.

"Was there something you wished to say to me?" she asked, toying with the braid edging his cuff.

Adrian shook his head. "Not here." He reached for her hand and brought the back of it to his lips. "Your mother has something to discuss with you."

She caught his hand when he let her go. "What's going on?"

Emotions flitted across Adrian's face, almost too many to count. "I'll see you tonight."

He strode away before she could say anything.

Muffled voices sounded from inside the chamber. One of the guards opened the door. Yves stood at the doorway. "Your Highness, please come in."

"Mother, you wished to see me? Would you tell me what is happening?"

Isabeau looked up from the expanse of the table covered in charts, drawings, and maps. "Yves was showing me something new. He has a theory of who started the fire. Have a seat."

Sidony sat, crossing her ankles under her chair and tapping the toe of her slipper against the soft carpet.

"We have confirmation that Zara is with the rebel leader," Yves said.

Sidony nodded.

"It is not clear if she is being held against her will or if she is aiding him. Knowing your sister, whichever she thinks would irritate me more would be her course of action."

"Mother, *please*."

Yves rearranged the same sheaf of papers and smoothed a particular section of the map repeatedly.

"We've had no communication from the rebels." Isabeau rubbed her forehead. "I do think your sister would have tried to send word."

Sidony nodded. It was an acknowledgment, one her mother rarely made, of her sister's consideration.

"Perhaps it couldn't get through," Yves said from the corner of the room.

"What makes you say that?" The queen sat again, her posture perfect. A slight frown swept over her face.

"There have been troops scattered between Mondelac Castle and where the king's men said they believe she's being kept. It would be difficult to breach that. Princess Zara may have tried to send an envoy."

"Odd then, that the Emburians told us they hadn't heard anything from the rebels either. Not after stealing my daughter away right out from under my nose. Excellent point, Yves. That will be all."

Yves bowed and left the small council room.

Isabeau moved a marker on the map in front of her, her expression contemplative. "I'm beginning to think your sister is somehow involved in her own disappearance."

Exactly what Sidony was afraid the queen would figure out too.

"That's ridiculous. Zara wouldn't run away."

"She didn't want to marry Torwyn at all, really. I think her note was a way for her to find time to leave the castle."

"But what about the rebels?"

"Your sister could have been working with them."

For a moment, Sidony wondered if her mother could pluck these thoughts from her head. She hadn't let Zara's secret slip out, had she? What possible reason would the queen assume this now?

"Why would Zara do that? Whatever disparaging things you say about her, please remember that my sister is loyal to you and to L'Ortagia. She would never do anything to jeopardize that."

"True." Isabeau sniffed. "It doesn't explain the lack of ransom request."

"Maybe that's not what they want."

Her mother waved a hand over the table. "As you know, your sister's wedding was one step toward a greater alliance with Embury. Without her here, we cannot proceed with our plans."

"So what happens now?" Despite her going willingly, Sidony worried for Zara the longer she stayed away.

"You know I'm concerned about her. Regardless, without her here and without any hope of her being returned soon, we have no choice but to proceed with the arrangements in a different fashion."

Sidony tapped her foot on her chair leg. What had Torwyn and her mother arranged while she'd been gone?

"Please don't tell me you mean for me to marry Prince Torwyn. Mother, I cannot."

"King Gracchus has requested *your* hand as a replacement for your sister."

Tap, tap, tap.

Her insides quivered like the rolling motion of a carriage. "No."

The queen waved her hand wearily. "Betrothals are not easily broken, so the marriage would be to his nephew, Prince Adrian. You two have developed a fondness, yes?"

Every muscle in her body stilled. Sidony could barely nod. Her slipper slid off her foot.

She was to marry Adrian.

"Unless you have a strenuous objection, I intend to accept on your behalf."

CHAPTER TWENTY-ONE

*A*n hour past sunset, Adrian knocked on Sidony's door. The rest of the castle knew what he was doing, since he'd asked for supplies earlier. But the hallway was empty. He stretched out his senses, pleased that he could send them farther and through more barriers than he had before he'd met Sidony.

The path to the lake was clear. They could be alone.

When Adrian had stood with Sidony outside the small council chamber earlier, he'd stared at the tall doors and been struck by the formality of their arranged marriage. It was what was done given their rank and status. Documents would be drawn up with all the details, the bride and groom, if they were young enough, not generally consulted about much.

With Sidony, he wanted a moment for the two of them. And he wanted to ask her himself. So much of his life had been given over in service to the king. Marrying Sidony would not only be a willing act, as he had accepted once he'd torn apart a straw-filled form, but he'd make it a meaningful one as well.

His powers picked up a shift in the wind outside the castle.

Would a breeze help or hinder what he had planned for tonight?

"Adrian?" Sidony stood in her doorway, tousled and gorgeous. He hadn't seen her since early this afternoon. Her green eyes shone with surprise.

"What are you doing?" she asked.

A tremor rippled up his spine at the thought of failing her. He straightened his shoulders. "I'm breaking you out."

"Is it my turn?" She gave him a tiny smile. "So serious. Are we going swimming or something you like to do for fun? Sword training?"

He tried to relax. "I have something to show you."

"When will you and I ever get any sleep?" She pretended to yawn.

"I hope this will be better than sleep." Perhaps he should have found a way during the day. He had never had to woo a woman. What if he made a mess of it?

What gave him hope was that when it came down to the two of them, past the suspicions and formal graces, it was easy. Sidony softened his edges. He hoped he protected her fire and sweetness.

"Give me a moment." Sidony made a face at him then closed the door behind her.

He kept his senses firmly in place, though he was tempted to watch and listen, discover a clue to her reaction about their betrothal. His unaltered hearing managed to pick up on her muttering "better than sleep."

Sidony emerged from her rooms, hair pulled back and wearing shoes. "What's going on? We have things to discuss."

He offered his arm and she took it, curling her fingers and leaning into his side. "Since you showed me how to have...what did you call it? Fun?"

"Yes, fun." She poked him in the ribs.

"I decided to repeat the experience, only with a couple of

146

changes." He tilted his head and looked at her. "But I'm not certain it will work."

"You need my help?" She tucked a curl behind her ear.

"Only yours."

"Oh."

And then the normally chatty Sidony was silent on the way out to the lake. It helped him rehearse what he was going to say and ask.

Are the stars brighter tonight?

He didn't remember seeing them sparkle across the water last night.

"Have you developed a fondness for nighttime swimming?" Sidony teased.

"Most definitely." He scanned the area, spotting only a few nocturnal creatures in the surrounding woods. He pulled in his powers, needing to save his energy for the night ahead. He was confident he could keep them safe on the water.

"Swimming in the moonlight and sword practice at dawn? When will we sleep?"

Adrian chuckled and led her over to a small boat nestled on the sand. Yves had left it for him. "Please. Get in."

"A skiff? No swimming, then?"

He shook his head. Sidony stepped in, carefully holding her skirts until she was seated on the bench. There was another bench across from her, and after pushing off, Adrian climbed in, balancing the boat quickly.

"Are you settled?" he asked.

"Yes, though I'm curious about what you have back there." She tried to peer around him, but he'd covered the packages with a tarp.

He grinned and rowed past a tree overhanging the shore.

"It's too dark to see. Don't bother peeking." Adrian laughed as she crossed her arms over her chest.

"You have an elaborate means of fun."

"I thought I'd bring you some place special." He kept rowing, almost there.

She pursed her lips. "You want to try diving out into the lake?"

"I hadn't planned on getting in this time."

Her mouth turned down in mock sadness. "Did some water nymph ruin midnight swimming for you?"

"The opposite, in fact." His attention had been on the water and the shoreline, but now that he'd rowed out to the point he'd figured earlier in the day, he sat still, taking in the feel of the gentle waves hitting the side of the boat.

"It's peaceful out here." She trailed a hand in the water.

"It's nice to have it to ourselves." He'd detected Yves on the parapet a few moments before. The safety of bringing Sidony out like this was questionable, but Adrian detected the magics that kept the inlet lake hidden from the outside. It was a matter of tuning in to his senses in a different way, of knowing what to look for.

Once they were on the water, they would be undetected by outsiders, and he could relax.

"It's lovely." She glanced up at the sky. "I feel better knowing Zara sees the same sky, wherever she is."

"That she does. We'll get her back. The rebels won't hurt her."

"Even after this long? What if they tire of her?"

"I don't think that's possible. My guess is that your sister will find a way to bring them in line."

Her eyes flashed to his face. She hitched her shoulder but didn't speak further about her sister.

He checked the water, still surprised at its warmth. A small river ran through this side of the lake, and he needed to be close enough to the current for what he planned.

He rubbed his hands across his thighs. "I have something for you."

"What is it?" Sidony grinned.

Searching behind his seat, he grabbed a narrow taper. He gave it to her and lit it. He reached again and brought forward one of the silk lanterns he'd put together this afternoon.

"What's that?"

"It's for wishing," he said softly. "I thought you would want to wish for your sister's safe return." He held out the lantern, showing her how to light the wick inside. The red silk glowed in his hand.

"What do I do with it?" Tears shimmered in her eyes. Her hands fluttered in her lap.

"We place it on the water and make a wish." He slowly turned the lantern to show her the painted side. The first depicted two women holding hands.

Sidony stared at it, running a finger along the top of the frame.

"Oh. They're *sisters*." She took the lantern, gently setting it in the water next to the boat. "Like this?"

"Yes. The current should take it downstream to Cadeau."

Her eyes widened. She stared at the lantern then glanced back at him. "That's wonderful. That's why we went out to this side."

He nodded. She seemed to like the first lantern. He'd kept her at bay for so long, he wanted to draw out the proposal. He wanted her to know it was about her and not merely that his king commanded him.

She closed her eyes, and when she spoke, her voice had a catch in it. "I was thinking how much Zara would like these floating into the city. She would want to share something so fine. How long will it stay lit?"

"A good hour or two. Here. Make a wish." Adrian gave the lantern a push in the water, and it floated a few feet away.

"I wish for Zara's safe return and for a message from her to our mother." Sidony sighed, and Adrian thought he detected a hint of frustration.

Again he had the notion that she knew more about her sister's kidnapping than she let on. He needed to press her about it, but now was not the time. He reached back again.

"Another?" The second lantern had a painting of a woman holding a book. On the other side, her arms were lifted above her head in a dance step.

"This one's for you." He held the lantern out to her and she lit it, turning the screens in a full circle before setting the lantern in the water.

"I love it. But I made a wish already."

"Wish for anything you want. You don't even have to tell me." So far, it was going well. The hardest part was coming up. Adrian rolled his shoulders.

Sidony closed her eyes. "There." She pushed the lantern, and it floated away, trailing in the wake of the first. "Thank you. Was that me holding a book of plays?"

"Yes. Your mother's hostess, patroness of the arts, and trusted diplomat. L'Ortagia is lucky to have such a devoted princess."

"I…thank you." Sidony looked like she hadn't heard that about herself before.

"One more." He turned back to her with a third lantern.

"Ah, for you?" she asked.

"For us," he said, and tilted the lantern to show her the sides.

"Let me see that." Sidony took the lantern and turned it, awed by the scenes of a couple together. On one, they danced. On another, they stood, surrounded by flowers. On the third side, two figures stood together on a beach. On the fourth side, they sat in a boat across from each other, holding hands, almost exactly as they were doing now. A breath caught in her throat, and she was overwhelmed by tenderness toward him. There, on those four silk panels, were images of their time together.

"Oh, Adrian. Did you paint these?" The designs were beautiful. How had he done all of this?

"Yes, although I had help."

"By the style of the paintings, I'd say they were all done by the same hand."

Though it was dark, the lantern provided enough light to catch the flush across Adrian's cheeks.

"Yves delivered the skiff and candles. He was surprisingly dexterous in fashioning the frames. I wanted to do this tonight."

"Thank you. They're lovely."

She waited for him to say more, but he grew quiet. He had said she brought him a sense of fun. Maybe he needed it now.

"Hmm, Adrian? This side is hard to see. Could you hand me the candle please?"

Brows raised, he passed it over.

"Ah, there," she continued. "They're fishing. Clever."

"Uh. They're fishing?" he asked.

"Yes, but I can't seem to find their fishing poles. But, yes. Definitely fishing." She squinted at the painting, holding it up. "Is that why you brought me out here?"

"Not really." He frowned. "I suppose they could be fishing."

"What shall we wish for then?" She lit the wick and moved to set the lantern in the water.

He reached out and helped her push the lantern downstream. "Fishing? It looks like fishing?" He blew out the taper, laying it under the tarp behind him.

"Well, now. Not necessarily." She let him take her hands. "What are they doing?"

"They're doing this." He leaned forward and kissed her

softly on the lips. When he pulled back, it was as if the cork had been popped off the bottle. "Sidony, since the moment I met you, you have affected me like no one else. You came into my life unexpectedly. You are everything that has been missing—things I didn't know I needed—and dear to me." He adjusted his grip on her hands. "Will you marry me?"

"Adrian." She flushed with pleasure. "Yes, I will."

His lips curled, and he kissed her again. "Sidony. I don't deserve you, but thank you."

She laced their fingers together and tipped up her face for another kiss.

"I like being out here on the water with you." She rested her forehead against his cheek. "So tell me about the fishing scene."

He chuckled and shook his head. "It could be fishing. But they're us, out here on this boat tonight." He swallowed and met her gaze. "They're falling in love."

Oh, this man.

"Then that's what I wish for. For us." Sidony watched the lantern float away, the procession of three casting a warm, red glow over the lake.

Adrian leaned forward, and this time she met him halfway, kissing in the middle of the boat. Her heart was full, aside from worry for her sister, but she would take this man, the choice in front of her, and build a life with him.

"Adrian, do you think we can be happy?"

"With each other, yes. Absolutely." He kissed her again, one hand slipping behind her neck, fingers tangling in her hair. The little boat rocked in the water. "Do you?"

"I hope so."

"Isn't this what you wanted?" There was a tinge of fear in his eyes.

"I wanted us to have a chance," she said softly. "And now, we do."

His lips slid down to press along her jaw. She rubbed a hand up under his coat, feeling his heartbeat against her palm. She held him close and gazed up at the night sky. The sweetness of his proposal soothed the heartache she'd carried with her these past few weeks of wondering when they'd have to part.

"Did you make a wish for us?" Sidony's fingers drifted over his hair, sifting through the ends tucked back in his queue.

Adrian rested his face against hers and gazed out at the lights trailing along the water. "Mine already came true. We'll have to go with yours."

CHAPTER TWENTY-TWO

*S*idony stroked her thumb along the edge of Adrian's waistcoat. The starch of his shirt and a sharp note of paint mixed with the delectable scent that was his alone, tickling her nose. The boat rocked in the water, drifting farther out into the lake. They could be in their own world. This was really happening.

He's...mine?

As if hearing her thoughts, Adrian turned back to her, holding her close. Angling her head, she kissed him. On a whim, she sent out a quick burst of her amplifier, just enough that she felt a pinch along her temples. The boundaries along the edge of the lake somehow sharpened and Adrian relaxed against her. Had it worked? Perhaps she'd try again later. For now, she wanted to be in this moment with him.

A sweet ache built in her chest. She kissed him with purpose, as if they'd kissed each other a thousand times and knew how their mouths fit together.

Adrian's chest was warm under her hand. So different from other times she'd touched him. Last night, they'd been able to cool off in the lake. Tonight, although her dress was light-weight due to it being summer, she was melting.

She pulled off her fichu, having grabbed it for modesty.

His mouth moved over hers with a firm pressure, and she shivered. Hot, cold. She squirmed on the bench, making the boat sway.

Adrian ran his hands down her arms and clutched her waist. She inched closer, wanting to launch herself at him. As it was, her skirts impeded her legs, and her sleeves pulled at her arms.

She forced herself to still and sat up. "Adrian, I love that your proposal was out here. I wish we could..." She waved a hand in the space between them.

"I know. Me too." He ran a thumb over her cheek. "Shall we head back?"

She loved knowing he was in a similar state of frustrated desire. She hated for their time out on the water to end.

"I'm not ready to go yet."

"Then let's talk," he offered and leaned back on his hands.

She turned her head to get another look at the floating lights. "The lanterns are beautiful. I've never seen anything like them. Thank you."

Adrian put a hand over hers. "They're from my homeland."

Sounds of the night settled in around them. Crickets chirped and frogs croaked from the shore.

"Was that a traditional Daeson proposal?" She met his gaze again, his dark eyes intent.

"Not among royalty. Those are usually still arranged. The lanterns are part of a festival." His thumb rubbed along her wrist. "That's where I used to see them, in Sinchon. I thought you'd like them."

"I do." She smiled at him. "What was it like growing up in Daeso?"

Adrian picked up the oars and began rowing them back where they had first set the lanterns in the water.

"We had a house outside the village of Sinchon. We'd go fishing almost every day. My father was terrible at it but kept taking us because he knew we loved it. My mother taught me to read. She has a beautiful voice, perfect for storytelling. She'd have me and my sister gasping for breath, we'd laugh so hard when she'd read to us."

Sidony couldn't imagine her mother doing such a thing, but the joy that lit Adrian's face as he talked about his family was infectious. "They sound like they loved you and your sister very much."

His gaze met hers. "Yes."

"Tell me more."

"When my father was alive, he talked to us about Embury a lot, explaining the traditions, the shifts and relationships between royal houses and noble families. Before he died, he made me promise that I'd see his homeland." Adrian's voice grew ragged at the end. He toyed with the handle of the oar before continuing. "After he was gone, we stayed in the house I grew up in."

She frowned. "Wouldn't his family have offered to have you live with them after he died?"

"Silvius, my father, was estranged from them. They didn't understand why he chose to be a scholar, or how he could marry someone..."

"Outside of Embury?"

"From the other side of the world, according to him." He met her gaze again. "My father's funds were cut off once he made it clear he would not be living in Embury as a minor prince. He had aspirations to see more of the world. He traveled the Silk Road, earning a small fortune. He eventually settled in Daeso, met my mother, and married her."

"Was her family more accepting?"

"My mother's from a noble family," he continued. "They were apprehensive at first. After I was born, they softened."

"That's good. That they accepted you. How often do you get to see them?"

They sat for a few moments listening to water hit the side of the canoe.

"I haven't been back since I came to Embury as Gracchus's heir. The king needed me." Adrian had softened when talking about his parents and his life in Sinchon. When he brought up Gracchus, he again retreated. His native accent disappeared completely when he spoke of the king, sounding like he'd lived in Embury all his life. She and Zara had been grilled on elocution lessons, so she recognized a practiced way of speaking.

"That must be so difficult, to be away from home—even your second home—and family."

He was utterly still but for the toe of one boot bobbing up and down.

"I owe much to my uncle. And I had a cousin I didn't know. Gracchus made a promise of sponsorship to my family when I agreed to come with him." His eyes glittered in the darkness.

"When was the last time you saw them?"

"When I left Sinchon."

It was as if a stone had been dropped into her stomach. It'd been years since he'd seen them.

CHAPTER TWENTY-THREE

A haunted look crossed Adrian's face.

Sidony squeezed his hand, waiting for a cue from him as to what he needed in this moment. She shook her head. Her husband-to-be had so many secrets and so much pain.

"Sidony," he said in a low, faraway voice. "When I stopped getting their letters, I feared they were dead."

"Oh, no." Sidony tucked her fichu back into the front of her dress. "Is there anything I can do?" Sidony asked, startled at his shuttered look.

"No." Adrian stared at her, some warmth coming back into his expression. "I miss them."

"That must be terrible."

Again he paused, as if choosing his words. "I used to think that if I just left for Sinchon, I could find them."

"Did you ever try?"

He laughed, the sound brittle in his chest. "Once. I was gone for a week. The passage I'd purchased was delayed long enough for Marlowe to find me."

She swallowed. "And what did he say?"

"He said that visiting…wouldn't bring them back. That I had a purpose here."

"Adrian, it's almost as if they died."

Somehow that broke something free in him, and his eyes snapped to hers. "I wondered about that for a long time. But they didn't. And someday…we'll be reunited."

She smiled at him. "I have every faith that you will. I look forward to meeting them."

He looked shocked but quickly checked his reaction. "I'd like that too."

The lanterns had drifted farther down the lake from where they floated, like tiny stars on the water.

"Sidony, despite how we…met, I wouldn't change what's between us."

She hurt for him, thinking about how he had such responsibilities he could only answer her carefully. "Would you repaint the scenes from the lanterns on something for me to keep?"

"Those?" His surprise was genuine.

"Of course. They were lovely."

A side of him she rarely saw came out, and he took to the oars again, bringing them closer to the shore. "Don't you have powerful friends in the L'Ortagian art world?" he teased.

Muscles bunched in his shoulders as he pulled the oars through the water. Each stroke effortless and masterful. "Yes, I do. Someone who'd pay to have those as part of my…I mean, *her* personal collection."

Once they were back on dry land, he pulled her close, his face inches from hers. "I'm glad I asked you myself." His gaze landed on her lips.

"Adrian, can we celebrate our betrothal tonight?" Before he could answer, she went up on her tiptoes and met his mouth with hers.

"WHAT DID YOU HAVE IN MIND?" Free from the confines of the boat, Adrian bent his head and kissed her collarbone, pulling the edge of sheer fabric aside to bare the upper swells of her breasts. She was lush and tempting.

"Something like this."

He kissed the tops of her curves and slid his finger along the edge of her bodice. She shivered and clutched at his hair. He tugged on her dress, revealing more honey-colored skin, her breasts straining against her thin shift.

She was his.

Words of praise flowed out of him. He'd wanted to say them last night but couldn't. Now, being able to return her affections made him ravenous for her. He wasn't sure how he could wait a moment longer. He was keyed up from their proposal and all the kissing they'd done on the boat. Talking about his family had only sharpened his sense of loss. Kissing her, touching her, was *real*. She was exactly what he needed.

"Why don't we go inside for this," Sidony said. She stepped back, toward the castle, and he followed, hands dropping to her waist.

"You're right." He turned his head. Soft grass grew along the edge of the small beach. "Although this wouldn't be the worst spot."

She laughed. "Adrian, come to my room."

He trailed her up the bank and a few steps into the grass before stopping. A tightness seized his chest. He was so used to holding in his emotions, keeping his thoughts to himself, that he felt raw now. He squeezed her hand.

She squeezed back and smoothed her hair, turning to him. "Despite what happened last night, I don't want to be observed when we do this."

Torches lit the parapets behind her. To the left and right of the path, the forest was dark, the trees too dense to see through.

"No one's watching." Adrian hadn't used his sensory powers for another sweep of the area, but he could. He thought he'd felt another boost of his nocturne senses out on the lake, but that might have been the intensity of the moment.

Under the stars, with the sounds of the water lapping at the shore, it would be romantic.

She tapped a finger against her lips. "You would protect me, wouldn't you?"

"With my life."

It was another honest admission she had somehow gotten out of him. He'd kept her at arm's length because he couldn't bear to bring another person into his chaotic world. Earlier, he'd wanted to confide in her, but he couldn't bring himself to put them both at risk. He'd told her as much as he dared.

She pulled him down for another hot kiss. "You make me feel safe. Wanted."

A warm slide of satisfaction coursed through his body at her words. Getting what he wanted was so unfamiliar, it took him a moment to respond. "Then let's stay here."

He spread his coat on the ground and scooped her up, laying her down. She fluttered her hands against his chest. Cool fingers loosened his neckcloth with impressive efficiency. He pulled her skirts higher, sliding a hand behind her knee and caressing her silk and lace garter. His cock pounded against his breeches. He wanted to bury himself inside her.

He had to do a quick sweep to ensure their safety because if they went much further, he wouldn't be able to focus on anything but her.

She undid the buttons on his waistcoat and pulled at his shirt. He groaned at her touch, anxious to feel her hands on his bare chest.

Adrian notched his knee on the ground between her legs and lifted his head to make sure they were alone. Sidony's eyelids were half-lowered, and she squirmed against him.

He closed his eyes, swept out his senses, and discovered two bodies about to breach the cover of the trees along the east side of the castle. *Shite.*

Sidony trailed her fingers low on his abdomen.

"We have to leave," he whispered in her ear.

She stopped her teasing caress. "What's wrong?"

"Someone's out there."

CHAPTER TWENTY-FOUR

*A*drian refastened his clothing, then stood and pulled Sidony up. The two people hiding along the edge of the forest moved closer, keeping parallel to the tree line. He drew his sword quietly.

"Wait," Sidony whispered. "It's probably a guard. No one would hurt me on castle grounds."

"They aren't guards."

"How do you know? I don't hear anything."

He didn't answer. Neither looked familiar to him. He squeezed her shoulder and tucked her behind him.

"Keep behind me." There was a chance they wouldn't attack, but he wasn't taking it. Sidony, thankfully, was silent. He cast out his senses.

"They spotted us. We should head back," a whey-faced male said.

Both figures were dressed in rough woolen clothing resembling crofters, but their boots and weapons were finely made.

Mercenaries, then. Likely nocturnes too.

"We follow through with the plan. Surprise was preferred. Not necessary." The soft feminine voice carried almost no timbre. Glancing at her back, Adrian spotted a quiver of arrows.

He had to get Sidony out of there.

"Let's go. We need another way into the castle." Adrian urged her to precede him into the woods, moving west. He'd debated charging the two in order to end the threat of attack, but he couldn't risk getting hurt and leaving Sidony vulnerable. He'd spotted one of the castle guards on the parapet when they were getting out of the canoe. Any others doing their rounds wouldn't return for another half hour. Despite his strengthened powers, his range did not extend to the castle past the personal apartments. He couldn't reach the guard tower at the front gate either. He was simply too far away to get help before the mercenaries would attack.

"I'm sure there's another entrance. Zara would know. I...I don't. I'm sorry." Her breaths came faster. There was no time for reassurance.

"Lead me through the woods, and we'll double back around." She would be safer in the woods, since the darkness would make it harder for the archer to aim.

"I've never been out there in the dark, other than along the path," Sidony whispered.

"We'll find a way." It was difficult to keep his focus, but for the first time, he'd been able to keep his powers trained on the two mercenaries, while also holding a conversation. His powers were expanding. He cast Sidony a sharp look, again confounded by her effect on him.

This was simply not the time to discuss it.

Once into the line of trees, they had to walk slowly, stepping over branches and low shrubbery. They made it twenty yards before Sidony stumbled. He helped her up, grimacing as she took a limping step.

"The woman will slow him down. Let's go," the archer said.

Adrian's powers were stretched thin, but he heard them

even as the distance widened. He sheathed his sword. It was too big a weapon to carry into the forest. His dagger was better.

Sidony walked without complaint, but she moved more slowly.

The two mercenaries followed, clearing the tree line on their side of the path, racing to the brush that edged the beach.

He made a choice. "Let me, princess."

He bent down and flung her over his shoulder. Her teeth ground together, but she didn't issue a protest. Keeping his senses on the mercenaries, who were gaining ground, he strode deeper into the woods, stepping over logs, wincing at the crunch of his boots against the dry forest floor. It couldn't be helped. Thankfully, nighttime creatures croaked and hooted, and above their heads, branches creaked as they tossed their boughs in the evening breeze.

Adrian's vision adjusted to the dark, and his nocturne-enhanced senses helped him navigate each stray tree limb and root. Running was impossible. He felt along Sidony's leg until he got to her ankle. It was already swelling. She would have been hobbling beside him. He kept moving, one hand ready with a dagger, the other tucked over the back of Sidony's legs.

He took a step, and his toe crashed into a rock. He hopped once and regained his balance, taking a small step to the side. An arrow landed in a tree trunk a few inches from where he'd been standing. Perhaps a lucky shot.

Sidony squirmed on his shoulder. "What was that?"

"An arrow."

He ducked, pulling a large branch out of his path, and the zing of another arrow zoomed over his head.

Thunk. A third arrow. This one whizzed by his ear. That level of accuracy was beyond luck or talent. Their pursuers could see in the dark. Definitely nocturnes.

It wouldn't be enough to get away from the mercenaries.

They needed to be stopped. Whoever had hired them wanted him, Sidony, or both of them dead.

Adrian stepped behind a tree and eased Sidony off his shoulder. He put a finger to her lips. She nodded. He pulled out another dagger from his boot. The mercenaries drew closer, and finally, that became an advantage. He aimed and threw the knife, using his powers to push it farther than he could normally throw it.

By the squelching sound, and a quick scan of his expanded sight, he'd hit the male in the throat. He had seconds to stop the archer. He repeated the action, nudging the dagger with his powers. The archer crouched down low. Instead of stabbing her between the ribs, she'd twisted at the last second, and the dagger sunk into her arm. Given her choice of weapon, it would disable her for a few days, or at the least, throw off her aim.

He grabbed Sidony, holding her close to his chest, and took off through the forest, angling left, so he'd get to the castle wall. He broke through the trees into the narrow strip of land adjacent to the castle. The torchlight from the parapet blinded him momentarily, and he stopped, blinking his eyes to adjust.

"Are they coming after us?" Sidony clutched his neck and peeked over his shoulder.

"Not yet. We'll be safe along the wall." At least he hoped. Left would take them to the guard gate, but they risked going past the lake. The remaining mercenary could also double back to wait for them rather than chase them through the woods.

Adrian went right. The headache from using his powers so intensely pounded against his temples.

"Sidony, is there anything back here? An old gate, the backside of a tower?"

She made an exasperated sound. "I don't know. I know all the hidey-holes on the *inside* of the castle. Zara knows more about the castle's defenses."

The wall was endless. They made a turn and reached the edge of the woods. Finally, there was an irregular pattern in the stones—not uncommon for an aged castle—but when he reached out to touch it, he felt wood, not stone. It was painted a stark gray to blend in.

He set Sidony down beside it and used his senses to see what was on the other side. Small, dark—likely an old guard station for patrols. Sidony waited, keeping her weight on one foot. The wind whipped around this section of the castle wall, creating an eerie sound. The door had a sturdy lock, which he opened from the inside. He helped her into the narrow room, coughing at the dust.

"Here." She held up a lantern she'd grabbed from a hook by the door.

"Anything to light that with?"

"This." Sidony held out a flint. "On a shelf."

He lit the lantern. "That was handy."

"Ha."

He shut the door, barring it with a nearby chair. It wasn't the sturdiest defense, but they could rest here for a while. He glanced around the room, searching. *There.* He grabbed an old, empty sack and laid it along the base of the door to block the light to the outside.

Secure for the moment.

Sidony sat on a bench, her skirt pulled up so she could see her ankle. Her hair was a curling mass around her shoulders. Elegant, even while disheveled. He ran a hand through his hair, smoothing it back into place.

He hunched down in front of her, kicking up dust from the floor. Tears welled, but she wiped them away before they could fall. She met his gaze with a determined one.

"Two things. First, thank you for getting us out of there."

"You're welcome. You were brave." He offered his hand, palm up, and she placed hers in it. He kissed the back of it, catching a whiff of the floral scent she wore at her wrist. His senses were on overload in the tiny shed.

"Hmm." With her other hand she plucked at her bodice, adjusting it, though she already had it back in place.

"What else?" His gaze swept her for other injuries, but he couldn't find any. She was safe. He'd gotten them away from the mercenaries. His relief eased the pounding in his head.

She smoothed her skirt over her crossed knees, the hem brushing his boots as it was lowered to a more appropriate length. "How did you navigate a forest in the dark, dodging attacks, and taking out the people chasing us? I couldn't see my hand before my face. Are the rumors true?"

CHAPTER TWENTY-FIVE

*B*lood drained from Adrian's face, and his shoulders dropped. Was that fear, or relief? Sidony could relate to the blood-draining sensation. She'd hung upside-down longer than she had in the entirety of her childhood.

As she'd regained her equilibrium against a tree and watched her betrothed throw daggers into the darkness with grim determination, she focused on what she'd observed. And, given her own powers of amplification, she'd helped to enhance. Without knowing his specific powers, she had no idea what, if any, nocturne powers she'd expanded.

Adrian had known they were being watched and hunted. He'd been able to navigate through a dark forest. Twice, he had successfully hit targets with assailants who were so far behind her she couldn't hear them.

Sidony had sensitive hearing. Her former music teacher had been impressed by her ability to tune instruments. She could detect which ones were out of tune within a group of instruments. Her hearing was fine. Adrian's hearing and sight were better than anyone's she'd ever heard of. Even in the dark.

Unusual, but not impossible. There was one conclusion: *He has powers like my sister.*

"You're a nocturne," she said.

"Yes." He gave a short nod.

She appreciated his honesty.

All the better since we're to be wed.

It actually made sense, now that she considered other times she'd noticed strange things: the unfocused way he'd looked at her when they first met—she knew she tended to use her powers unintentionally when she was tipsy; the way he jumped across the banquet table before the windows exploded; and everything he'd done tonight. She'd attributed her fantastical perceptions of him as simply a product of her infatuation. He must have been using his powers.

"When were you going to tell me?" She fussed with her skirts in agitation.

"I don't know." He narrowed his eyes. "I wasn't sure how you'd react."

In an effort to find a sense of calm, her gaze strayed from his intent one. She assessed his broad shoulders, her body aching in places from having been tossed over one of them. His strength was obvious. She couldn't stop the rush she felt at taking in his full, muscular form. That form had bravely whisked her away from danger, holding her close while they sought safety.

Stop it. Explanations first, then fawning over his gorgeousness.

She shook her head. "What do your powers entail?"

He stood and stepped back from her. "I can project my senses outside of my body. At any time, and from increasing distances. My senses help me see in the dark."

So, no mind control. Mind reading?

He stared at her, arms crossed over his chest. *Probably not, then.*

He wouldn't need to use that power with her. Usually when she was around him, she spilled every thought in her head.

"What have you used with me?"

He rubbed his finger over his lip, his brows furrowed. "I've used my powers around you, like you witnessed tonight. I use them often. I smelled the fuse before the explosion. I tracked where our assailants were tonight and again to see in here." He pointed to the door of the shed. "But I haven't used them on you directly."

She frowned.

"Except once or twice. My apologies. I checked on you after I'd bade you to leave the day before the wedding. I also watched you clutch my shirt the first day we met that morning in the library."

Her cheeks flamed. "Did you see me through the water last night?"

He held up his hands. "No. Never."

"Don't you use them as the king's spy? After all, that's one of the stories about you."

He closed his eyes. "Yes. That's why he brought me to Embury. But I don't use them to…" He waved his hands, indicting her body. "I was raised to be a gentleman. I don't use them to observe your…state of undress, though I have been tempted."

"Hmph."

She should have known from the start. Nocturnes lived more openly in Embury under the newer king. What she'd thought was a rumor had been the truth. And even in L'Ortagia, with the explosion, she'd thought it strange that he was bounding over the table, but it made sense once the windows exploded. Only now, she realized he was the first person to react to it because he'd *sensed* the fuse burning seconds before the blast. She shook her head slowly. He'd hidden his extrasensory skills well.

"Why didn't you tell me? Did you think I would scorn you?" Why hadn't he trusted her?

"The practice of nocturne powers is unlawful in L'Ortagia. In Embury, magic is more accepted." His expression was considering, as if he had more he wanted to say.

"I accept nocturnes. I've been around them since I was a child."

He dropped his chin. "So you finally admit to being a nocturne."

"Yes," she said easily.

"A princess of the realm is a nocturne in a region where the practice is outlawed. Is this an open secret?"

"No, not at all. My mother forbid it when I was a child. She was afraid."

"Afraid of what? Nocturnes are rare, but we exist."

Zara would have appreciated his earnestness. "We exist but are not understood. She feared the lack of acceptance meant nocturnes could be harmed. Or that somehow having a nocturne as a daughter would weaken her reign."

Adrian shook his head in bafflement.

"She doesn't know that I use my powers." Could she trust him with Zara's secret? The fact that he'd hidden something from her gave her pause. It also wasn't her secret to tell. She seemed to be racking up several of her sister's secrets.

"Your power must be expansive, like a boost to my own. You've magnified mine several times." He stared at her then rubbed a hand across his brow. "How many people do you use your powers on unwittingly?"

She winced. "I can't always control them. They work best on other nocturnes, but they enhance human performance as well."

"Sidony, you've helped me more than you know. I haven't brought it up because...well, for lots of reasons. Mostly, I feared someone using you. In a culture more open to your powers, you would be highly sought after."

Her eyes widened. "I would?" Then she crossed her arms. "I guess it's good we're having this conversation. Were you ever going to tell me?"

"I thought...some time after the wedding." He said it like a soldier, all seriousness.

She wanted to be angry, but the heat of it wasn't there. She closed her eyes, remembering their time on the lake, the look on his face. If he'd been through anything like her sister had, with powers more obvious to an outside observer, he would have taken pains to hide them. The widespread fear of the nocturnes, especially in L'Ortagia, was real. Views of witchcraft and sorcery had changed over the years. Although there hadn't been public trials in decades, accusations of *maleficium* continued. It wasn't a charge anyone wanted levied against them, as charges could lead to imprisonment or worse. Particularly not a prince raised in a foreign land...or a princess in hers.

"What do Gracchus and Torwyn know?" she asked.

"They only know about my powers," he said, his expression grim. "But they suspect you're a nocturne too."

"Adrian, tell me."

"They only suspect you." His gaze darted briefly. "They don't know my powers are changing, that the distances I can reach are expanding."

"He makes you use them on his own people?" The truth of how much the king used his nephew hit her.

Adrian grimaced. "He has me use them to get information. I don't want to talk about him." He cleared his throat, smoothing his expression. "This is between us."

Very well. She could drop the subject for now. "When did your powers start to change?"

"The night I met you."

A knock sounded at the door, and they both startled.

"Your Highness? Prince Adrian?" Yves called from outside the door.

She raised a brow to Adrian. "Can you check?"

He leveled his gaze on the door. "It's him. He's with six other guards, all L'Ortagian. None of them are the mercenaries —nocturnes too—who were after us earlier."

She beamed at him, impressed.

He went over and removed the chair and the sack from the door, opening it for Yves. "How did you find us?"

"One of the guards spotted you leaving the forest and going along the wall." Yves entered the small room and eyed Sidony.

"I'm fine." She lifted one foot. "We sought shelter here after I twisted my ankle."

"We also found this at the edge of the trees by the lake." Yves held up an arrow. From the grim set of Adrian's mouth, it was one of the arrows that had narrowly missed them.

"Did you search the grounds?" Adrian asked.

"There's a search going on now. Come. Let's get you both back on the other side of the wall. Prince Adrian, do you know who would be coming after you? Is this the work of the rebels?"

CHAPTER TWENTY-SIX

"It's a shame the guest list is so small." Lucia fussed over Sidony while she stood at the doorway of her chambers, preparing to leave for the ceremony.

"With Zara gone, we can't have a grand wedding. I wouldn't want one without her here anyway."

Lucia adjusted Sidony's necklace. "She would want you to be happy and Prince Adrian makes you happy."

"That he does." Sidony sighed. These few days with Adrian had flown by. Their betrothal was announced, the ceremony planned, and each had their own responsibilities to attend to. She kept busy with her patroness duties, which were bitter-sweet. The Gilded Rose players were readying *The Marriage of Figaro* for a mid-August debut. Sidony wasn't sure when she and Adrian would leave for Embury, but she hoped to convince him to stay for opening night.

While her betrothal made her happy, two aspects were rather thorny. The first was Zara's continued absence. It cast a pall over everyone at Mondelac, including the queen. The strain of keeping Zara's secret, that she'd gone with the rebels willingly, was wearing on Sidony.

The second was having to leave L'Ortagia within mere weeks. She and Adrian had yet to discuss their plans in detail, but she knew they'd spend most of their time in Embury. Zara would eventually return and resume her place. Sidony wouldn't have to fill in for her.

So her days as patroness, at least in her home country, were coming to an end.

"Are you ready?" Lucia asked.

Sidony nodded, and they left her suite, trailed by a set of guards.

"King Gracchus is in the chapel," Lucia said.

"Yes, he delayed a trip to Marenburg and is here for the ceremony."

The king's presence was startling, as he had not been expected. A letter announcing his visit had arrived only a day ahead of him. Sidony imagined he made the trip in order to assure himself that a wedding uniting the two countries would indeed occur.

She and Adrian had had no time to be alone together once their betrothal was announced. After the attack at the lake, Yves had forbade any late-night swimming. Not that Sidony would have considered it. Each of them had been assigned additional personal guards. What privacy they'd once had was gone. They had stolen a few kisses, but nothing else.

Sidony was more than ready for her wedding night. She'd been ready for it weeks ago. She supposed she should be nervous, but when it came to their physical attraction, each time Adrian had kissed her or touched her, all she could do was anticipate more. Still, it was one thing to look forward to marital congress and quite another to know it would be happening on the same day.

She giggled at the thought.

"Are you all right?" Lucia asked.

"I'm fine." Sidony sought for a more sober expression. "Just thinking how different this day is from what I had anticipated."

Lucia nodded but didn't seem convinced.

She and Lucia walked toward the family chapel, taking the route that led to the main entrance. Once they arrived, a footman opened the door. The assembled guests surprised her by applauding at her entrance. She nodded and curtsied, unusually self-conscious.

Isabeau and Gracchus were deep in conversation in a far corner. Torwyn stood off to the side, his gaze straying to his father. He smirked at Sidony, tilting his head as if to indicate his approval. She ignored him, her attention snagged on Adrian's uncle. The king was slightly shorter than she'd imagined, with a full head of salt-and-pepper hair. He gave off a robustness like that of a favorite uncle. As she watched him, his expressions ranged, but never into a hint of a smile.

A somber officiant stood to the side, a leather-bound book clutched in his hand. The short rows of pews strained to fit the nobles and select courtiers, though not all had taken a seat. The stained-glass windows glowed, their colors somehow richer. The scent of heavy perfumes and candlewax permeated the space. A wave of dizziness came over her.

Where was Adrian?

"Is there a protocol?" Lucia asked in a low voice.

"Not until the ceremony starts." Sidony surveyed the room again, hoping she'd missed him. He wasn't there. "Let's greet my mother and the king."

"He's probably on his way."

Sidony smiled at Lucia's encouraging words, trying not to let her nervousness show. "It doesn't bode well after my sister missed her own wedding."

"True."

As she made her way over to her mother, Torwyn pulled the king aside and spoke to him.

"Sidony, darling," her mother called to her.

Gracchus scowled and pointed down. Torwyn left, his shoulder brushing hers as he made his way past her down the aisle. Sidony shivered.

Where was Adrian?

~

ADRIAN AND YVES had nearly completed their ride along the perimeter of the castle grounds when Adrian spotted a rider.

"Stop here." He held the spyglass to his eye to continue the ruse of needing it.

Yves pulled his horse to a halt, his gaze scanning the low hills before them. "What do you see?"

"A young man on horseback carrying a large satchel." Though the satchel was plain and worn, it had a distinctive marking branded into the leather. It was the insignia of the House of MacKinnon, the family who ruled before Gracchus took the throne. The rebels had begun using it too. "Could be a messenger. Let's go."

Since Zara's disappearance, Yves was suspicious of any travelers from Embury, so they intercepted the rider before he got much closer to the castle.

"State your business on this road," Yves said, his voice gruff.

"I bear messages for the queen and the princess." The youth tugged at the cap on his head. Shaggy blond curls hung over his face. He could be harmless, but Adrian was still wary. He knew not to underestimate the rebels.

"I'm the queen's Captain of the Guard. You'll give it to me." Yves held out a hand and brought his horse closer.

The young man took out a packet tied in string. He handed it to Yves and looked nervously between the two men. "Here."

"Are you to wait for a reply or was your mission merely to delivery it?" Adrian asked.

"To see if the queen wished to send a reply." The youth's eyes widened, his gaze fixed on Adrian. He sucked in a breath and bowed, removing his cap. He spoke with a stammer. "Yer one of the princes."

"Yes," Adrian answered.

The bells tolled, and Adrian grimaced. He was late for his wedding. He had come out with Yves in the hopes of finding some word about Zara or the mercenaries who had attacked him and Sidony.

Yves read the first note then passed it to Adrian. It explained the rebels' mission and that they would return Zara soon. Callum had signed it. Frustratingly, he'd made no demands, so there was nothing to negotiate. All they could do was wait for Zara's release. The second letter was addressed to Sidony and Isabeau. The handwriting was different from Callum's, so Adrian assumed it was from Zara. He used his powers to read it while it was still sealed. The letter was brief, confirming Zara's safety.

"Prince Adrian, a word?" Yves asked.

They took their horses a few paces away from the messenger, who hadn't been able to take his eyes off Adrian.

"I'm assuming you want to take this young man to the castle for questioning, yes?"

Adrian nodded.

"Let me speak with him. He's a farmer's son who took some coin. I want to see what he knows and send him off. You go on, I'll bring the letters to the queen after the ceremony."

"Thank you, Captain." Adrian was already late. A distraction of this magnitude could postpone the wedding. He wanted to be well and truly married to Sidony before something else could come between them. As it was, he wasn't sure how much time he'd have with his wife anyway.

"You'll be a good husband to the princess. There's been enough upheaval. Go."

Without Yves's help, he wouldn't be able to marry Sidony this morning. By him delaying the letters' arrival and the presence of the messenger, Adrian knew he'd be in the captain's debt. He nodded at Yves in thanks.

Before he left, Adrian addressed the messenger. "What is your name?"

"Edwin." The messenger bobbed his head, his hands fidgeting with the reins. It wouldn't do to have him afraid of the L'Ortagians or himself.

"Edwin, you are under my protection. Now tell me, did you see Princess Zara?"

"No." The youth swallowed nervously. "They hired me to do this job. I'm not...I'm loyal to the king."

"Yes, I'm sure you are. We'll need to take you back to Mondelac to deliver these messages. Captain Yves will have more questions for you."

"I don't know who hired me, Highness. We lost nearly two dozen of our sheep last year. They offered me a fair bit of coin. I couldn't turn it down."

Yves crossed his arms.

"But I did ask about her. Because we heard the rebels had Princess Zara."

"And?" Adrian asked.

"They said..." Edwin averted his gaze. "Pardon, but it's quite an insult."

"What did they say?" Adrian asked.

"They said the princess was happier with a true prince. That the usurper's line would end with him." Edwin's cheeks flamed.

As far as insults went, Adrian had long ago become immune. Edwin was lucky he shared it with him, as Gracchus and Torwyn would likely take offense.

"I need to get back to my wedding."

The boy swallowed. "Is there a message I'm to take back?"

"Come with me," Yves told Edwin.

Adrian rode back to the castle, thoughts churning over the news about Zara and the message from her. There was no time to tell Sidony since he was already late. If he told her first, he'd risk the ceremony being postponed, perhaps indefinitely. If news spread of Zara's letter, Isabeau might stall the wedding. Though he didn't know what his future held, or where he would live, this was his only chance to marry Sidony. Too much stood in the way before.

Yves's words stayed with him as well. He rushed to change clothes and get to the chapel. Maybe he could say something to her privately.

When he entered the wood-paneled room, Sidony was talking to Lucia. His bride was breathtaking. She wore a crimson gown, with wide bands of gold along her sleeves and skirts, embroidered with silk thread. When she turned, a tightness squeezed his chest. Her face and hair had been lightly powdered, but she glowed beneath it, her cheeks pinkening as she met his eyes. He'd never seen her so formally and regally attired.

He nodded at the assembled guests and hastened over to her, kissing her cheek. "I'm so sorry."

Sidony clutched his sleeve, her brows pinched with strain. "Are you all right?"

"I'm fine." He patted her hand, aware of the many eyes on them. "You look radiant."

"Adrian, let's get on with it. You don't want this one to slip away." Gracchus's expression was neutral, the rebuke in his tone aimed at Adrian.

"Uncle. Your Majesty," he greeted Gracchus and Isabeau. "Apologies for my lateness."

Isabeau lifted her chin. "Are we ready to begin?"

It was effectively a command. Adrian's news would have to wait. Relief coursed through him as the ceremony started.

The officiant stood in front of the altar and performed a

simple but binding ceremony. Sidony stood to Adrian's left, her hand on his arm. Her head nearly rested on his shoulder, they were so close. As they repeated their vows, weeks' worth of tension eased from him.

When it was time, Adrian slipped a ring on her finger. It had a large pink diamond. He also gave her a smaller ring with a jade cabochon. He wore his father's ring.

Sidony made a soft humming sound once the ceremony was complete. Adrian turned to her and bent down, meeting her lips with a tender kiss.

In spite of the applause, he couldn't tear his gaze away from his bride. Her peridot-green eyes were wide, as if in shock. "We are wed, my darling." He brought her fingers to his lips.

"Finally," she said on a rush of air.

She leaned closer and kissed him again, her expression a mix of joy and relief, unforgettable. Lips curled, cheeks rosy, and a softness to her gaze when she looked at him. He tucked her against his side, keeping an arm around her. She felt so right. It was enough for now.

He pitched his voice low. "You're my Persephone now."

She raised twinkling eyes to his. "A willing Persephone, though."

Lucia hastily wiped a tear and even Isabeau's eyes were misty.

Sidony laughed softly. "I feel like I can breathe now."

"Me too."

They signed official documents, a small portion of the vast negotiations that had gone on between the two countries. He was again glad their proposal had been just between the two of them.

Guests congratulated them, including his uncle. Once there was a free moment, Adrian led Sidony over to one of the stained-glass windows.

"I have news about Zara. We received a message. Yves is verifying it before bringing it to Isabeau."

Sidony put a hand to her mouth. "Is she coming home soon?"

"I hope so. She sent you a letter." It was a relief to give her news about her sister.

"Did you read it?"

He spoke at her ear, as softly as he could. "Without opening it. It's brief. She confirms she is with the rebels and that she is safe." He pulled back, gauging her reaction. "Yves has it now. I assume he'll bring it to your mother first."

She swallowed, a range of emotions crossing her face. "This is good news."

With his expanded senses, Adrian sensed Yves walking toward the chapel. He tensed, anticipating Gracchus's anger that the messenger hadn't been brought to him right away.

Yves greeted the queen and pulled her aside, showing her the letters.

Isabeau paled, then nearly sank to the floor in a swoon before Yves caught her.

CHAPTER TWENTY-SEVEN

"Sylvie, that will be all." Isabeau's normally strong voice sounded faint from where she lay against a mound of pillows. The room was dim, the heavy brocade curtains drawn against the late-morning light.

"Someone needs to stay at your bedside, my queen," Sylvie said. She held the queen's hand, petting it lightly, from where she knelt beside the bed. Her aubergine-colored skirts pooled at her feet.

Her mother's response was too soft to make out the words.

The queen's lady-in-waiting stormed past Sidony, stopping in front of the doorway. "Find me when you leave," she said on the way out.

Sidony stood still, alone with her mother. The queen was rarely ill; it was mildly terrifying to see her so weak. Although Sidony had never told her, she admired her mother's presence. Isabeau could control a room with an expression. She would have been riveting on stage, not that Sidony would ever share that thought with the queen.

"Light the lamp." Isabeau's face was pale, her eyes tired.

Once Sidony lit the wick, her mother sat up. She clutched her midsection and let out a groan.

"What happened?" Sidony asked.

"I'm not entirely sure. You know I don't faint." She peered at the door.

"No, of course not. Was there something in the letters that shocked you?" Sidony pulled up a chair to sit next to the bed.

"Other than it doesn't sound like Zara is miserable and wants to come home," Isabeau grumbled.

"It was brief. I was surprised by that as well."

"Yes, well. It gives credence to the theory that her kidnapping is less about her and more about whom she was to marry. I still wonder that they haven't sent your sister home."

Sidony nodded, guessing her sister was deep in a plot with the rebels. "Mother, can I get you anything? How are you feeling?"

"You know how I hate to be fussed over. That's what I wanted to tell you." Isabeau checked the door again, a move completely unlike her. She had moments of paranoia, but her arrogance usually overrode any long-standing fears. "I've been fainting lately, usually in the morning."

Sidony's hand fluttered to her chest. "It wasn't the letters?"

"No. It wasn't. I've been having…digestive problems." Isabeau detested discussing anything physical, so it must have been extreme for her to do so.

"Have you asked the physician?"

Isabeau snorted. "And have him bleed me? No."

"Then what are you going to do?" Sidony asked.

"I don't think I have a disease. I think I'm being poisoned." She tilted her head as if the matter had been decided.

"What? Have you told Yves? How long has this been going on? Don't you have a royal taster?"

"Yes, I do. And she's perfectly healthy. It's been weeks." Isabeau sniffed. "Although she never tastes my tea and biscuits."

Sidony frowned. "Mother."

"I have several ideas, but that's the only thing that's different. No one else is sick."

"You should still see a physician. Surely Cadeau has dozens, what with the school there."

"And say what?"

"Mother. Don't be difficult."

"I could be dying," Isabeau said flatly.

"Don't. This is ridiculous. Bring in your taster to sample the tea."

"I can't. It's too awkward."

"You being poisoned is awkward, to say the least." Sidony checked an urge to roll her eyes.

Isabeau waved her hand. "Well, there you have it. I'd like to talk about your sister."

"Wait. I'm sending for a physician. And you need to...not drink your tea or eat your biscuits."

"Fine." Isabeau reached out and patted Sidony's hand. "It's nice to know you care."

Sidony was speechless. Her mother had been poisoned.

"Your sister's note changes little." Isabeau drew herself up, her cheeks flushing. "These rebels do not dictate when they'll release her. We are sending out a new search party tomorrow morning."

"Adrian assures me she will be unharmed." Sidony rested her hand on her chin, recalling her sister's letter. "Why didn't she talk about missing home or give any clue to where she was?"

Isabeau appeared to be deep in thought. "It doesn't appear to be a code for anything, though that would be unlike your sister. In truth, she doesn't sound distressed."

Sidony nodded.

"I've asked Gracchus about those rebels. He says they are royalists supporting the former regime."

More likely led by a member of that regime. "You met them, right?"

"Of course. We didn't have many occasions for a royal visit, but there was a memorable one. You'd have been too young to remember. Your sister, though, was quite taken with the middle son, as I recall."

"Prince Callum?" Sidony's chest felt light. She had a feeling about why her sister had been gone so long. Maybe it was all strategy, but maybe it was something more.

"Yes. He was a tall, strapping young man. Your sister fairly chased him around Blackthorne." The queen's expression was wistful.

"I cannot imagine her doing that."

"Well. She got a stern lecture from her tutors when we returned to Mondelac. A princess waits for a man to come to her."

Sidony rolled her eyes. Why her mother doled out such advice—that she herself didn't believe—was one of her exasperating traits.

"Did the prince return her affections?" Her heart ached for Zara. Her sister spent most waking hours trying to fit a model of behavior that was so rigid. For her to abandon that, she must have been quite fond of the prince.

"He may have danced with her or given her a posy." Her mother put her hand to her chest. "It doesn't matter. The MacKinnons were assassinated in the king and queen's bedchambers. That this rebel would call himself Callum is an insult to the former royal family."

"How can you be so sure?"

"My last visit to Embury was to attend their funerals." The queen paled. "One doesn't forget a country in mourning or the sight of five caskets draped in black." Her eyes met Sidony's. "The Lost Royals are a ghost story, phantoms of the imagination of a people still grieving."

"You think the rebel leader is an imposter?"

The queen shrugged. Her eyelids drooped, as if their conversation was wearing on her. "This is why the alliance was so important. That line of MacKinnons is dead. Your wedding, the hope for a new generation, will bring their people together."

Sidony wanted to pat her mother's hand, but knew she hated coddling. "Mother, how long have you been feeling ill?"

"A fortnight. The first was three months ago, but then, I felt better."

"Isn't that the first time you began betrothal arrangements with Embury?"

Isabeau tapped a finger against the coverlet. "It could be anything."

"But the timing. Why would someone hurt you?"

The queen huffed. "Too many reasons to list."

"We'll find out who did this and stop them. How long were you going to suffer like this?"

Isabeau's lips pressed together. "I was going to look into the matter more fully after you wed. I wasn't feeling badly until recently."

Sidony shook her head. "You're never the martyr."

"I'm not the martyr now." Isabeau brushed at the coverlet. "I don't need your help. I need your cooperation."

"Mother."

Isabeau yawned and waved her hand.

"You owe me, you know." Sidony stood and fluffed the pillow behind her mother's head.

"Do I?"

"Yes. For throwing me into all of Zara's duties with only a month or two of warning," Sidony huffed.

"I got you the groom you wanted."

"That you did." Sidony paused. "I never even told you."

"It was all over your damn face." Isabeau glared at Sidony, but without heat. Then she closed her eyes.

"Sylvie put laudanum in your tea, didn't she?" Sidony asked.

The queen snored delicately and fell asleep.

CHAPTER TWENTY-EIGHT

"When are you leaving?" Adrian asked Gracchus once they were alone. With Isabeau confined to her rooms and Sidony with her, Gracchus, Adrian, and Lucia had served as hosts of the truncated wedding banquet.

"This afternoon. I meet with the head of the queen's guard first." Gracchus leveled his gaze on Adrian. "You seem to have a good relationship with him."

"Yves, sire. And, yes. That was why you wanted me to stay here."

"Thanks to Zara's message, there's a new urgency for the L'Ortagians to find her. They think we know something." Gracchus grunted.

Adrian stayed silent.

"You did well today, nephew. The court has accepted you. They listen to you."

"Perhaps they approve of Embury and L'Ortagian aligning again."

Gracchus shrugged. "Then you've done your job well. The blond one suits you."

Sidony was the last person Adrian wanted to discuss with

the king. It was obvious from the ceremony how they felt about each other, so denial wouldn't help. What he needed to know were his uncle's plans so he could search Embury for his family. If he could find the orb, that would be all the better.

"She does," he said carefully.

"It would be a pity if something were to happen to her." Gracchus took a small pouch out of his coat and poured the contents on a nearby table.

"Meaning?" Adrian asked.

Gracchus exhaled and stared at the semi-transparent polished stones.

"It's never enough. You should know that by now," Gracchus said smoothly. He motioned for a footman to pull out his chair.

Adrian was never sure if Gracchus meant that about his ambition or the magics he fed to retain his power. He clenched his jaw, frustrated at Gracchus's demands after he had spent months maneuvering a wedding for the king. At least his marriage to Sidony should keep her safe. Torwyn had promised as much mere weeks ago. He could only trust his cousin and uncle so far.

"Now that you've secured an alliance, we need to turn our attention to crushing the rebels. Capturing the princess has emboldened them. Retrieving her will take away their symbolic victory."

"You know where they're keeping her?" Adrian sat across from Gracchus.

"They keep moving. I've sent men into the northern territory."

By his absence, Adrian assumed Marlowe had been one of the men sent to rescue Zara. He'd been hoping the baron would return with his uncle.

Gracchus picked up a light green stone and held it in his

palm. Normally it took concentration to scry, but his uncle had been a practitioner for years.

"How close have you gotten?" Adrian asked.

"We believe she has some sort of mystical protection. Something allows her to evade us."

"I'm sure the rebels are trying anything they can to keep her."

Gracchus dropped the stone and scooped up a piece of onyx agate. "If they hurt her, we could use the L'Ortagian forces to avenge her."

"Have you discussed that with Yves and the queen?" Adrian asked. He didn't want to encourage his uncle but at least it would help to know his next plan.

"They can't commit the number of troops I need."

This went back to the argument they'd had many times about whether and how to quash the rebellion. Gracchus and Torwyn argued for force, while Adrian favored the courts, which his uncle used to an extent. It was strange that his uncle avoided bringing charges against the generals in the rebel army. He'd been successful in limiting the rebels' ability to have Callum's case heard, but that had been accomplished through heavy bribes.

Gracchus had also restricted the rebels' movements within Embury's borders, and he'd kept them from gaining powerful allies abroad. Any allies the rebels amassed hadn't yet committed to sending troops to fight Gracchus. Despite the king's successes, the rebel army and loyalty among the people continued to grow. The king wanted to wipe them out entirely.

Gracchus swept the stones into his pouch again. Adrian refused to inquire about the outcome. He already worried his powers were indirectly allied with dark magic since Gracchus often commanded him to use them for him.

Adrian knew in his heart that his powers were good, or at least neutral. He had discovered them at a young age, when his mother had asked him to retrieve a book from their home. On his way, he had somehow seen into the room and known the book she wanted wasn't there. When he went back to his waiting mother and told her it was gone, she had scolded him for not bringing it back. She'd marched all of them back together, only to find that what Adrian had said was true. That night, as his mother had tucked him into bed, she'd asked him about it.

"Ah deul, tell me what happened today," his mother said, brushing the hair off his forehead. "You were scared when you came back to me. At first I thought it was because you hadn't returned with my book."

"Uhmuni, it was so strange. I got close to home and saw inside, but I was still outside." Adrian's heart raced at the memory.

"Then what did you see when you went inside?"

"The same vision. Uhmuni, what does it mean?"

She patted his chest, smoothing the blanket. "It means you have the gift. Like your grandfather."

"Do you have it too?"

She gave him a hard look, and Adrian worried she wouldn't answer. "Promise me you won't tell this to another."

He'd nodded eagerly.

"I don't have the same gift, of projecting. Mine is different."

He'd blinked, assimilating her words. "What is yours, Uhmuni?"

"I can see souls," she'd said softly. "And yours is beautiful, ah deul. In perfect balance." She'd kissed his cheek then blown out the candle beside his bed. He hadn't been sure how her power worked at the time, but he'd known he shared something special with his mother. The last time he'd seen his sister, Minah, she hadn't had powers. In the time he'd been with Gracchus, she could have discovered them. With his mother's help, Minah could have even developed them. If she had, they weren't enough to set them free.

Adrian used his abilities because he had to, for his survival and his family's. In service to his uncle, he had done terrible things. Edwin, the messenger, had looked at Adrian with fear in his eyes for good reason. When he was finally reunited with his mother, her magic would show that his soul had become tainted. If he'd done something often enough, good intentions wouldn't matter. His actions would.

One day Adrian planned to use his powers to help others, to right the balance. Now that he and Sidony had wed, he had a tiny spark of hope that he might be able to accomplish what he needed to do. Having her in his life made his urgency all the greater. He had to find his family, protect Sidony, and get free of his uncle.

"Are you going to Blackthorne?" Adrian asked.

"I may. It depends on how quickly my men can retrieve the rebel's prize."

"And then what?" Adrian wasn't expecting an answer, but he wanted to know.

Gracchus leaned his head back on the chair and closed his eyes. His hands rested on his thighs, rings adorning most of his fingers. Adrian used his powers to see if the orb was on his uncle's person or hidden in the room. He couldn't find it. That meant it could be anywhere, including back at the palace or with one of the king's trusted knights.

Gracchus was already on to discussing his future plans. "Then we begin to expand our dynasty. Perhaps your sister would bargain for her freedom. We could marry her off to a minor princeling in exchange. Would you like your sister to live a life of luxury?"

Anger burned in him, that his uncle would continue to bargain with his family, as if he hadn't done enough already, and would still threaten more if Adrian didn't obey his commands. He needed to be free of the loathsome man.

When Adrian spoke, his voice was calm, though it strained him to keep it that way. "I want you to release Minah and my mother. Even if you married my sister off, were you planning to keep my mother a prisoner forever?"

Gracchus laughed. "Give me a good reason to let her go. She's too old to marry again."

"My mother committed no crimes against you or the kingdom. Let her go." He'd already begged his uncle, but Gracchus wasn't persuaded by pleas. Only strategy or force would work.

"Hmm. No. Not a good enough reason."

For several heartbeats, Adrian considered killing him. Torwyn would then assume the throne. It would end his uncle's hold over him but merely continue the strife in the kingdom. But that plan couldn't guarantee his family's freedom.

As if the king could hear Adrian's thoughts, Gracchus opened his eyes. "You won't find them. Let us bargain, nephew. I'm in a giving mood. You won't believe me, but I value family."

"What do you wish to bargain?" Adrian asked slowly.

"An exchange of family members. Future for past, you could say."

"Uncle, no. I don't want to hear this." There was nothing Gracchus could offer that wouldn't have a steep price. Would he threaten to sacrifice Sidony again?

"Maybe you do. You know I need a legacy. Offer me a trade. Give me your firstborn. I'm not picky: boy or girl, it doesn't matter. Your firstborn for your mother."

Adrian felt like a tree had run him through. It would never stop. He should never have agreed to come to Embury with his uncle, not even for his father's sake. His father couldn't have imagined his brother was capable of this.

"I'm leaving." He strode to the door, but Gracchus stopped him with a hand on his arm.

"I wouldn't need you then, Adrian." He squeezed, not enough to hurt, but where Adrian could feel the slight pull, like a leash.

"Are you done?" Adrian's fists clenched. He jerked free, turning to glare at him with loathing.

His uncle made a *tsk*ing sound and shook a finger in the air. "Should anything happen to me, know that your mother and sister will forfeit their lives."

All of the heat that moments before had risen to the surface, evaporated, leaving Adrian frozen in place. Of course Gracchus protected himself. Killing him would only cause his mother and sister to die too.

"Enjoy your time with the princess and be quick about getting a babe on her."

CHAPTER TWENTY-NINE

*S*idony walked back from her mother's chamber, and Adrian met her in the hallway. He pulled her into a nearby room, shutting the door behind him. Once they were alone, he embraced her, tucking her head under his chin. "I needed to see you."

She put her arms around him, comforted by his embrace, and for the first time all day, alone with her new husband.

"Did you meet with the king?" she asked.

If possible, he held her tighter, burying his nose in her hair. "I did."

She tried for levity. "That eventful, eh?"

"You have no idea." She felt him sigh, but it didn't seem to bring him any relief. His body was fraught with tension. "The king will find your sister."

"Well, that's good news." She was frankly surprised that the king hadn't been able to find her sister yet. Even though Adrian was concerned about her, she didn't think his reaction had to do with her sister. Something else had happened with the king.

She stood with him, silent and unsure. As she leaned against him, she felt his hands shaking.

"Adrian? Is something wrong?"

He clutched her and shook his head. "Missing you."

She wrapped her arms around his back. "I'm here. We did it. No missing bride or groom this time."

He pulled away with a stricken expression.

Had she said the wrong thing? Sidony touched his face, running a finger across his brow. His brown eyes were filled with pain.

"Darling, what is it?" she asked.

His hands skimmed her sides then held her waist. She couldn't tell if he was going to pull her close or set her away from him.

"My meeting with the king went...as expected. I needed to see you."

It hit her that he sought her out for comfort, holding on to her like a lifeline. Something had changed between them these last few weeks. With the wedding, she had gained a husband, and also another monarch. She found King Gracchus to be eccentric, at times personable and then swiftly curt. He was an enigmatic man. One had the sense that before he was king, it would have been difficult to ignore him if he was in a room.

What had the king discussed with Adrian?

"Adrian, I'm here." She didn't know what else to say.

Adrian dipped his head and kissed her lips. Quick and hard. "I know. That's why I found you." He stepped back and ran a hand over his hair, flexing his fingers against a slight tremble. "I have to go. Where's Lucia?"

She waved a hand. "Nearby."

Adrian stared fixedly at the door. When he concentrated like that, he was using his powers. "She is. Keep her by your side today." He brought their hands together and kissed her fingers. "Promise me."

"Promise."

With his mouth set in a grim line, he took her to Lucia, kissing her once more before he left.

THE NEXT TIME she saw Adrian was when he sat down beside her in the partly refurbished banquet hall. Half of the windows had been replaced. The others were covered with white cloth.

Sidony smiled at him, relieved and hopeful about Zara as the day went on. Adrian smiled back, but it didn't reach his eyes. An air of agitation remained about him. She'd never seen him this way. Usually he was calm and cool.

She leaned toward him. "Recognize the songs?"

The same musicians who had played his first night at Mondelac performed music from Embury.

Adrian cocked his head, his fingers tapping the rhythm on the arm of his chair. "Our first dance."

Sidony patted his leg. The muscles tensed. Perhaps he needed to get through the evening in order to let go of whatever he'd discussed with the king.

As servants brought out the different courses, Adrian remained quiet. She reached for his hand under the table. He laced their fingers and set their hands on his leg, bouncing it slightly.

Sidony instructed the servers to refill Adrian's wine, but he refused, thus blocking another of her attempts for him to enjoy himself. She wished they had more time to be alone, but they would have plenty once the night wore on.

Sidony had arranged for performances by two of Cadeau's premier opera singers. Adrian paced between performances, almost missing the soprano's opening notes.

Finally, her new husband raised his glass and turned to her. Various courtiers rose to their feet, slapped each other on the backs, and raised their glasses to Adrian, which she took as masculine signs that her wedding night was imminent. She downed the wine in her glass, possibly her third or fourth of the evening.

Adrian stood and held out his hand to her. "To my fair bride, Princess Sidony. Let us bid our guests adieu."

Adrian bowed, and she curtsied in front of the well-wishers. The crowd cheered. Although playing to a crowd was familiar, Sidony blushed at their bawdy encouragement.

"Cheers to the bride!"

"May you sow your seed tonight!"

"Another heir for Embury!"

"Bed her good and bed her well!"

With a tight smile, Sidony tugged Adrian's hand, ready to make their way to her bedchamber.

Adrian swept her into his arms.

Her head spun with the movement. "What are you doing?"

"It's tradition." He held her up in front of him. The crowd's cheers grew louder, and she clutched at his shoulder.

"Don't brides get captured this way?" she asked. She'd heard stories of clan members stealing the bride after the ceremony, only to return her to her groom sotted. She'd nearly accomplished the sotted part at supper on her own.

"This is how it's done in Embury." He held her up one more time before sweeping her out of the hall.

CHAPTER THIRTY

*A*drian carried Sidony over the threshold and into the
bedchamber. She clung to him, her eyes glassy. He
brought her to the side of the bed and set her on the mattress.

He wanted to follow her down, get lost in her embrace, and
forget his uncle's threats.

Instead, he went over to the sideboard and poured himself a
drink. He had one swallow before setting it down and turning
to take in the sight of Sidony sprawled across the bed. Candlelight made the room glow and brought out the gold in her hair.
Her coverlet was white with a green pattern on it, depicting a
bucolic scene. The color and the style suited her: playful, feminine, and out of the ordinary.

Despite his efforts, his uncle's words reverberated in his
head. Here he was, blissfully happy with his bride, and yet
terrified the king would take it all away. Because Gracchus
could.

"Would you go away with me?" Adrian's words slipped
out. He'd held them in since Gracchus made his threats.
Adrian wouldn't trade family members for each other, so
there was nothing to consider. But Gracchus's pleasure at

his marriage hadn't gained Adrian anything. Sidony was safe for now, but he didn't know how long that would last.

"Anything to be alone with you." Sidony peered at him, slightly mussed and alluring. It was their wedding night. They should be making love.

"More than this. What if we were by ourselves?" He pulled out the black silk ribbon holding his queue and ran a hand through his hair.

"Wait. Do you mean leave for Embury tonight?" She sat up, color suffusing her cheeks.

His temples throbbed, and he gritted his teeth. "No, I… sorry. I just have this feeling that this could all be taken away from us."

Adrian sat in a gilded chair by the bed, his palms sweating. Making Sidony his wife meant that Gracchus would have greater access to her. It was only a matter of time before his uncle would use her to manipulate him. He had to get away from him before that happened.

Sidony slid down from the bed and padded over to him. She ran soothing fingers through his hair. "You've been like this since this morning. What is it?"

He leaned into her and wrapped his arms around her waist, holding her close. She was warm and soft and smelled delicious. If only he had more time. The longer it took to find his family, the more he put Sidony in danger.

"Adrian? What's wrong?" She ran soothing hands over his shoulders, down his back.

He inhaled to clear his thoughts. "It's too much."

"This?" She made a sweeping gesture, indicating the room.

"No. Not you." He pulled back and brushed his thumb along her jawline. "It went badly with my uncle."

"He's not letting you see your family?"

How much should he tell her? "No."

"Even after all that you've done for him? Even after our wedding?" She trailed her fingers along his temple.

"No. It wasn't enough to appease him. He's obsessed with destroying the rebels. He'll use whatever he can to accomplish that."

Her eyes widened. He wanted to focus on how good it felt to have her touch him and look at him with such care in her eyes. Guilt clawed his gut.

"Including you." Her tone was gentle, encouraging.

"Yes." He wanted to reach out and wrap one of her curls around his finger. He couldn't remember ever having the leisure to play with a woman's hair.

"You've had to deal with him by yourself, haven't you?" She tilted her head, and her curls tumbled across her shoulder, in invitation.

"Almost." He couldn't tell her of his friends and allies. Not yet. She was right, though. He had been alone for a long time. "There's Torwyn, but he generally sides with the king."

"Well, then." She grinned. "I'll have to stay close enough for you to remember that I'm here for you." She gave him a look under her lashes. Part mischievous and part lusty. "That shouldn't be too difficult now that we're wed." Boldly, she pushed the edges of his coat over his shoulders and down his arms. He shrugged out if it, letting it drop into the chair.

"Sidony," he started, uncertain whether he could go through with their wedding night.

Undeterred, she began unbuttoning his waistcoat.

"This part, tonight, is what we've been waiting for. You may be distracted, but I'll try to keep your mind on us." She worked quickly, pushing the garment from him while she spoke. She unfastened the two buttons that closed his shirt.

Adrian sat, awestruck that this woman kept reaching out to him. He flexed his fingers on the arms of the chair but made no move to touch her. He wanted to, yet his mind kept racing with possibilities of how Gracchus would harm her, or their child. Finally he closed his eyes, hoping to block out his thoughts.

"Do you want me to leave you be?" Her voice was a whisper in his ear.

He met her gaze, her expression troubled. She must think he didn't want her. "No." He was disgusted he'd let her think for a moment he didn't want this. He did. He had to get around his fear. Thankfully, his cockstand was undaunted.

He stood. "Please continue. I enjoy your ministrations."

She gave him a half smile. "I can tell." She tugged, pulling his shirt over his head. It made a soft thud on the pile of clothing on the chair. Usually he was meticulous, but in the mood he was in, it was all he could do to stand still. He dropped his chin, frowning as he tried to get his mind off the king.

Sidony moved behind him toward the sideboard, her footsteps shushing across the stones. There was something familiar about being in an old castle. Mondelac reminded him of the older parts of Blackthorne, which had also been built to be a fortress. There was nothing warlike about her, but maybe Sidony wasn't as fragile as he feared.

She plucked a grape from a bowl and ate it, her gaze focused and clear. She brought over his cup of wine and held it out to him. "I had plenty at dinner. You, however, drank sparingly."

He took it and held it to his ribs with both hands. She held up her hand, miming holding a drink, and he matched her motion. "To us and to this night. May we appreciate the unexpected, for that's what brought us together."

He touched his cup to her raised hand, then took a drink. "To you, for coming into my life when I needed you most. I promise to protect you." It was all he could promise her, but he meant every word.

"Serious tonight, aren't you?" She pulled his hand down and tipped his cup so she could take a sip as well. "I've learned to appreciate what life gives and to hold each moment dear." She kept her fingers on his. "You're dear to me. I never thought this night would come, with us, together."

"I know." He set the cup down, snagging her around the waist when he came back to her.

Her breath hitched, and tears welled in her eyes. What was he doing to his sweet bride? She was right. Her presence in his life was the greatest gift, save the freedom and safety of his family. He should cherish her, starting now.

He kissed her, brushing a kiss across her lips as if to rub off some of her boldness and surety. She tasted like wine and warm woman. Their kiss heated his blood.

Sidony's hands were on his waist, her fingers pressing against his abdomen for long seconds. He sucked in a breath, enjoying her touch. She found the front placket of his breeches and loosened two buttons. Reluctantly, he pulled her hands to the side, forestalling her progress toward removing his pants. Her undressing him had had the desired effect, and he was nearly fully erect, straining toward her.

He wanted her to feel just as undone.

Angling his head, he kissed her more deeply this time, rubbing his tongue against hers and savoring her soft moan. She kissed him back without hesitation, and again he thrilled at her passionate response. She leaned toward him, and her breasts pressed against his chest. He groaned at the feel of her softness, his arousal sharpening.

He eased his hand between their bodies to adjust his cock. Sidony pulled back and looked down. He moved the head to rest outside his waistband, two droplets seeping from the slit in hunger for her.

Sidony gasped and reached out to touch him. He almost pulled away and then shook his head at himself. Her touch was what had brought him back to life. He wouldn't deny her what she wanted. He groaned at the feel of her fingers running over the head of his prick.

"Here. Like this." He curled her hand around him, showing her how he liked to be touched, how much pressure to use.

"Oh. There?" She twisted her wrist, and he had to blow out a breath as a bolt of lust shot through him. She reached lower, squeezing. Sweat broke out along his body. Why had he ever stepped away from her after entering her chambers? He wanted her now.

"Damn these breeches." He unfastened the rest of the placket and pushed them down his hips, freeing more of his hardness for her. Sidony grasped him again, sliding her hand along his length. While part of him enjoyed standing before her nearly naked while she was in her gown, he knew that if they went much further, he'd end up tossing her on the bed and taking her with her skirts flipped up. Probably not how a royal lady imagined her wedding night.

"Sidony, a moment." Before he got too far gone to stop her, he pulled her hand away and spun her around. He helped her out of her gown, brushing his hands along her shoulders, waist, and hips as more of her was revealed. "So lovely."

She faced him again, and he sucked in a breath. Her breasts pushed against her stays, straining and full. She reached back and untied her underskirt, then kicked it behind her.

"This is so unlike us." She stepped back to lean against the bed.

"How's that?" He shucked his breeches. He wouldn't last, not at the level his arousal was now, and he wanted to last.

"Being this close to a bed." Sidony pulled up the edge of her shift, exposing her legs and giving him a glimpse at what lay between. "Adrian, be a dear and help me out of these stockings."

Adrian ran a hand over his mouth to keep from touching what was surely a moist, hot slit.

"What?" He struggled to follow her in their conversation. He went down on one knee before her and placed her foot on his leg, his attention riveted by the shapely length. He ran a hand up the back of her leg, feeling her muscles tense. Her skin was warm and smooth.

She put a finger under his chin, turning his face to hers. "My stockings. I've been waiting months for you to take them off for me." Her cheeks were flushed, her lips parted.

Chuckling, he untied her garter and slid it off her leg. Tugging gently, he rolled her stocking down, stroking the soft skin revealed. After removing the first garter, he switched and started the process with her other leg. "I hadn't dared to dream of taking them off you."

"You seem to have mastered the task quickly, then," she said in a hushed tone. One of her dusky nipples was visible through her ruffled neckline, already beaded and tight.

He stroked her exposed leg at the top of her thigh, his thumb drawing slow circles. He let his thoughts drift from alliances and duty to the warm woman standing before him. He could no longer keep her at a distance. He untied her second garter, dropped it to the floor, and worked the stocking down, then lifted her foot to his shoulder. She hadn't lowered her shift.

With lust bearing down on him, breaths tight in his chest, he let himself sink closer. His need for her went beyond a physical ache. Sidony stirred something in his soul, a longing he had pushed down so deep, he barely knew it was there.

"I wonder if the way to a lady's heart starts with her shoes, and then her stockings, and then..." He trailed off. He spoke the words to her lower half, completely overtaken by lust at the sight of her dewy, flushed sex. "I imagine something like this."

He kissed along her inner thigh, making his way to her quim.

"Adrian? Are you going to...?" Sidony's voice was breathy.

Adrian glanced up. "Is this the way to your heart?"

Her lips parted, and a bloom of color rose across her chest. He'd gotten her off balance. She could so easily do that to him. He moved closer, sliding her leg over his shoulder and clutching her hip. He stilled, waiting for her reply.

"Y-yes." She pulled up her shift another few inches, settling back against the edge of the bed.

He set his mouth against her, his fingers opening her for his tongue. She was so soft. He traced her, sucking at her inner lips before closing his mouth over the bud of her pleasure.

She moaned and spread her legs wider, sinking her fingers into his hair and pulling him closer.

He worked his tongue in small circles, carefully drawing out her arousal. She grew wet, her flesh heated and slick. He held her up, half balanced against the bed. She nearly melted around him, but he wanted her lost in pleasure. Using his powers, he reached for her breasts, cupping and squeezing them.

"How did you—oh!" Sidony cried out.

When he gently pinched her nipples, Sidony whimpered again, her quim even hotter. Adrian could not get enough. His need for her spiked fiercely, and he could sense she was close to her peak.

Adrian pulled back and stood before tossing her up onto the bed. He groaned at the sight of her. Her shift was tangled around her thighs, her skin dewy and flushed. He followed her down, settling over her with his weight on his elbows.

Sidony parted her lips. "I quite liked that." She traced a finger over his face.

"Mercy." He wanted to get right back to what he'd been doing. "I did too."

She gazed up at him with an openness he envied.

"Adrian." Her legs shifted against his, one opening to flank his hip. Everywhere she touched him, his skin blazed.

He tensed with anticipation, wanting to please her. Her breasts beckoned to him. Pulling her chemise down, he freed both, feeling a fresh surge of lust at the sight of her ripe flesh. He cupped her, sucking at the tip of each. She arched into his hold, her head thrashing on the bed.

"Touch me again," she begged.

Adrian knew he'd been given a rare gift. Not only was his new wife beautiful and kind, but she was a woman who would demand her pleasure. He was more than happy to give it to her. He slipped two fingers into her sheath and shuddered as she clenched around him. He worked them partway then stopped. She was aroused but tight. Though he ached to fill her with his cock, he wanted her to be more relaxed first. Softer. So it could be better for her.

"Sidony, I'm going to bring you off with my mouth." He uttered the words against her neck, sucking at her skin. He pulled her shift low and her pert breasts were almost his undoing. Her nipples were tight, rosy with passion. He rolled each one between his fingers, lips curling as she moaned.

"Ah, yes. Now." She raised her head, her eyes glazed. "I need you. I need this." She cupped the side of his face, and he turned, kissing her palm.

"So do I." He moved down between her legs again.

CHAPTER THIRTY-ONE

*S*idony was going to die from the pleasure of Adrian's mouth against her. She arched up to his touch, sensitive and aching. With her legs spread, she felt exposed. But Adrian clearly enjoyed kissing her this way. His earlier distraction was long gone. He focused solely on her, on giving her sensations she'd only felt fractions of before. And he responded to what she liked. Each time she moaned, he'd pause then repeat whatever he'd done. The only words she'd been capable of speaking while he touched her were "yes" and "more."

"I can't quite tell if you like that," he said from between her legs. His voice was a low rumble, and she shivered. His hand came up to cup her breast, and she held onto his fingers there for a moment, her whole body tight. Adrian had slowed down his frantic pace, and her tension ratcheted up until she thought she would break.

She panted, struggling to find words. "I do, I do."

He chuckled and did it again. She arched her back, pressing her breast into his hot hand. The twin stimulation of having him tweak her nipple and suck and lick along her sex were almost too much. She wasn't sure if she wanted to hold off or let go.

Her hand got lost in his hair, slipping down to his shoulder as he angled his head. She couldn't take much more. All of her concentrated on how good he made her feel.

"More."

He sucked at her clitoris, running his tongue on the underside. "More of that?"

She moaned, her head pressed hard into the bedding.

"Or maybe you want this?" he asked as he pressed a finger to her bud of pleasure, circling her.

"Ah, yes. Please." She arched against him, striving for more contact.

He switched again, drawing out her pleasure until she pulled on his hair. She wasn't sure if he had been teasing, but she was done, about to burst out of her skin with desire.

"Now, now," she panted.

Her remaining clothes felt tight, and she longed to be naked and rub her skin along his. She strained against his hold, writhing on the bed beneath her. Adrian groaned again. His hand left her breast to clutch at her hip, effectively holding her still for him. Glimmers of heat built in her sex.

"Breathe. I've got you," Adrian said against her. She huffed out a breath, trying to relax, and suddenly felt herself go over. The wave rushed up at her, tingling across her nerves, and spreading intense pleasure in its wake. Her body tightened in response, and she cried out. The sensation went on, centered in her lower body, where she felt the most delicious throbbing.

Adrian's hand cupped her hip, his thumb rubbing softly, and she felt anchored to him. She had imagined him touching her intimately, but the real thing was so much more. She felt like a puddle on the bed, satisfied and in awe. He was so thorough, so giving. The worries from his talk with his uncle that surfaced once they'd been alone no longer bothered him. It was heady to have his attention like this.

Sidony stretched and stroked his shoulder. The furrow between his brows was back but not as deep as it normally was. He'd propped his head in his hand and trailed his fingers along her inner thigh.

"You're quiet again."

"Just watching you." He met her gaze, and his earlier strain was lessened. She certainly felt as limp as one of her discarded stockings.

He touched her lightly, and she squirmed. His lids lowered, and she thrilled as he petted her again, more firmly this time. He turned his hand and pushed a finger into her depths. The ache at her core started again, but this time she wanted more.

"Adrian." His fingers wouldn't be enough. "I need you." She squeezed his shoulder, wanting him to just take her.

That seemed to be the cue he waited for because he straightened and removed his hand. She propped herself up on her elbows to watch him, excitement replacing her earlier languor. He was gorgeous. Strands of his hair hung along his cheeks. His chest was one long slab of chiseled perfection, calling to mind the work of a master sculptor. His shoulders and arms were muscular but lean. She didn't think she'd ever seen a more finely made male.

Adrian pulled her hips to the edge of the bed. One leg dangled over and the other rested against his hip, her foot propped on the bed for balance. He positioned his cock at her opening, but teased her with it first, running it along her sex. She moaned. She'd never had a lover take such time with her. Not that she'd ever let a lover do all of what Adrian had done with her tonight. They usually had her touch them and were done all too quickly. Sometimes she got off too.

But Adrian kept the focus on her, showing her a new appreciation for her own body.

Right now her attention was on him and how he was barely nudging into her with the head of his cock. She ached for more, wriggling against him with impatience. One slim black brow went up at her actions.

Anticipation gave her voice a breathless quality. "I need this. Don't keep me waiting."

His lips parted at her words, and he surged against her. "Here." He pushed in a few inches. "Have me."

She panted as his thick knob spread her. "Oh." She squirmed at the sense of fullness, tracing a finger down his belly. Adrian didn't move. Her gaze shot to the point where their bodies were joined. Not possible. He had more to go.

Sidony peered at him through her lashes. Sweat beaded his brow and a vein pulsed in his neck. He went slowly for her. The realization struck a chord in her. She doubted he even knew how tender he was with her.

Her eyes burned and she blinked away the tears.

It got better. Sidony moaned at the feel of him. "Adrian, yes."

"Not too fast for you?" He sank a few inches deeper, and spoke through gritted teeth, his cheeks flushed. "Sidony, you're so wet."

She blushed, helpless with need. She shifted her legs, bringing her knee up and back. That got him going because he bucked inside her, lodging farther.

Leaning over her, he braced a hand behind her on the bed, and held her hips with his other hand. His face dipped down, and he kissed her, sweet and soft. Finally, he pushed the rest of the way into her.

She let him kiss her, feeling like he was taking her sex and her mouth at the same time. Once he was fully seated, he thrust against her and licked into her mouth. She felt so full, stunned with the sensations. She'd waited for this, wanted him so much, and it was better than she'd dreamed it could be.

He pressed deeper, and Sidony squeezed her eyes shut, overcome with desire rising again. Adrian's hips swung back and he thrust into her again, angling to press against the spot of heat at the apex of her thighs.

She arched her neck and moaned. "Oh, yes. Like that."

"Sidony." He kissed her neck, his hips churning. "I never want to leave you." He moved faster, sparking off nerve endings and amplifying her arousal. He kept at her, working a steady rhythm, and she found her peak again. She cried out as the orgasm rushed through her.

Adrian stilled. Their eyes met and satisfaction glowed in the dark depths of his gaze. Before she came down fully, he surged against her. Pleasure wound tight once again, and she bit her lip while she hung on.

His thickness reached nerve endings she didn't know she had. She tried to meet his thrusts, laughing softly when he clutched her closer. He jerked and groaned, giving in to her with focused intensity.

"Ah, Adrian." He drove her mad with want.

He raised himself up on his hands, his hips pounding, a look of stark hunger on his face. She tilted her hips down slightly and surprised herself with how quickly she reached her peak again. Adrian slowed, drawing out her climax almost unbearably.

The swirling of their magics together must be heightening their pleasure.

"Like heaven," he crooned to her.

She was amazed he could even talk. She was drowning, her body enveloped in satisfaction. He resumed his rhythm, kissing her hard on the lips. When he pulled back, rising above her, she watched him work his body for her. He caught one of her legs in the crook of his elbow. She quivered, glorying in his thrusting cock.

His gaze swept her body, his look covetous. She cupped her breasts, holding them up.

Adrian's eyes blazed with heat. That must have been the end of his control because a flush darkened his cheeks.

"Sidony," he moaned. With one last thrust, he held himself still for a moment. Then he eased through his orgasm, clutching her to him, his head against hers on the coverlet. He kissed her softly, his lips featherlight against her sweat-soaked skin. After long seconds, Adrian pushed up on his elbows and ran a hand through his hair.

"That was…ah, poets write sonnets about what we did."

She laughed, pleased he enjoyed their coupling as much as she had. "Yes, they do."

His lips curved in a smile. The expression made him seem younger, as if she were getting a glimpse of a more carefree prince. In a husky voice, thick with the accent of his homeland, he said, "You are everything to me. I don't think I could ever let you go."

She brushed a lock of hair off his face, struck by his possessive tone. She felt the same way but sensed there was more to his words.

"You'll never have to. I'm not going anywhere."

A shadow crossed his face, but it disappeared quickly. "Was that too much? Did I hurt you?" he asked, all solicitous.

"No, it was perfect." She stroked his shoulder and slid her hand down to his chest, his muscles tensing at her touch. "I can't believe we waited to do that."

"Didn't I tell you it would be better on a bed?" Satisfaction lit his features. Ah, he was the picture of masculine beauty.

"That you did." She patted him, wincing slightly as he eased out of her. "Though I'm not relegating this to only a bed."

"Of course not." He kissed her lips softly then stood grinning at her. "I love your adventurous spirit."

She stretched and sat up, contentment coursing through her.

Adrian grabbed a dressing gown that was draped across one of the chairs by the fireplace. With one arm through a sleeve, he froze, the green silk trailing down his back. He tipped his head toward the door. Something had caught his attention outside, but Sidony heard nothing. Was he using his powers to check that the hall was clear of guests?

Sidony clenched her jaw and directed her energy toward her new husband, hoping to utilize her own powers. In the past, they'd been reflexive, and she was not always able to tap into them.

As she admired Adrian's lithe grace and the masculine way he seemed to take up space, she focused, wanting to give his senses the expansion they needed. A tension built across the top of her head. When it had happened in the forest, she'd attributed the tingling to having been upside-down. Now, it seemed to be a signal she was directing her supernatural ability.

Adrian's shoulders tensed, and he shot her a quick look before turning back to whatever had caught his attention.

Wonderful.

The sooner his task was complete, the sooner he could join her in bed. She crawled up to the headboard and leaned against it, content at having aided him.

Adrian snapped to attention and tossed the other robe to Sidony. She held it to her chest, enjoying the sight of him walking across the room.

Then Lucia's voice sounded outside the door, her tone chastising. Probably another reveler wandered too close to the wrong side of the castle. Sidony couldn't make out their exact words, but her new husband clearly could. He dropped his robe and pulled on his pants and boots.

She patted the space beside her. "Darling, Lucia can handle it. Come back to bed."

"In a moment, love." He walked over and pressed a kiss to her lips. "Wills has a message for me."

"Maybe it can wait for the morning?" Regretfully, Sidony pulled the robe over her shoulders.

Again, Adrian's gaze snagged at the doorway. "I appreciate you helping me with... Thanks to you I read the message. I'm sorry, but it's urgent. I'll be back."

He left, pulling his shirt over his head.

Sidony sat in shock for a long moment before angrily pushing her arms into the sleeves and wrapping the robe tight around her chest.

My husband left our bed mere minutes after we consummated our marriage?

CHAPTER THIRTY-TWO

"Your Highness, sorry to interrupt. A letter arrived for you." Lieutenant Wills waited just outside the door, a hand over his chest.

"Yes, I know." Adrian didn't bother tucking in his shirt as he held out a hand for the missive. Less than a quarter of an hour had passed from the time he'd been so out of his mind for Sidony that the entire rebel army of Embury could have been at Mondelac's gates and he would have paid them no mind.

Then he'd sensed the lieutenant walking down the hall. Scanning nearby rooms and searching for possible threats had become almost a reflex once his powers had expanded. Moments ago, Sidony strengthened his powers again. In seconds, he'd read the letter Wills carried. Despite the awkwardness of the timing, he had to speak with the lieutenant.

Lucia waited behind Wills, her eyes wide, lips pinched.

He and Wills needed to go somewhere private. "Follow me to my chambers."

As they left, he was aware that Lucia knocked on the door

and checked on Sidony. There was nothing for it. He'd hopefully make it up to his bride within the hour.

They got to his room, which was blessedly empty. Adrian lit some candles, enough to read the letter again. Wills waited, his expression anxious.

"When did you get this?" Adrian broke the seal. It was from Marlowe, written in code.

"Barely a quarter hour ago. Seemed urgent."

In his succinct hand, Marlowe had written that Songbird House, a small estate only three days' ride from Mondelac along Embury's border, would be worth a visit. Marlowe, in his careful code, hinted Songbird House could be where Adrian's mother and sister were being kept. Unfortunately, Marlowe needed to stay with the king since his absence would be deemed suspicious.

Finally, Adrian had everything he wanted nearly in his grasp.

He touched a corner of the letter to the flame and carried it over to the hearth. He set it on the grate, making sure the fire swallowed every piece of Marlowe's script. He crouched down, using a poker to nudge the letter's ashes into the existing pile.

"Your Highness, is there anything you require?" Wills asked.

Adrian stood, his thoughts swirling. He could get to his family and help them escape while the king was traveling in the other direction. Aside from Wills and possibly two or three other soldiers, he would be on his own. And it would mean leaving Sidony behind.

He needed to leave in the next hour. But with guests in attendance, he wasn't sure he could and not raise suspicion. He was so close, and this was his best opportunity to find them. In order to rescue them, however, Adrian would need to be able to trust Wills.

"Lieutenant, how many soldiers do you have who are loyal to you?" There wasn't an easy way to ask the question.

Wills regarded him, brows raised. "Loyal to me? Or to you?"

Adrian rubbed his lip. "Both."

Wills met his gaze. "Three, possibly four men."

"I don't want possibly. Three it is."

"Four then, including me. What do you need us to do?" Wills asked.

"We'll be on a retrieval mission."

"For you?"

"Yes. The king would consider it treasonous. Tell your men the barest detail," Adrian cautioned.

"Certainly."

He'd give it another day, which would allow them more time to prepare, and then he'd leave for Songbird House.

"Ready your men to leave in two days' time."

"Yes. Do you want the rest of the men to remain at Mondelac or to head on toward Blackthorne?"

"I need them here. Once we travel back to the palace with my wife, I don't want to leave us with fewer guards." For now, Adrian would stick to the plan of returning to Embury with Sidony. Depending on what state his mother and sister were in, he wasn't sure if he'd ever go back to Gracchus.

Adrian would have to find a way for Yves to put additional guards on Sidony while he was gone. She'd be safest here, though he was loath to leave her.

When Adrian returned to Sidony's room, she was curled on her side asleep, her cheeks wet with tears. He felt like a cad leaving her so abruptly. He wanted to reassure her he'd only done it out of urgency, not any desire to be away from her.

He tucked his body around hers, pulling her close. She stiffened, and for a moment he worried she would pull away. Instead, she tugged the hand he'd draped across her hip, up to her chest, holding him to her.

He didn't deserve her. And he was only going to break her heart when he told her he'd be leaving again, this time for a sennight, and he couldn't tell her why. He had given her pieces of his past. He wasn't ready for her to know what he had allowed Gracchus to do. In loyalty to his father's memory, he'd trusted someone who hadn't deserved it. And after years of service, he and his family had been betrayed and exploited. How could he tell her that?

Though he was beginning to trust Sidony, he wouldn't put her in the position of knowing where he went or why. He couldn't take the chance that she would tell someone where he was. He didn't think she would try to stand in the way of his rescue, but he knew they each had divided loyalties. Their bond to each other was tenuous and new.

He'd tell her when he returned with his mother and sister.

BY THE TIME Adrian woke up, Sidony had already left their bed. She spent most of the day avoiding him, entertaining guests, and keeping close to Isabeau. It was disconcerting, since he was used to her trailing him throughout the castle.

They'd been seated across from each other at luncheon, and she'd been polite, but only polite. She blushed at jokes about the bedding ceremony and gave a saucy toast praising him for a memorable wedding night.

But between the two of them, she was impersonal. He'd never seen her like this. They were so busy with guests, he couldn't get her alone to explain what had happened.

By midafternoon, they stood in the courtyard together, saying their farewells to the guests. The clip-clop of horses' hooves along the courtyard, along with the soft whine of the wheels, gave him a moment's privacy amid the noise.

"I'm sorry about last night," he said at her ear. "About leaving like that."

"It must have been important," she said, her voice crisp.

"It was," he said honestly. But the words made him cringe, for she pressed her lips together, clearly hurt and angry. "You were asleep when I came back, so I couldn't explain."

To his own ears, he sounded like he was making excuses.

"Will you be repeating that every night?" she asked.

The two of them stood arm in arm, speaking through clenched teeth. He'd observed many nobles doing this. Inwardly, he'd scoffed at them. He finally understood that while some things needed to be said, there was only one way to do it in public without causing a scene. It didn't make it any easier, though. Nor were public arguments anything he ever thought he'd have with a wife.

"Sidony, I'm sorry. It was urgent."

"Is everything all right?" She met his gaze, her brow knitted with concern.

"No. I have to leave for a few days."

She muttered, "Unbelievable." Her hold on his arm loosened. "Will you at least tell me what is going on?"

"I can't." He laid his hand over hers. "I'd tell you if I could."

She blinked. "What shall I tell everyone?"

"Tell them that I got called away. Some royal duty," he said.

"Is that what it is?"

"Might as well be."

"So you won't tell me or you won't tell me here?" Her voice had softened, and he wished he could confide in her as to where he was going.

"I'll tell you more when I return."

Sidony let go of his arm and stepped away from him.

He needed to tell her more.

"Wait," he said before she took two steps. "Have faith in me." He bent close to her ear. "It's for my family. That's the only reason I'd leave. Remember that."

Her shoulders relaxed. "When do you leave?"

"As soon as enough guests have, so as not to call attention to my absence," Adrian said.

"Then hurry back to me." She turned to him and went up on her toes, pressing a kiss to his lips. Although it was urgent and quick, it had no less of an effect on him for its brevity.

His body tensed, shocked she'd bestow affection like that in public. Relief had him bowing his head. He'd soothed her, and this was his reward.

CHAPTER THIRTY-THREE

*T*he first night after Adrian left, Sidony struggled to fall asleep in their bed. She read a book of poetry, reciting the lines to herself until her thoughts got foggy. She'd nearly drifted off when there was a knock at the door.

Had Adrian returned?

She grabbed a robe before opening the door.

Sylvie, her mother's lady-in-waiting, stood on the other side. "The queen requests your presence."

Sidony wrapped the thick robe tighter around her body. "At this hour?"

"Yes." Sylvie's lips pursed with impatience. "Her Highness's words were, 'Fetch my youngest daughter immediately.' This isn't a court appearance."

"Fine." Sidony slid on her slippers and shut the door behind her. "What's happened?"

"It's best if the queen informs you herself," Sylvie said as if she'd been warned not to say much of anything.

"Of course."

The castle was quiet at this hour of night, with only a few

servants in the corridors. She kept up with Sylvie's brisk pace, her anxiety heightening with each step.

The queen's apartments were located near the small council chamber. As they approached, the doors opened from within, startling the guards posted outside. At the entrance stood her sister, Zara, hands outstretched, as if she'd been the one to open both of the heavy, iron-laden doors.

While her face was clean, Zara was pale, and her hair looked to be hastily tied at the back of her neck. She was also clearly in a borrowed gown, for it looked to be tight at the shoulders and the hem was so short it showed at least two inches above her ankles. Whatever it was, was important enough for her to forgo her own wardrobe.

Zara gave Sidony a tentative smile. Sidony rushed toward her, enfolding her in a hug.

"Zara?" Her sister smelled like she'd been traveling for days.

"Good," Isabeau said from her chair. "Now that you are here, Sidony, we can begin. Sylvie, that will be all."

The lady-in-waiting turned and left the room, her hands clenched tightly together at her waist. Zara waited for her to leave, then held up her hands, and the doors swung shut. Sidony hadn't seen her sister employ her little-used powers that overtly in years. Perhaps never. She must have opened the doors that way as well.

"That's enough dramatics for the evening, Zara. Please, be seated."

Before following the queen's command, Sidony touched Zara's arm. "I've been worried about you. Are you well?"

Zara opened her mouth, but before she could answer, the queen spoke again.

"Yes, that's the question we'd all like to have answered. Be seated. You called this meeting in the middle of the night. There'll be time to catch up with one another later."

Their mother was at the head of the table, with Yves to her

right. Her other advisors sat along the side, including Daven, Master of Swords, Emmanuelle, Chief Diplomat of Foreign Affairs, and Lord Forrenti, Exchequer of Coin and Currency. Zara straightened her shoulders and strode to the chair opposite their mother, indicating a spot to her right for Sidony. A man she didn't know had the next seat over.

The entire room was dressed for a formal meeting of the council, save Zara and herself. Sidony, in her sister's absence, had gotten used to these meetings, though this was the first held at such a time. She sat, back straight and head held high, like she did for each one.

"Let me begin with introductions," Zara said. There were circles under her eyes, and her hands rested on the table in front of her. Outwardly, her sister retained her elegant manners, but she had clearly been through an ordeal. "To my right is General Jeffors Millerton. He leads the army of whom you would call the Embury rebels. In Embury, they are royalists."

Silence greeted the general as Zara's words sank in. Sidony nodded and smiled at him, trusting Zara, but wary. The general was tall and quite handsome. His dark brown hair was closely cropped, his skin a shade lighter than his hair.

"Thank you, Your Highness. I'm pleased to meet all of you." The general's presence at Mondelac Castle could be dangerous for him. Whatever he was there to do must be important enough to risk his arrest, even though the king and prince had left. Yves watched the general warily but made no moves to arrest him.

Zara completed introductions around the table. The L'Ortagians were polite but barely. Yves spoke through gritted teeth. "You snatch her from her own home and then sit here as if nothing has happened?"

"Yves, hear them out," the queen said.

"Yes, Highness."

"Jeffors is under my protection," Zara warned.

"It's to be expected." The general met Yves's glare. "We were desperate to stop the alliance between L'Ortagia and the usurper. I urged Callum to abduct your princess."

Yves shot to his feet, but the queen rested her hand on his arm.

"I promised my heir that I'd hear her out. She's here now. We can decide on the rest later."

The captain sat hard in his chair, a flushed anger creeping from his neck to his hairline.

"Why antagonize him?" Zara frowned at Jeffors.

"If we are to sway the council to our side, they need to know with whom they are dealing. From what you've told me about the captain, I thought it best to be honest." Jeffors folded his hands in front of him on the table and looked to Zara.

"You understand him perfectly." She inclined her head at the general.

She smoothed her hair and took a deep breath. "Thank you all for agreeing to meet. My purpose for this meeting is to protect L'Ortagia. During my time with the rebels, I learned that one of the supposedly deceased heirs, Prince Callum, has been living in hiding since the assassinations of his family and King Gracchus's rise to power. The rebels seek to reinstall King Angus's heir to the throne of Embury. We need to support them in this cause."

Sidony's eyebrows shot up. What else could she proposed could involve L'Ortagia in a civil war.

"You called this emergency meeting before we could discuss what happened to you, where you've been, and how you are returned to us." The queen's tone was icy. "How am I to know that this man isn't somehow coercing you?"

"General Millerton is my guest. He helped bring me home," Zara said. "I'm under no coercion from him or anyone else."

"Princess Zara, are you asking us to believe that after weeks of captivity, you returned unharmed? There was no ransom, no assurance of your safety, aside from a letter we received from you mere days ago. Do you know why you were kidnapped?" Daven's dark eyes fixed pointedly on the general.

Everyone's eyes turned to Zara.

"It was in order to stop my wedding," Zara said. "I assure you that I was unharmed during my time with them."

Sidony fiddled with the tie on her robe. Her sister had been too late to stop the alliance from moving forward without her. With her wedding to Adrian two days ago, L'Ortagian had solidified its ties with Embury, possibly for the worse.

"You are aware that your sister has wed Prince Adrian?" the queen asked Zara.

"I heard of their betrothal." Zara turned to Sidony, brows drawn. "The wedding already happened?"

"Yes. The day before yesterday." Sidony's cheeks heated. She wished she could have spoken to Zara alone, but clearly her sister or her mother had orchestrated this public reunion. Sidony wanted to offer a reason why their marriage was beneficial. "It was a love match," she said matter of factly.

Zara's eyes widened, and she stared in silence at her sister for the span of several heartbeats. Sidony twisted her hands in her lap, wishing she could explain.

"Things moved forward without you. And you were gone for so long."

Zara raised a shaking hand to her chest and addressed the queen. "Were the terms the same as my arrangement?"

"Better, in fact. I managed to maneuver a few changes since Gracchus was unable to rescue you."

Zara's face had grown paler than before. "Then I'm too late. It's done. I couldn't stop it."

Sidony leaned forward. "I wanted to wed him."

Zara shook her head. "That's not possible."

"Oh, but it is," their mother said, her eyes on Sidony. Her

expression hardened when she turned to Zara. "Would you like to hear how much she wanted to? You insisted your sister attend this meeting. Let's hear what she has to say."

Sidony had thought she was dragged out of bed as part of her role on the small council. But it seemed that she was right back to being used to score a point in the match between Zara and her mother. Usually she rooted for her sister's side. Now she didn't want to be stuck between them at all. There were much larger things at stake.

Sidony faced her sister, tucking her hands in her lap to conceal their shaking. "I wanted to marry him. Prince Adrian is kind and thoughtful. I believe we are well-suited."

Zara gave her a pitying look. "The prince can be quite charming. He even tried to protect me from Callum, fighting for me. But he's his uncle's lackey. Everything the rebels said about the king's spy is true. He's surely involved in the king's misdeeds. Perhaps it's not too late to seek an annulment for you."

Sidony's pulse throbbed in her ears, recalling that before his cousin's wedding to Zara, Adrian warned her away from Embury. "I only know his character from what he has shown in his treatment of me and others. Since you were gone for weeks, without any word, we needed the alliance, and I agreed to the marriage. Willingly. Happily. Adrian is a good man."

"Yves said the prince left." Zara looked genuinely puzzled, and Sidony was grateful that her sister was trying to understand her position. "Shouldn't he be by your side?"

"He had something urgent to attend to." Under her breath, she cursed her husband for not giving her more information. His absence only made him look worse.

The council members whispered among themselves. The queen said something quietly to Yves. Adrian must not have told them much more than he'd shared with her.

Zara shook her head slowly. "Sidony, this brings me no joy.

I tried to get here to stop the wedding. Prince Adrian serves at the usurper's command. I know you think he's a good man, but he isn't."

Sidony's forehead pinched with frustration and fear. She remembered the haunted expression on Adrian's face the times he'd spoken of the king. There were secrets there—each royal house had its own. Whatever he'd done had likely been under duress.

"What are you accusing him of?" Sidony asked.

General Millerton spoke, his tone conciliatory. "The prince is a trusted advisor of the king. The usurper uses him to rout threats against the crown."

"Every man and woman serves at the pleasure of their monarch. Why is this any different?" Sidony asked.

"Because the rebels assert that Gracchus had the previous regent—including his queen and three children—assassinated," Zara said.

"There have been rumors of this for years," Isabeau said, breaking the silence that followed Zara's accusation. "And the assassinations happened when Gracchus and Adrian were out of the country."

"Whatever Adrian did was done out of loyalty to family. He gathers information. He would never hurt anyone."

"How could you marry him when you've heard the rumors about him?" Zara asked. "You could barely stand to talk to him when you met him at Peletierre."

Finally, her mother weighed in. "Prince Adrian has spent weeks in my court. I'd know if he had such defects of character, as you're suggesting. If the man who took you is who he claims to be, why hasn't an Embury court reinstated his title? His throne?"

"The usurper bribed the courts, Your Highness," Jeffors replied.

The queen threw up her hands. "I didn't call this meeting in the middle of the night to debate legal issues in a neighboring kingdom. My heir is returned, and I want to know where she was and why she was gone for so long. If the prince serves the king, then at least he has his priorities in order, which is more than my heir can accomplish."

Zara winced, looking tired from the argument. "I'm afraid it's all tied together, Mother."

"You can't be serious," the queen said.

Sidony waited for another strike to land against her husband. Her staid sister quirked her lips. After a pause, she said, "I also came back on behalf of Callum MacKinnon, one of the Lost Princes of Embury."

"The one who kidnapped you? Who you seem to be defending?"

Zara nodded. "Though I'll not have the rebels charged with kidnapping because I went willingly."

Relief flooded her that Zara's secret was out. "He kept you long enough to convince you to help his cause."

"Aye," Zara said, sounding like a native of Embury. "Though I'm not pleased with his methods. That's what I'm here to improve upon."

"Did they hurt you?" the queen asked.

"The rebels didn't." Zara's lips pressed into a tight line. "In many ways, Prince Callum was good to me."

In what ways was he not? Sidony wanted to ask.

General Millerton spoke. "Your Highness, one of the soldiers who was tasked with bringing a message to the court as to the princess's safety was captured. It was weeks until we knew you hadn't received word. My apologies."

Daven nodded slowly. Their mother was anything but mollified.

"As if being kidnapped—or rather, inelegantly snuck out of her own home—isn't bad enough. We'll have you examined to determine your health, daughter. I don't want any surprises in the coming months." The queen's voice was perfectly modulated, her expression stern.

"I am petitioning the council for recognition of Callum MacKinnon as surviving Prince of the House of MacKinnon of Embury, and to offer L'Ortagia's support for his claim of sovereignty."

The small council argued and questioned Zara as to why she thought it would be in their country's best interest, particularly since they had recently allied with Embury. But her sister also had a bold plan.

"Callum has been captured." She smiled. "Though not by Gracchus. I intend to travel to Marenburg to negotiate for his release."

"It's too bad you didn't get here two days ago. You could have traveled with the king," the queen said. Her green eyes were bloodshot, and it was clear she was still feeling the effects of the poisoning.

Zara ignored their mother. "He typically goes by the name of Ash. He lived in hiding for a few years and then among the rebels. Is it that surprising the rebels would rally around him?"

Sidony detected a note of pride in her sister's voice.

"How would I know the inner thoughts of a rabble band of vagrants?" the queen said.

"Mother, you go too far. Callum is Angus and Maeve's son." Zara's hands were laced on the table. "We've neglected the turmoil our neighbors in Embury have endured since the royal family's deaths. We can no longer stand idly by."

"It is quite a leap you are asking us all to take, Zara," Sidony said softly. Zara had been with a displaced prince all this time. Where did Adrian fit into all of this? He'd been so guarded about Gracchus, she wasn't sure how deep the cracks were in his loyalty. But she also couldn't recall him talking about his future with Gracchus or Embury.

"The usurper plotted to kill the royal family." Zara spoke with utter conviction.

"What evidence do you have?" Daven asked.

"Those are serious charges against a king, Your Highness," Yves cautioned.

"The stories of the Lost Royals are true?" Emmanuelle's mouth hung open in shock.

"It is one thing to state that a dead prince has returned. It is quite another to make such accusations." Her mother finally raised her voice.

Forrenti lowered his head as if in prayer.

Sidony imagined a curtain being pulled aside, revealing things Adrian had hinted at, alluded to. He'd been so careful, so guarded when he'd first arrived. It was no wonder, since clearly there were strong reasons to suspect the king had had a hand in making his ascendency to the throne happen in the worst possible way. Adrian had benefitted from the king's actions.

"Enough," the queen said. "The courts have already cleared Gracchus of any involvement in the royal assassinations. The matter at hand is Zara's return and our involvement in our neighbor's budding civil war."

If what Zara said was true, Sidony's own marriage served to legitimize Gracchus's rule.

"Zara, why didn't Callum bring you home earlier?" Sidony asked. "Why not stand by your side and make his case to our mother weeks ago?"

"He had his reasons. I don't agree with them, but you have to understand his position. And as he's being held prisoner in Marenburg, he's unable to speak for himself now." Zara stared at each member of the small council in turn. "I won't have L'Ortagia aligned with a false king. Prince Callum needs to be freed. We have to take this step."

The next hour passed quickly as negotiations and arrangements were discussed. Zara wanted their mother's help to free

Prince Callum. Isabeau clearly wanted to avoid antagonizing a new and dangerous ally.

"Mother, both of your daughters are now a part of Embury," Zara's calm voice rang out. "I refuse to let us be pulled into a war and be on the wrong side. L'Ortagia will side with the rightful king."

Sidony dreaded what that would mean for her husband.

"Then you need to leave tonight," Sidony said to Zara. With her hands in her lap, she twisted her wedding ring on her finger. "You should leave for Marenburg right away."

"You support his claim?" Zara's voice was incredulous.

"I support L'Ortagia and my family." Sidony couldn't allow Zara and Adrian to be at Mondelac together. She had her own questions for him. Having her sister there, with her accusations, would only drive a wedge between them, possibly even endangering Adrian. "You have to leave before my husband returns."

"Go, Zara," the queen said. "Go save your prince."

Zara blinked back a tear and nodded. She and Jeffors stood. Emmanuelle did too, as she would be joining them on their trip.

Sidony hugged Zara before she could leave. "Be safe."

"I will." Zara squeezed her back.

Jeffors straightened his coat and escorted her sister from the room.

CHAPTER THIRTY-FOUR

They'd been on the road for three days. Adrian was certain they'd find Songbird House before midmorning. He hadn't sent out a rider because with his expanded powers, he made a better scout. He tried not to worry about Sidony, but his mind drifted to thoughts of her. He'd done his best to ensure her safety before he left.

The morning of his departure he'd met with Yves in his gatehouse.

Yves had crossed his arms. "Must be awfully important to leave your new bride."

Adrian pinched the bridge of his nose, fighting off a wave of guilt. "It is. That's why I need you to keep her safe."

Yves squinted at him from behind his desk in the gatehouse, a pair of spectacles perched on his broad nose. "I'll increase the number of her personal guard. Why not take her with you?"

"Speed and safety." He wasn't sure what he'd find at Gracchus's estate, and bringing Sidony into that situation seemed like a bad choice.

"Can you guarantee your own?"

"Yes, and that of my men." Adrian wasn't sure why it

mattered, but he wanted the queen's guard to trust his judgment on this.

"How long will you be gone?" Yves made a note on a sheet of foolscap.

"A week, more or less." Adrian stood, waving for Yves to stay seated. "If all goes well, I'll be returning with guests."

"Anyone I need to clear with the queen?"

"No, but I'd be happy to introduce her to them. Please take care of my wife."

"Certainly. Hope it's worth it," Yves said. "Not the best way to start off a marriage."

Adrian had nodded. He didn't normally question a decision once he'd made it, but Yves's words stuck with him. Being able to search for his family helped ease the strain he carried over their imprisonment. But he regretted leaving his new bride. "It's unavoidable. Sidony understands."

Yves's bark of laughter had echoed down the stairs as Adrian left.

The timing was terrible. Hopefully, turning up with his mother and sister would provide explanation enough. Though if he found them, he wasn't sure how long they could stay in L'Ortagia, especially given Isabeau's recent alliance with Gracchus. The king would request that they be released to him. Adrian shook his head. He had to find them first, then he would decide where they could go.

The tension knotting up his neck and shoulders was stronger than it had ever been. The weather was warmer than usual, and the route had been first northern, and then it continued along in a westerly fashion. Patches of forest spread out over the land, and the terrain was rough going in places.

Maybe it was the wind rustling the trees, but a memory of running through and around the trees that grew along the eastern side of his home in Sinchon came to him. Back and forth, he and Minah would chase each other, trying to be stealthy, but failing due to laughing at each other's antics.

He shook his head as feeling swamped his chest. He had to get to her.

They entered a valley, and Adrian swept out his senses. He searched for the small estate he'd seen in Gracchus's orb. It was just over the next rise.

"We're close," he said to his men.

They nodded and straightened in their saddles.

He pulled his senses back. He hadn't detected any threats, no guards posted along the perimeter of the property either. Songbird House was quiet. He recognized the courtyard. He could have swept the house, but he wanted to see them without using his senses. He tried to imagine how Minah would look, how he'd run to her and swing her around. He took the image Gracchus had shown him of his sister and tried to change it, imagining a slight, dark-haired woman laughing. She was grown now, but still young. As children, they'd been easy playmates. Whatever it took, he'd make it up to his mother and sister and never let Gracchus harm them again.

Adrian nearly lost his seat when his horse reared. His teeth clacked together, and he scrambled to keep hold of the animal. A shaggy black-and-white dog raced from the side of the road, looping close to their horses. It yelped at the horses' reactions and ran off in the direction they were headed. Some guard dog. He wasn't sure why it had gotten so close, but he was rattled.

A rise in the road allowed them a glimpse of the estate. The farmhouse had been built in the last century, sturdy but it hadn't had much upkeep. The road leading up to it had deep ruts and was overgrown with vegetation. A couple of windows were boarded up. Aside from the dog, there were no other animals. Adrian scented that a few horses had been there recently.

He rode up the front drive and dismounted, handing his reins to Wills. Dust from the road swirled, making him cough.

The front door swung ajar, hanging on one hinge. His heart sped up. If his sister and mother were still here, they weren't being guarded closely. After all these years he was so close.

Maybe they'd been attacked. Maybe someone had tried to hurt them. The farmhouse looked vacant.

"Stable's empty," Wills called out.

Adrian searched, his senses scattering out around him. He couldn't detect anyone on the property. He swallowed hard.

No, no, no.

"They aren't here." His voice cracked.

He stormed up the steps and slammed the door wide. His boots thudded along the wooden floor. Dried rushes muffled his sounds in the kitchen. He searched a pantry, needing to see with his eyes and not his powers that the place was abandoned. Adrian's footsteps echoed through the rooms. Whoever had lived here had left beds, chairs, and a few tables, probably anything that couldn't go on a horse or in a carriage.

Dusty, faded curtains blew in the breeze from the front door. Adrian paced the house again. His fingers were numb. He kept walking, treading up the stairs and back down again. He even went out into the root cellar, wondering if they were trapped there.

They were gone.

His men were silent. Wills wandered in, but didn't say a word.

Adrian finally sat on one of the beds. Minah and his mother must have been kept in the same room. There was something neat and tidy about the one at the end of the hall, the one with light green curtains. Long, black strands of hair lay across one of the pillows. They had to be Minah's.

He gripped the coverlet, wanting to shred it. They were gone. He was too late.

"Sir." Wills spoke from the doorway.

Adrian didn't trust his voice. He stared at the wall, imagining the hours and days his family had been prisoners in this shabby room. It was a far cry from the luxury of Blackthorne or the comfort of his family's home in Sinchon.

"Sir, I'm sorry. Is there anything I can do?"

"Leave me." Adrian's face felt tight. "Go back to the inn we stayed at last night. I'll meet up with you by nightfall."

"I'd like to leave a man with you."

Adrian couldn't bring himself to look at Wills. He needed to be alone.

"No. Leave me."

The young officer hesitated before clearing his throat. "As you command."

Wills left, calling to the men outside. They rode off within minutes.

Adrian's shoulders shook, and his jaw trembled though he tried to clamp it shut. He slumped onto the bed, raw sounds coming from his throat.

Minah and his mother were gone. He'd missed them, by what looked like mere days or even hours. He clutched at his chest and squeezed his eyes shut, tears wetting the coverlet. Who knew what they'd been through in this room? He'd seen evidence of his sister being beaten, his mother's expression one of resignation.

But he was certain their leaving had been hurried. The king did not leave loose ends. Songbird House had been left unsecured, with food still in the pantry.

Someone had tipped off Gracchus's men that Adrian would be coming.

CHAPTER THIRTY-FIVE

*S*idony crossed her mother's sitting area to her favorite settee, putting herself across from the queen.

"Yves told me your husband is expected to return tomorrow." The queen took a sip of wine and offered a glass to Sidony with a nod of her head. "We need to discuss strategy."

Sidony had been dreading this talk since Zara's visit. She reached for a glass. "I'm assuming you have a new taster?"

"I do."

"And they're tasting *all* of your food?" Sidony asked.

"Yes, all." Her mother winced. "Yves found a nocturne who can detect poison without harm to herself. She has a heightened sense of smell or other such ability. Quite useful."

"They can be." Helpless not to, Sidony sniffed her wine before taking a sip. "Who was the culprit?"

"That has been the more difficult task. Yves and Sylvia are looking into the matter. They disagree on who they suspect."

"Mother, are you taking this seriously? Usually you're more decisive."

"It's hard to feel threatened by a slow poisoning."

Sidony nearly choked, which did nothing to calm her fraying nerves. "Mother, please."

Isabeau set down her wine and clasped her hands in her lap, right over left. The large emerald and pearl ring on her right hand, a ring passed down from queen to queen, reminded Sidony of the tumultuousness in the kingdom the past couple of days.

"It's being handled, Sidony. Now, we need to discuss your husband's return."

Her mother would expect her to remain loyal to L'Ortagia first, which was also how she felt. Wasn't it?

"I don't like keeping things from Adrian." It had taken a lot for her husband to confide in her, and she wanted to be able to do the same. She knew he had more he needed to tell her, but she still wanted to give him a chance to explain.

Her mother moved to sit next to her, pulling one of Sidony's hands between her own, the burnished gold band warm against her hand. "You barely know him. You have greater loyalties."

Sidony had rarely seen her mother this fierce. "I will agree to give Zara time."

"You owe your sister more than that. You can hide the fact that she returned from him. Your loyalty is to your family and to your country."

"Zara is in no danger from my husband. I also have loyalties to him." She gestured in the space between them, pulling her hand out of her mother's grasp. "We have loyalties to Embury. What do the rebels even want?"

"You said that Adrian acknowledges that Callum is alive."

"Yes, I did." Sidony took another drink from her glass. "Supporting their cause against a sitting regent is tricky. Do you really think Adrian could be caught up in what Zara is accusing? What if Adrian doesn't know anything about this? What if he has no idea what Gracchus has done?" Her words sounded gullible to her own ears. She only wanted to defend Adrian. Wouldn't she have sensed something was off about him? She knew that Gracchus made him use his powers, but she didn't know for what purpose.

"He knows." Isabeau got up and returned to her favorite chair. The embroidered rose silk had two spots that were well-worn, but the queen refused to have it recovered. The original fabric had been a gift from an admirer.

"What convinced you of that?" Sidony asked.

"Your husband knows the inner workings of Gracchus's court and his policies. In terms of his character, I still don't see it. Gracchus? Who can say? He's ambitious, cultured." Manners always went far with the queen. "He understood power. Obviously, being king gives him more."

"Gracchus found Adrian the year before he took the throne. He went to Daeso to get him. They weren't in Embury during the assassinations." It was horrifying to think of what Gracchus was accused of. Adrian couldn't have been a part of that.

Isabeau shrugged. "That is precisely the problem. Neither was in the country at the time of the assassinations. So we focus on the now. If your sister is to succeed, she needs to be able to get to Marenburg without anyone warning Embury that she's there."

Sidony felt guilty, not wanting to put Adrian in a position to lie, but also not wanting to keep secrets from him. Her sister's safety, however, won out. "I won't tell him until Zara gets back."

"No, you won't. You won't tell him you saw your sister alive. You will go back to your chamber and lie in bed, acting like nothing happened that night."

"Why even have me at the small council meeting, then?" Sidony asked.

Her mother smiled grimly. "You earned that role, and because your sister wouldn't speak without you there. She had some misguided notion that your life revolved around hers, and she was protecting you."

Sidony stood, exhausted. "Do not throw my relationship in her face. Zara didn't deserve that."

"No, she didn't. Your marriage certainly makes her affair all the more complicated."

Sidony ignored the stab of guilt.

Isabeau finished her wine. "You are in a tenuous position, especially as my de facto ambassador to Embury, for the time being. Your new husband—whom you bravely defend—has left your bed for days now. That you have lost his attention this fast is quite unbelievable."

"*Mother.*" Her mother usually saved her crueler remarks for Zara. That stung. "I gave you my word. Good night."

CHAPTER THIRTY-SIX

*S*idony climbed into her carriage to return to Mondelac after another long day of her patroness duties in Cadeau. She'd been able to focus her nocturne power today, hopefully with greater accuracy. She'd been practicing daily since Adrian left. She traveled into Cadeau without incident, although Yves had insisted she take her expanded personal guard with her. It was bittersweet for Sidony, because she would be leaving soon.

He'd left after two days of marriage. She trusted Adrian enough to believe his reasons were urgent. She wished she knew what they were. They hadn't had time to talk about their life together. And she clearly did not know enough about his relationship with his uncle. What she wanted was for Adrian to come back to her and for them to begin their married life together. Except now they'd have even more secrets between them.

As the carriage rode along, Sidony's stomach tightened. Each day she returned to Mondelac, she hoped he would be waiting for her. And each day she was disappointed, but it meant she could stay another day in the castle and the town that she loved.

Soon after Adrian returned, they would leave for Embury, to a new home. She'd left Lucia in charge of packing her things. With a possible shift in her own country's stance on his uncle's reign, Sidony wasn't sure what that meant for them. How long would they stay in Embury? How could she find out what Adrian felt about the rebels and Callum's—and Zara's—claims?

Adrian had said he'd be gone for about a week. That meant he was due to return any day now. Though she wished she could behave as if his absence hadn't torn at her, she couldn't. They'd barely had hours together before he'd left. She pulled the curtain aside and glanced out at the countryside. They were nearing the castle. The gate was open, and she spotted commotion in the bailey.

Was he back? Was it merely a delivery or a visiting noble?

When she got out of her carriage, she frowned at the Emburian soldiers in the courtyard. Had Adrian returned? The men avoided her gaze, save for the solemn-faced young officer. He was familiar, but she couldn't place his name. When she caught his attention, he approached and bowed.

"I'm Lieutenant Wills, Your Highness. The prince has retired to his apartments."

"Thank you, Lieutenant." She pressed a hand to her mouth, momentarily overcome with relief at Adrian's return. "Will you escort me?"

"Aye." Wills offered his arm and they walked into the keep, Sidony's guards trailing them.

They were on the stairs, and Wills still hadn't said anything.

"How did the mission go?" The men's demeanor in the courtyard hadn't exuded victory, but she was more aware than ever of the complexities involved in her husband's endeavors.

"Partly successful and partly not, Your Highness."

That was a lot of nothing. Odd that Adrian wasn't there to

greet her. Was he injured?

"Did something happen to the prince?" she asked, trying not to panic.

Wills coughed. "You'll need to ask him yourself. He forbade me from discussing the details."

"Well, then." Save her from reticent men.

He walked with her, keeping his steps measured, his glance nervous.

"Lieutenant, whatever it is you wish to say, say it now."

Wills put a hand over his heart and lowered his voice. "I don't know if he confides in anyone. My hope is that he could confide in you."

Sidony felt a stab of pity for Adrian. She'd certainly offered to share his confidences, but he had given them sparingly. "He could."

"I've never seen him like this. He was like a haunted man on the journey back."

LUCIA WAITED in the corridor and handed Sidony a set of keys. "I sent the prince to his former rooms. They were available, and we were in the middle of packing. He's not quite himself."

Sidony picked up her skirts and hurried toward the set of rooms Adrian had occupied for most of his time at Mondelac. She'd had a few of his things moved to her room, but most of it was how he'd left it after their wedding.

She knocked on the door. "Adrian? It's me."

No answer. Maybe he was sleeping?

She used her key to unlock the door and let herself in.

Adrian sat in profile to her, in a chair by a window, facing the lake behind the castle. He seemed to be staring at nothing. She wasn't sure he'd registered her presence until he spoke.

"I would have come for you when I was fit company." He

gripped the arms of the chair, face pale and exhausted. His coat had been tossed on the bed, but he still wore his boots.

She hesitated, wondering if she should leave him alone. The image of his men's faces and the urgency in Wills's plea helped her decide.

Sidony padded closer to him and stood by his chair. "Darling, when did you get back?"

He squinted up at her, twin lines of strain bracketing his mouth. He seemed to have aged a few years in the span of a week. "Less than an hour ago."

She stroked the back of his hand, and he turned it, capturing her fingers. She squeezed back. "Have you eaten today?"

"No. Needed to get back to you." His eyes were bloodshot. Dust from the road coated his boots and streaked through his hair. Though his expression was flat, he winced. "It didn't go as planned."

Her heart ached for him. "I missed you," she said as she traced a line over his thumb. "Whatever happened, you're here now. Tell me what I can do."

"Wine," he said in a low voice.

"Certainly." She went over to the sideboard. A small decanter sat next to two glasses. She filled one and took it over to him.

He grunted in thanks. Sidony crossed her arms and stood by the window. The late afternoon sun made the lake shine. Adrian took long swallows of his wine then set the glass on the floor next to his chair.

"Adrian, what happened?" she pleaded. She'd never seen him so unreachable.

He closed his eyes, fingers pressed to his sockets, his face in shadow. "I can't...I was too late. I failed them again."

She hated seeing him like this, nearly distraught. "Oh, no. You left as soon as you could."

He cut off her words with a shake of his head. His eyes were dry, the depths as dark as she'd ever seen them.

"I don't deserve your comfort, but I'll take it anyway. Come here." He held out a hand, and she went to him, settling into his lap.

She curled up against him, one hand pressed against the middle of his chest, as if she could hold him in place.

"I missed you," she said softly. "Every day I returned from the Gilded Rose, I'd look for signs that you'd come back."

He pulled her tighter against him. "I missed you too."

"Will you have to leave again?" she asked. Was this a hint of what their life would be like together? Would Adrian disappear for days at a time, unable to tell her why or when he'd be back? Had he been on a mission for the king?

"I needed to do this." A shudder went through him "And it's not over."

Sidony stroked his chest, cringing at the inadequacy of the gesture. She'd hoped that once they were reunited, he'd be back to his old self. Serious, but attuned to her. He still seemed far away. She recalled the thread of his earlier words. "What were you late for?"

Adrian said nothing for a while. His voice cracked when he finally spoke. "The letter I received told me where I could find my mother and sister. I found the estate where they'd been kept, by the king, but they were gone. At most, I missed them by a couple of days."

"To come so close." He hadn't seen them in nearly a decade, and he was hurting. She tipped back to look at him. "Any idea where they went? Could they have escaped?"

Surprise flickered across his features. "I hadn't considered that, but no, I don't think so. And no, I don't have any clues to where they could have been taken."

"You're sure they'd been there?"

"Yes. I've seen glimpses of the estate. Gracchus has an orb

that can show me their location. I didn't know where the house was, but I'd seen the courtyard."

Sidony took a moment to digest that information. "Another nocturne gave the king the power to do this. Where is it?"

"Possibly Blackthorne. It wasn't on him when he was here for our wedding."

The pieces fell together, both her sister's accusations, and Adrian's disclosure. "This is how he makes you do things for him, use your powers for him?" she asked, though the answer was clear. And it wasn't just Adrian who he used. "Gracchus plots to use every nocturne he's ever met."

He nodded, his eyes sparking with life. "I've helped him rout spies in the kingdom, stop rebel plots against him."

Here was her moment, where she could tell him she knew about his uncle and what he'd done to gain a kingdom. But she'd promised her mother she wouldn't say anything to him yet. She was such a fool to have made that promise.

All she could manage was, "The king uses nocturnes to hold the kingdom."

She'd *known*, but she hadn't understood the depths the king had gone to.

His face nestled into her hair. "Yes. And I've let him."

"WHAT CHOICE DID YOU HAVE? You thought your mother and sister were dead, yes?"

He raised his head to look at her.

"You've been looking for them since you knew they were alive, doing everything you can. You mustn't blame yourself."

He nodded, overcome. She rubbed his shoulder, waiting. She had more patience than he did.

"He's the most powerful man in the kingdom," he finally said.

"And he...he's quite threatened by the rebels." She pulled at his shoulder, willing him to look at her. "If my mother knew, she'd never let me go to Embury with you, would she?"

He cupped her cheek, his gaze desperate. "No. I don't know where you would be safe."

She gave him a half smile, refusing to be terrified. "I'm safe with you."

He sat back, sliding down in the chair. He propped his feet on a low table and pulled her up his chest. "With me, you are."

She ignored the warning in his voice and moved one leg across his body. He was warm and solid, more real than any of her dreams the past few nights.

"I should leave you here." His hands roved across her back and hips. "I should never have dragged you into this."

"I don't recall there being a choice." Reaching up, Sidony brushed her fingers across his lips. "You can't leave me here without the king being suspicious." She didn't add that Gracchus would become suspicious of a lot more than Adrian trying to rescue his family.

"He's suspicious of everyone." There was a tone of both defeat and exasperation in his voice, an edge she hadn't heard before.

Her mother's plea that she not alert her husband of the changes in L'Ortagia nagged at her.

"Gracchus is expecting you to bring me home with you."

He tipped up her chin and met her gaze. "You don't have to do this. Let Yves keep you safe."

"We tried being apart. My week was miserable. How was yours?"

He leaned against the chair again, arms looped around her back. "The same."

"So I'm going with you to Embury." Sidony rested her head on his shoulder, the matter settled.

She desperately wanted to confide in him but held her tongue, aching at the secrets between them.

CHAPTER THIRTY-SEVEN

*T*hey lay like that for a quarter hour before Sidony got up. She tugged at Adrian's boots but he brushed her hands away, yanking them off himself.

"Why don't you get in bed? I'll send up food for us."

"Too tired to eat." His words ended on a yawn. He rose and took off his shirt on the way over to the bed.

"I'll let you rest, then." She brushed the wrinkles along the front of her gown in futility before turning to leave. When she was two steps from the door, something touched her shoulder. She looked back at him, brows raised.

Her husband was propped on an elbow, his eyes half-closed. He must have used his powers.

"Sidony, hurry back." He let go of her, but his eyes burned bright. The man needed her, whether he'd admit it or not.

"Fine, but I'm having food brought up."

"As you command, sweet wife." His head dropped back against the pillow, and his eyes slid shut.

"I'll be back." She stepped into the hallway and had one of the guards take her request down to the kitchens. When she returned less than a minute later, Adrian was asleep. She sat next to him, her hand in his hair, and stroked his face while he rested. The lines of strain on his face eased except for a furrow between his brows. That's probably how she'd looked those nights without him.

How long would it be until he decided to leave again without her? They needed to trust each other. With secrets piling up between them, that could get harder and harder to do.

Her breath caught on a sob. She blinked and took deep breaths, willing the tears to stop.

She was saved by a knock on the door. Two footmen brought trays of food. She instructed them to leave the trays on the desk, which was the right size for a dining table for two. She fussed at the table, trying to make herself busy with anything other than her worries for them.

"What did the cook send up?" Adrian asked from the bed. The sheets rustled, and she hastily wiped her eyes.

He cleaned his teeth and splashed water on his face. When he walked up behind her, he put his arms around her, peering over her shoulder. She lifted the silver covers.

"Meat and bread and cheese. Cook said that's what your men asked for. If you'd rather have something else…"

Adrian pulled away from her and sat. He took a healthy bite of bread with a slice of beef, rolling his eyes in delight.

"Or perhaps this will do?"

He nodded and pulled out a chair for her. She filled a plate for herself and sat.

"Did you ride all morning to get back or was the fare not as good wherever you went?"

"Both. Mostly stayed at inns when we could." He spoke between bites, eating with relish.

She realized they hadn't dined alone together before. It was intimate. Nice. The right husband made all the differ-ence. He hadn't donned his shirt, and she wasn't about to remind him of that fact. She quite enjoyed the sight of his bare chest.

"Let me get our wine." Adrian pushed back his chair and went over to his discarded wine glass on the floor. He refilled his and brought a glass over to her, dropping a kiss on her neck before taking his seat again.

"Thank you." She touched the spot that burned from his lips. The days and nights without him had been so long. Her stomach growled before she could contemplate trying to get the half-naked man sitting before her back in bed.

She took a bite of bread. "Did you stay with anyone?"

"No, we made camp when we had to," Adrian said matter-of-factly. He refilled his plate. "How did you keep busy while I was gone?"

"Mostly with the theatre. The play opens in two weeks." She hadn't had time to ask him if they could stay for the opening.

Adrian paused, his fork in midair. "I'd planned for us to leave tomorrow."

"With your leaving, I wasn't sure what that meant for our timeline."

Adrian sat back and regarded her. "Gracchus will be gone."

"So you can search more freely. Of course." Sidony took a sip of her wine.

She waited, and he went back to eating. She hated being in this position. Her irritation at her mother's agreement grew, blossoming in her chest, along with the knowledge that Adrian was keeping things from her.

He finished his wine. "The king's abroad."

"He could be gone for weeks," she said. "Where did he go?"

"More wine?" He got up and refilled his glass, keeping his back to her at the sideboard. "He's following a lead on one of the rebels. Any word about Zara?"

"Mother is convinced it's any day now." There. A truth, for her mother did hope that Zara would be able to report back that she was able to secure Callum's release. But otherwise, she'd done as her mother commanded and lied to him.

How could a few days—and a few more secrets—make such a difference? Their conversation was stilted and awkward. Her husband was evasive. And now she would miss opening night?

Sidony stood, brushing nonexistent crumbs off her skirt. "I need to tell Lucia to be ready to leave. We can send for more of my things once we're settled." She started for the door.

"I thought you wanted to go with me to Embury," Adrian said from behind her. Apparently, he'd followed her to the door bodily this time.

"I do. I just hoped to see one more performance." It shouldn't matter to her, but it did.

"Is this the play you were reading all summer?"

"One of them." She rubbed her temples. "They'll have to make do without me soon enough."

Adrian put his hand above hers on the door, penning her in with his body. He'd moved faster than she thought he could, but it wasn't his powers. This time it was the man. His chest was against her back, touching along a few points.

His other arm slipped around her waist, and she held still.

"If I could, we'd stay and I'd escort you."

"I know." Turning her head, she peered at him. "I'm anxious to see Blackthorne."

His forehead dropped against her shoulder, and he sighed. "Remind me when all of this is over, and I'll take you to a play. We can go every week."

Relief bubbled up in her chest, making her giddy. She smiled, sliding her fingers up the door to touch his palm.

"Thank you. Will I really have to remind you?"

"No." He kissed her ear. "Now, why is it that I'm gone for a week, and it's like we barely know each other?"

"I wondered the same thing." She wanted to talk to him like

she had before he left, to tell him about her sister's return, to ask him all the questions she'd been saving up.

"Thank you for welcoming me home." His rumbling voice made her shiver.

"Is that what I was doing? More like questioning you to death."

He pressed a kiss to the side of her neck and her knees nearly buckled. "You've more tenacity than I knew." His lips slid lower, and she arched her back, pressing her bottom against his front.

"You have no idea."

The hand at her waist slid up until he'd reached the top of her bodice. He pulled her fichu loose, dropping it on the floor.

She had to know one thing before they went any further. "Adrian? While you were gone...were you with another woman?"

He froze. "I probably deserve that for leaving so soon." He stepped back.

She turned and leaned against the door, wanting to see his face. "Is that a yes?"

"No. There's no one else. There couldn't be." Adrian ran a hand through his hair. "I don't want anyone but you."

She believed him. He kept secrets from her, but he hadn't lied outright. "Good."

"Sidony, when I promised to be faithful, I meant it." His thumb brushed across her cheek.

"I know. But when you left...I didn't know...I wasn't sure with how we left things between us." She shrunk back, feeling small in her uncertainty. Though she'd tried to dismiss them, her mother's words about how she'd lost Adrian's interest so quickly flickered through her thoughts.

"There wasn't time to explain. I'm sorry for that, sorry to give you reason to doubt."

Sidony put a tentative hand on his chest, needing to feel

him. "It's not you I doubt. When it's just you and me, we're fine. It's everything and everyone else. I wish we could go away together."

His eyes widened, their color reminding her of the lonely nights she'd spent without him. The light was fading, casting long shadows in the room, though the sun wouldn't set for another hour. They had so little time left at Mondelac.

"I want that too."

Adrian was starting to get that lost look again. She ran her fingers across his forehead, trying to chase the shadows away. "It's like you aren't all the way back."

SIDONY'S WORDS released something inside him. He didn't want his past to stand between them. Gracchus had wedged himself into nearly every corner of Adrian's life. He couldn't let it happen again. Not with her.

"I'm here now." He bent his head and kissed her. Not quite long enough to be a proper welcome home, but long enough to make his point. He knew he was making it more to himself. He wasn't sure what the future would hold, but in this moment, he didn't want to be anywhere else but with her.

"Turn around," he said, his voice rough with feeling.

She did as he asked, and he loosened the ties to her gown, slipping it off, along with the layers beneath. He kissed along her back and shoulders, anything revealed by her divested clothing. He dropped to a knee behind her, pressing a kiss to her hip and the tender skin of her waist. She wore simple hosiery and garters, the ribbons the same shade of celadon as her eyes.

She stepped out of her shoes and bent, reaching for one of the ties but he stopped her. "Leave them."

Sidony laughed. "Fine."

He wanted to take her tenderly, savoring her, but control over his desire was slipping.

"Hurry," she said, spurring him. She didn't reach back to touch him, but her fingers flexed at her sides.

With an arm slung low across her belly, he tugged her close, cursing at the feel of her skin against him.

"I wanted to take you when you first came in the room. Toss you on the bed and show you how much I missed you." He spoke low against her ear.

She moaned and pushed back, pressing her lush bottom against his groin. "Hmm. It didn't seem like it. You looked like someone had walked across your grave."

She was right. When she'd come into the room, he hadn't had the strength or the will to greet her. He'd still ached for her, though. "I'd needed your comfort first."

She rested her forehead on the door. "I can do that for you."

He brushed a kiss across the nape of her neck. "You did." He trailed his finger from the spot on her neck, across her shoulder, and down her arm. Her breath hitched in her chest. "Let me make that up to you."

He would not mess this up. Somehow, when his life had started cracking at the seams, he'd been given the gift of her as a wife. He would find a way for nothing to be between them. Tonight, at least, he could show her with his body what his intentions were.

He drew the pins from her hair, scattering them on the floor. Gently, he dug his fingers into her mass of curls, easing the honey-colored strands loose until they dangled down her back. He clasped her hips, ready to bring her close again but she wriggled free.

Sidony turned and leaned against the door. "At least let me see you."

He stood still while she made her perusal, pleased at the gleam of excitement in her gaze. He made short work of the fastenings on his breeches, pushing them down his thighs. She gasped when his cock sprang free. He hardened further at her attention.

"You're sure that isn't for the tray of food you had earlier?" Sidony brushed her hair off her shoulder.

His eyebrows shot up, and a laugh burst from his lips. How had he managed to stay away from her for a week? He caught one of her hands and pressed it to his shaft. "I'm quite sure this is for you."

She squeezed him gently at first, then her grip got firmer. She drew her hand along his length, making him groan. She nearly undid him, as she had whenever they were together. He'd barely let himself think of her when he'd been gone. His cock shot hard when he had, which was a most uncomfortable way to ride a horse.

Sidony licked her lips. "Adrian, I want to try something." She pushed him back a step and went to her knees before him.

"What are you—?"

"Hush." She grasped him with one hand and brought him to her mouth, pressing a kiss to the head of his penis.

"Sidony, wait." He rubbed a hand over his face. She waited, her lush lips mere inches from his cock. "You don't have to do that."

"But I want to." She slid one hand around to hold him in place, and then she closed her lips around him.

Any coherent thoughts he'd had fled; he couldn't remember why he was stopping her.

The heat of her mouth was incredible. She stroked her tongue against him as she took him deeper, wetting his flesh. He closed his eyes for a second, focusing on the feeling of what she was doing. Desire coursed through him. His thighs tensed, bracing against the pleasure she wrought.

"So good," he praised her.

Her hand moved down, holding him at his base, then slowly

squeezing upward. He couldn't hold out much longer. Her cheeks were hollowed with her motions, her hand twisting up to meet her mouth. He almost lost his seed. Strands of her hair caught some of the last rays of sunlight and glowed, giving her an ethereal look.

Adrian wondered if he'd died; it was all too much.

Voices in the hall reminded him where they were. If they continued, he'd take her against the door. He checked the hall with his powers. A few servants bustled between rooms. He wasn't in the mood to be overheard by them. Sidony was all his.

He pulled away before he spent himself in her mouth.

"Wait. I wasn't done," she cried.

He pulled her up and cupped her face, kissing her fiercely. When she stepped closer and her hard nipples brushed against his chest, he groaned. The bed wasn't far, but he couldn't wait.

He picked her up and backed her against the door, her legs on either side of his hips. He dropped kisses from her shoulder to her neck, trying to slow the beat of his heart.

On the other side of the door, two maids were in a heated discussion of the best soap to use for laundering bed linens.

Sidony giggled. "Shall I dismiss them?"

"Gods, no."

She arched closer to him, sliding her thigh higher. Her skin was so soft. All he wanted to do was impale her on his cock. Her nails dug into his shoulder. "Adrian, don't make me wait any longer."

He shook his head. Not like this.

Inspiration struck. He could try something new. "Never leaving your side," he promised.

At the end of the hall, around the corner, Adrian projected his voice. He wasn't exactly sure what he said, but it was something along the lines of "Princess Sidony has requested the upstairs maids report to Mrs. Dowds." He was almost sure that was the chatelaine.

The earnest squabbling outside the door ceased, followed by several other footfalls, and then they were truly alone in this wing of the castle.

Sidony arched her head back, baring her neck. "Did it get quiet out there? Did you have something to do with that?"

He brushed his lips down the column of her throat. "Don't know how I managed it."

"You're clever, that's how."

She laughed, and he kissed her, thrusting his tongue in her mouth, and rubbing it against hers. She matched his motions, angling her head to deepen their kiss. She pulled at him, twining her leg around his waist. His shaft ground against her mound. He was ready, but he wasn't sure she was. He slipped a hand between them, feeling along the folds of her sex. She was wet but tight. He rubbed the heel of his hand against her, keeping to a narrow circle, thrilling when she gasped, "Adrian, please."

Her eyes slit with desire, and a flush rose on her cheeks. He dipped his head to her breast, lifting her higher against the door, and inhaled her sweet honeysuckle scent. She squirmed against him. She was a goddess about to take the sweetest mercy on him. It was one fantasy he'd allowed himself while he'd been gone.

"I'll make it good," he promised.

He hitched her up and positioned his cock at her entrance. He wanted to bury himself inside her, but instead, he made himself be patient, working slowly in and out of her. Her breaths came in pants. At last, she took his entire length, and the warm clasp of her body caused a slow heat to climb up his spine.

He held still for a moment, watching her face. He cupped

her breasts, loving how hard her nipples were against his palms.

"Did you miss this?" she asked.

"I dreamed of you."

"I couldn't sleep without you."

He kissed her for that, wanting to make it better.

He'd waited as long as he could. When he began moving, she sucked in a breath. He did it again, holding her with a hand under her arse. Her expression didn't change, though her gaze flicked over his face. He went faster, bracing a knee against the door. When she moaned, he knew he had her right where he wanted her.

He held her, snapping his hips up to grind against her with each stroke. She braced a hand on the door above her head, pushing her body back to his, moaning in his ear. He clutched her closer, murmuring words of praise, of how good she felt, of what he wanted to do to her. Her body turned liquid and fiery hot, squeezing him as she found her release.

His mouth on her shoulder, he let her catch her breath, and then he did it again, pumping up into her clutching depths. She gasped his name, and he kept going until he felt her stiffen and cry out. "Adrian, yes, yes."

This time he didn't wait, following her down after she reached her pleasure in his arms. He filled her with his seed as the spasms continued, wrenching a groan from him. Finally, he relaxed his grip on her.

Sidony was draped around him, spent and languorous. One of her stocking-clad legs shifted against the back of his thigh, a sweet caress that brought him back to where he was. He recalled the knocking sound of the door, hitting the hinges as he'd pounded her against it. He'd completely lost control, been so impatient to have her he'd taken her against the door.

Hot tears landed on his chest, and he leaned to the side, trying to see her face. "Sidony, what is it?"

"It's nothing." She wriggled, and he released her legs, setting her down. Her gaze was troubled and focused on his chin. "I don't know how I can feel so close to you, our bodies finding such harmony, and yet…"

He didn't know what to say to reassure her. He felt the same way, sensing the distance that had crept between them these past few days.

"Let it be enough for now." He kissed her, wanting the feeling to linger for as long as possible.

At least they could find pleasure in each other.

CHAPTER THIRTY-EIGHT

*T*hey'd been on the road for several hours the next morning when it started to rain. It was long past the rainy season in L'Ortagia, but the steady downfall was insistent. Sidony had ridden in strained silence with Adrian and Lucia. Adrian was on edge the moment the first raindrops fell. He'd spent an hour in the carriage, but had been so antsy and agitated that he'd gone outside to ride alongside his men. It was not how she'd imagined her honeymoon.

She supposed the morning conversation she'd had with her husband had been to blame.

"I need to ask you about something your mother mentioned at dinner last night," Adrian had said while they hastily ate breakfast in his room.

"Certainly." Her mind had raced, wondering if they'd talked about Zara and Callum. She smiled, feeling the stiffness in her cheeks.

"It stuck with me." He took a bite of toast and peered over at her as if to gauge her reaction.

"Oh?" She sipped her tea, hating that she felt guilty.

"The queen mentioned you and Zara leaving your old life to

start a new one. It seemed like an odd phrase for what Zara's going through."

Sidony blinked at him, at a loss for words.

Adrian tilted his head, frowning slightly. "Is there something I should know about your sister?"

"Adrian, I can't talk about it." There. She admitted she was keeping something from him. She should have made something up.

He dropped his head, then stood and grabbed his coat. "I know the feeling," he said at the door before walking out.

So here she sat, in the cold, traveling to her new home, sure she'd put more distance between herself and her husband than was already there. She looked out the window, hoping to spot Adrian, then sat back dejectedly when she didn't. She let a bitter laugh escape.

Lucia, who'd been dozing in her seat across from Sidony, sat up abruptly, nearly dropping the embroidery she'd held on her lap. "What is it? Are we there?"

"I'm sorry I woke you."

"The rain is getting to you too." Lucia yawned.

Sidony gestured to the window. "This isn't what I would have wanted for a honeymoon."

"Your first week apart, the next stuck in a carriage with me." Lucia picked up her hoop and set to work with her needle again. The needle struck her thimble when the carriage bounced, but somehow Lucia avoided injury.

"It could be worse."

Lucia narrowed her eyes. "There was quite a buildup to your marriage. You two seemed happy together, then he left. Has he made it up to you?"

Sidony fiddled with the book in her lap, running her finger over the leather binding. "We have this pull between us, it's so strong. And then we each have...secrets. There's nothing he needs to make up to me. Some things can't be helped." Sidony wanted to believe her own words. She hated the awkwardness between them.

"Hmm."

"This alliance is still tenuous. I refuse to let my marriage be." She looked out the window again, still not seeing him but trusting that he was close. "You must be exhausted from last night."

Lucia pulled a small set of spectacles from a pocket in her apron. She wrapped the thread around her needle three times, then held the string as she poked the needle through, leaving a nubbin of thread. "We were mostly packed."

"You managed a royal wedding on just over a week's notice too. You are a skilled woman, Lucia."

"My father would have a fit of apoplexy before he'd ever let me earn a wage, but I like having options. Maybe matrimony isn't in my future." Lucia made another knot and chuckled. "Have we crossed into Embury yet?"

"I don't know how much the rain has slowed us down, but Adrian said we would before the end of the day."

Lucia turned up the lamp. "Then I have a couple hours of daylight left."

THE ROAD they'd chosen was well-maintained, so while in L'Ortagia, the rain hadn't slowed their progress much. They'd changed horses and eaten, but pushed on.

"I'm crossing at Anjou," Adrian told Lieutenant Wills.

It was a border town they'd avoided when they'd searched for his family.

"Are you worried about a rebel presence there?" Wills asked.

The messenger who'd delivered Zara and Callum's letters had been hired from outside Anjou.

"It's the shortest route to Embury, and in this rain, I doubt they'd stage much of a protest." He needed to take the fastest route to the palace. "Besides, the rebels wouldn't harm my wife."

"How can you be so sure?" Wills asked.

"Her sister was taken by them, and they haven't harmed her."

"Sir, I need to talk to you about that."

"What is it?" Adrian steered their horses away from the group, riding behind the carriage. The steady rain helped cover their conversation.

"While we were away, Princess Zara returned to Mondelac."

"How did you hear that?" Adrian asked.

Wills cleared his throat. "Last night...I was with one of the maids." Though his cheeks turned red, he continued, avoiding Adrian's gaze. "Anyway, she asked me about the rebels because the princess had returned. She came back the night we left."

"How long was she at Mondelac?" Though their time had been short, Sidony had had opportunities to tell him about Zara. He'd asked her twice about her sister, and she'd either changed the subject or told him nothing.

"Less than a day. Molly didn't know where she went. She just said there was a middle-of-the-night meeting with the queen. It was all to be hushed up."

As the words sunk in, Adrian stared at the back of his wife's carriage. To know that she'd kept something so big from him hurt. He kept secrets from her too, perhaps too many, though he had intended to tell her about his plans once he found the orb. And he'd told her more than anyone else besides Marlowe about his family. "Where is Zara now?"

"I believe she's on her way to Marenburg."

Then she really had gotten in deep with the rebels. And she was about to run into Gracchus. "Who's with her?"

"I don't know. One of the L'Ortagian diplomats was unable

to meet with me before we left, but I can't be sure it was because she was gone."

"Emmanuelle?"

Wills jerked his head. "Yes."

"She's probably with her." Adrian steered his horse around a larger rut in the road. "Did Molly say anything about the princess's condition? Was Ash with her?" Why hadn't Sidony told him?

"She returned unharmed. The rebel leader was not with her, but one of his representatives was. Jeffors."

"Was he there in Ash's stead? There could only be a few reasons why he wouldn't have accompanied her. He's likely caught up in this Marenburg mess too."

"True. He seems to have that knack." Wills steered his horse around a large puddle in the middle of the road. "I would have told you this morning, but I didn't trust anyone else with the information."

Adrian shook his head. "No, it's fine. I couldn't have done anything about it earlier, and it wouldn't have changed our leaving."

His mind reeled with the news of Zara's secret visit home. The fact that her return had been kept secret from him could only mean a few things. First, the L'Ortagians didn't trust him, even with Gracchus gone. That might be why his wife hadn't told him about her sister's visit home. He could understand the predicament that put her in.

But it also meant that during Zara's time with Callum, he had convinced her to help him. "She chose the rebels' side."

CHAPTER THIRTY-NINE

To Adrian's relief, crossing into Embury went smoothly. Gracchus's loyalists manned the bridge and had bowed to their new princess as her carriage rolled by. If there had been a rebel presence at Anjou, they hadn't shown themselves. Perhaps they simply didn't hold the border town. It was just as well. Adrian would not have wanted to fight them. Learning of Zara's new allegiance only strengthened his urge for peace with the rebels. If he had his family back, he'd be tempted to join their side against Gracchus.

It was another reason he hadn't confronted Sidony yet about Zara. Not only did they lack the privacy for such a discussion, part of him didn't blame her for keeping it a secret from him. He had his own secrets to contend with.

Once they were free, Minah and his mother would have to decide whether to return to his extended family in Daeso, assuming they would be protected from the king, or seek sanctuary in another country. He wasn't sure if he'd have a place in Embury. Now that he had a wife, he had to take Sidony into consideration too. As the days passed, his urgency at finding a way for them to stay together grew.

He continued to ride outside the carriage, occasionally talking with Wills. The weather was warm, the roads drier than normal. It made his return to Embury bittersweet. He'd felt out of place many times since coming to live with his uncle. In those early years he'd worked hard to fit in, to look and sound like a prince of Embury. He'd spent hours with tutors, learning to hide his accent, to sound like a native.

Maybe it was because Daeso was so far away, maybe it was because of the way his uncle had assumed the throne, but Adrian had wanted the people of Embury to be proud of him, to see him as an heir. Gracchus was the usurper, but Adrian never wanted to be seen as an interloper. Early on, he had wanted to be an asset to his uncle. Years later, after his uncle's deeds had severed any loyalty he'd felt and Torwyn was firmly ensconced as the royal heir, Adrian had at least wanted to serve the people as best he could.

Though he hadn't been born in Embury, he felt a connection to his father's home, and his adopted homeland. He hadn't resented what he'd chosen to do until that day Minister Lin had visited and called him by his birth name, Haemosu, which he'd politely declined. The king would have found a way to punish him or his family if he'd let the diplomat call him that. His uncle only tolerated Adrian's speaking Daeseon because he needed him to. But rejecting his family name had shifted something inside Adrian.

Now that he was contemplating his last days in Embury, there was a palpable sense of loss. The wide stretches of heather and even lichen-covered rocks had become such common sites. The miles passed quickly as his unfocused gaze wandered across the rocky countryside. He never truly believed that someday Gracchus would die, and his cousin would assume the throne. That didn't mean that giving up a land he'd called home for the past nine years was what he wanted to do either. Unless Gracchus was removed from power, Adrian didn't see a way for him and his family to stay in Embury, regardless of whether the people would still accept him as a prince.

Adrian pushed those thoughts to the back of his mind as they crossed a drawbridge and were finally on the palace grounds of Blackthorne. There was a buzzing sensation at the back of his skull. Nothing painful, more like an itch. He sent out his powers, checking to see if Gracchus was somehow in residence. This was the first time he'd been able to use them so extensively at the palace. He had Sidony to thank for that. Their strength, range, and ease increased as the days passed and she was in his life. She helped him focus and open up abilities he'd had but couldn't tap into. She made him stronger in many ways.

As he searched the rooms, it seemed that his powers were working normally. Adrian didn't find his uncle. Since it was early evening, Gracchus would have been in meetings with his field commanders. He maintained a tight schedule, nor would he have ever been in hiding at the palace. His uncle was still in Marenburg, as expected.

Adrian considered the buzzing again. He'd never felt anything like it, though his muscles sometimes got tight along his shoulders. Perhaps his lovely wife would help him work out the tension. That must be what it was, as his senses were working fine, including his expanded benefit of reach. He'd been able to search the entire palace in mere moments. Perhaps in the coming days, he'd go back to the drawbridge and see if he felt the sensation again.

Gracchus had expanded Blackthorne since he assumed the crown, and therefore since Sidony had last visited. While parts of the old keep were still in good condition, his uncle had had the king's apartments, as well as the family wing expanded, and added long galleries connecting the two.

During Adrian's search, he found the orb locked in Gracchus's rooms. His senses had practically pulled him toward it. He wanted to snatch Sidony out of the carriage and race into the palace. It was almost too easy. Relief rushed through him. It was here; it was in reach. Tonight, he would find his family.

Adrian dismounted his horse and handed off the reins. He went around the side of the carriage and helped Sidony down. She smiled at the servants, who all greeted her with polite curtsies and bows from where they stood in neat rows before the palace steps. Despite the king's absence, the palace remained a dangerous place. Gracchus would be watching their movements through his spies. While Adrian knew who many of them were, he was sure his uncle had more.

"Welcome home, cousin." Torwyn greeted them from the top of the staircase in front of the line of assembled servants. His hawkish features were smoothed into a banal expression.

"You aren't with the king?" The prince rarely left the king's side.

"He bade me to stay at Blackthorne while he is away." And in an uncharacteristic move, Torwyn congratulated them on their nuptials.

Adrian barely concealed his shock. The false manners were for Sidony's benefit, surely. He inclined his head anyway. "Thank you, Torwyn. We'll see ourselves inside."

"Welcome to our remodeled palace, Sidony," Torwyn said, as they passed him.

"Thank you." Sidony's gaze trailed over her shoulder for a long moment before she turned back to the rest of the servants.

Torwyn kept a respectable distance, saying nothing during the introductions to the staff. He left when Adrian and Sidony walked toward the entrance, saying only, "I'll see you at dinner."

Although they'd had dignitaries and visiting royals, it had been many years since a female royal had been in residence. When he had first come to Embury with Gracchus, Adrian had anticipated his mother and sister visiting him, but Gracchus never allowed it.

Sidony's floral gown, though wrinkled from her hours in the carriage, trailed the scent of honeysuckle. Adrian wished she could trace a path through the entire palace and erase his uncle's stain in her wake.

"Would you like a tour?" Adrian offered his arm as they ascended the steps.

"Only if you're in the mood to give it. It's been a long journey." Sidony squeezed him discretely.

"When the king is at the palace, dinners are served at eight. Torwyn will be keeping to that schedule."

Sidony took in the immense front hall with its sweeping double staircases. The walls gleamed against black-and-white marble tile set in a harlequin pattern on the floor.

"It's elegant," Sidony said softly. "The floor reminds me of the newer section of Mondelac."

"It was completed less than a year ago. It's stunning."

"It doesn't feel like the same place." Sidony wore a half frown.

Adrian decided to make a show of loyalty to the king in case his palace spies would report back to his uncle. He motioned the butler over and requested a small repast to be brought to their rooms. He then asked the housekeeper to notify the cook that they'd be eating a formal dinner at the usual time.

"Let me show you some of the improvements my uncle has made. The royal residence is an entirely new wing of the palace." Adrian offered his arm to Sidony again, and she took it as they ascended the stairs.

"Adrian, you spent most of your time in this residence, correct?"

"Since coming to Embury, yes." He never thought of it as home, but as they walked down the long gallery to the royal wing of apartments, he began telling her stories of growing up here, places he'd played and trained. For a short time, he could pretend that this was a home he was proud of. He leaned down and pressed a kiss to her temple.

She tipped her head against his shoulder while they strolled into the next room. "Tell me more of your adventures living here, my prince."

∼

THEY'D HAD A HARD JOURNEY, a lengthy tour, and then a formal dinner. Thankfully, there hadn't been any foreign heads of state to entertain. Having lived a life in the public eye under the scrutiny of a royal court, Sidony was used to being on display. But she had been able to be mostly herself. In Embury, she was not sure who she should be. And while she had Lucia and Adrian with her, she did not know whom to trust.

Several courtiers and their ladies sat at the long table with them, along with Torwyn. The women were bejeweled, powdered, and dressed beautifully. Many of the men—and all but a few of the ladies—also wore powdered wigs. Both Sidony and Adrian did not, though for different reasons, but the fact reminded her of how out of place she and her husband were. Sidony worked hard to converse with her guests, some of whom she'd met at Mondelac before her sister's wedding.

"More wine?" Adrian gestured to one of the footmen to refill her glass.

"This will be the last one, then." She was certain he had a reason for keeping her glass filled at dinner.

They'd eaten several courses, each served with impressive efficiency and deportment. Sidony thought her mother was exacting, but Gracchus's household staff was impressive.

"Has your sister been found yet, Princess Sidony?" Lady Moira asked. She'd invited Sidony to hunt with her at her nearby estate once the weather got cooler.

"Not yet. We are hopeful she'll be returned soon."

"Were there extra measures in place for your wedding so you wouldn't get stolen away?" a duchess seated farther down the table asked.

"Yes, I believe so. Our wedding was much smaller."

"But no less a royal affair, dear wife." Adrian raised his glass to her from the other end of the table.

The questions went on into the evening. Courtiers asked about her sister, her mother, their wedding, all pertinent and mostly polite. They'd caught Adrian up on the goings on in the palace while he'd been away. But the strain wore on her. Finally, when the last course was cleared, Adrian stood.

This was their agreed upon signal, so she did her part and yawned delicately behind her hand.

"You are all welcome to continue the evening's entertainment. We'll be retiring for the night." Adrian set down his napkin.

The guests murmured their gratitude, and Sidony stood, nodding to the footman who pulled back her chair. Torwyn tipped his glass to them but didn't say anything.

Adrian met her at the end of the table and escorted her from the formal dining room. Once they were on the stairs, she released the pent-up breath she'd held since the meal started hours before. Everything had gone as planned. They'd been the dutiful heirs, now properly married and returned home to await the king.

CHAPTER FORTY

*S*idony leaned into Adrian's side as they walked down the hall to the grand staircase. She tipped her head back when they passed under the ormolu chandelier, noting the smoky hue of the crystals. Wine and exhaustion from days spent traveling slowed her steps.

"The chandelier is breathtaking when all lit up."

Adrian glanced up at her words then gave a slow shake of his head. "I never noticed that before."

She hugged his arm to her chest. "Maybe you got used to it, passing under it every day."

"Perhaps." He led her to the marble staircase. "You have that effect on me. I see things, notice details."

"What sorts of details?"

As they rounded the curve, her head swam and she wobbled in her shoes.

"Steady, love." Adrian put his arm around her, his thumb stroking her shoulder. "Beautiful ones."

She smiled. The warmth of his body had her curling closer to him. She shivered at his touch, recalling how for the past week they'd lacked the privacy to do anything but sleep.

"I've missed you." She laid a hand on his chest, her fingers sliding against the subtle embroidery on his lapel.

Adrian bent his head toward her. "And I, you." So discreet. He was much more cautious at Blackthorne. Although he'd warned her the Embury court could be vicious, she hadn't seen evidence of that at dinner. Their guests at the table had been perceptive and guarded. She'd find out soon enough if they'd use any of what she'd said tonight against her.

When they reached the top of the stairs, their footsteps were muffled by the lush carpets running the length of the hallway. Here was her moment. After several days in the carriage, she'd had plenty of time to reflect on her new marriage, and she'd come to a few conclusions. Their first night in the palace together should begin without any secrets between them. She would tell Adrian about Zara and take a chance on trusting him more fully. He might be angry that she'd kept the information from her for over a week, but she'd done so because of a promise she'd made to her mother.

The issue of Adrian's loyalty to Gracchus gave her pause. She put a hand to her forehead, rubbing against the growing ache. That was the crux. Despite the tensions between Adrian and the king, she didn't know how far her husband would go, what he would consider a betrayal. If it came down to her or the king, whom would he choose? They were bound by matrimony, but Gracchus held a tight rein on her husband. Adrian would defend and protect her, but Zara's meeting with the small council had immense repercussions for all of them. Sidony had never given the grand scope of politics much thought until recent weeks. Zara's kidnapping had changed that forever.

Over the course of many miles and long hours, she'd realized that despite their different backgrounds and loyalties, she and Adrian truly only had each other. Secrets would drive them apart.

She was wary of marriage after having watched her parents' miserable one. She'd gone from not wanting to be used as a bargaining tool to being made aware of a larger role she was being asked to play. Her desire to maintain her patroness responsibilities seemed simple now. Where did she and Adrian fit into the conflict brewing between their countries? Despite the rocky start to her marriage, she wanted it to be better.

When they reached his suite, Adrian dismissed the attendants at the door. Sidony had seen his rooms on the tour and again when she changed before supper. Gold-framed paintings hung on the linen-colored walls. The four-poster bed had a navy blue coverlet with similar accents, all of which shone in the candlelight that graced the tables and sconces in the room. Elegant but understated. Almost spartan in comparison to other parts of the palace. It suited her husband perfectly.

She was ready to tell him about Zara's return. But when he strode past her, she hesitated. As if he were a marionette whose strings had been cut, he visibly relaxed once the door closed behind them. His hands flexed at his sides, and he drew in a deep breath. He hid it well, but she was learning his signs of tension. Here was the first moment she'd seen any tension ease from him since crossing into Embury.

The words caught in her throat. What she had to say could make him pensive and worried again. They'd already had enough of that.

She stalled and slipped out of her shoes. "I like your rooms, Adrian."

He stripped off his coat, tossing it on a nearby chair before striding over to her. "I like you in them."

"So." She fidgeted with her hands, searching for courage. "We're finally alone."

"That we are." His gaze dropped to her mouth.

She froze, reading the intent in his expression. Heat rose in her chest. "We have things we need to discuss." Her voice came out breathy, and she shook her head, trying to dislodge the sensual turn her thoughts were taking.

"Go ahead." He started unfastening his waistcoat. His lean fingers slid the buttons free, and her flush deepened. She couldn't concentrate but she tried.

"I've been thinking. Now that we're here, let's make a fresh start."

His gaze swept over her cleavage. "Fresh start?"

He tossed his waistcoat on a nearby settee. The white linen of his shirt contrasted with his sun-kissed skin and nearly black hair. There was no reason she couldn't touch him while they talked.

She stepped closer, skimming a hand up his chest. "Yes. We spent nearly two weeks apart."

"I am sorry about that." He pulled at his neckcloth, unwinding it and sending it to land nearby.

The skin revealed at his neck distracted her. She wanted to bury her nose there and feel his arms around her. She couldn't stop touching him. He was so warm and hard. He loosened his shirt, and her hands crept underneath, feeling the ridges of muscle. What was she saying?

"I don't want there to be anything between us."

Adrian pulled his shirt over his head. She no longer cared where it ended up. Her own clothes felt restrictive, hampering her movements.

"Neither do I." He cocked his head at her. His hands were on his hips, the move accentuating his fine form.

She touched his abdomen, her fingers coasting along his flesh. She wanted to press her lips to his skin, to taste him. Her lips parted, but the words wouldn't come out.

The thought of discussing their family, obligations, and loyalties seemed less urgent. Heat suffused her skin, making her languid. Maybe it was the sexy way he moved. Maybe it had been too long since they'd last made love. Standing in front of her half-naked husband, she cared naught for politics.

She rubbed her palm up over his heart. "I need you."

Adrian snapped into motion. He leaned down and cupped her face. A breath before his lips met hers, he muttered, "Talk later."

He kissed her fiercely, slanting his lips over hers again and again. Her arms went around him in sweet relief. This was what she wanted, what she needed.

His hands slid around to the back of her gown, working to unfasten it. Without turning her, he managed it. Likely with his magic. Pieces of clothing fell to the floor until she was down to her thin chemise.

He stood before her in his tight breeches and boots. She had eyed the bed when she walked in, but before she could get there, Adrian pulled her over to stand by his desk.

"I'm assigning you a personal guard." He sat at a nearby chair and pulled off his boots in quick succession.

"Why?" She started to pull the string at her neckline, but he stood and brushed her hands away.

"Embury can be a dangerous place." He rent the garment in two.

She knew she should be affronted at her torn chemise, but she didn't care. She loved him like this. Loved that she was the one to get him to that point.

After shrugging out of the remains of her shift, Sidony was left standing in her stockings and pink beribboned garters. She bent and slipped out of them too.

"Fine." She shrugged, grateful for the extra protection.

"Come here."

She tugged on his breeches with one hand. "I don't want to be anywhere else."

Adrian cupped her breasts and kissed her neck. He found a

spot that sent shivers through her. She squirmed, on fire for him.

He bent and slipped his arms behind her thighs, picking her up and holding her along the front of his body. She loved being held by him, feeling his strength. He set her on the edge of his desk and captured her mouth with a kiss. His hands cupped her face, and she felt treasured.

Sidony reached for the fastenings on his pants. Her fingers fumbled on the buttons, so she reached inside and cupped her hand around his hard cock.

Adrian groaned against her neck. "Harder."

She gave him a squeeze, pulling her hand along his length. He kissed a spot behind her ear, trailing his lips down her neck. She smiled, committing to her task. Soon he was panting against her, groaning when she hit a sensitive spot.

He'd gotten even harder in her grip. She wanted his breeches off. "Adrian?"

He still had a hand behind her neck and another cupping her breast, but the placket on his pants loosened. The fabric slid low on his hips. Ah, his magic.

His erection sprang out, and she closed her hand around his hot length. Adrian captured her wrist and brought her hand to his mouth.

"Like this." He licked her palm and wrapped her fingers around him again. She immediately felt the difference. She repeated his action and squeezed again, her hand sliding along his skin with a delicious friction.

Adrian's forehead dropped against her shoulder. He groaned, his breath gusting across her breasts. She arched her back, needing his touch there too.

He obliged her, his hand holding her breast, teasing at the peak.

She held on, working his cock, her need rising so that she

lost her rhythm. He chuckled in her ear. "Enough. I'll spill on the floor."

She let go, reaching for his shoulders, his chest, his abdomen, needing to touch him. She traced the lines of his body, feeling like she couldn't get enough. Desire coiled low in her belly, and she moaned, her arms curling around his neck.

Adrian leaned her back and spread her legs farther, wrapping one around his hip. One hand tipped her up to him, the other clutched at her hip. His mouth dropped to her breasts; he kissed and sucked at her nipples. Her head fell back against the desk, and she nearly cried out from the pleasure. She tried to draw him down to her with her knee sliding along his side. She bucked her hips against him, but still he held back.

What would it take for him to be inside her?

She felt his hardness along her inner thigh, though he made no move to enter her. He kept tormenting her with his mouth on her chest and neck. "I thought you missed me, husband."

"Not yet." He reached between them and petted her soft folds. She tightened her hand in his hair when he parted her and slipped a finger inside.

"I am ready now." She sucked in a breath when he added another one, then used his thumb to caress the bud of her sex. She tightened around him, her body tensing and her breaths coming faster.

"One, Sidony." He lifted his head and stared into her eyes. The heat in his expression nearly caused her to climax right then, but she held back. She struggled to keep her eyes open the pleasure was so strong. "For me."

His voice was low and the command too hard to resist. She clutched his shoulders as she climaxed on his fingers. He worked her through it, drawing out her pleasure. She moaned low when he kept going.

"I need you, Adrian."

Adrian lifted her leg higher, angling her open for his first thrust. She didn't think she would ever get used to the feeling. A breath caught in her throat as he eased inside, filling her. She gave a cry when he drew his length nearly out of her.

"Mine."

His words thrilled her. "Yes, yours." It was like he'd pulled the thought from her fantasies. "Yours."

He pushed his heavy cock into her again, so slowly this time that her eyes screwed shut. She hitched her leg higher, and that seemed to give him permission to pound away at her. His hips slammed into hers, over and over. She clutched at him, squeezing with her inner muscles.

The desk slid across the deep carpet and Adrian let go long enough to pull it back. He swore but kept at her. She felt her body stirring again, the sensations streaking up her thighs and across her sex. She moaned his name when she broke apart. Her body's reaction seemed to send him over the edge. With a hand under her ass, he angled her closer. She wanted to wring his orgasm from him. She squeezed and exalted when he gripped her tightly then exhaled on her shoulder, his cock pulsing inside her.

They stayed like that for long moments. Finally her legs slipped down. Adrian adjusted his breeches and handed her a scrap of linen from his pocket. He braced his hands on the desk.

"You wanted to talk." His eyes blazed into hers.

Sidony sat up and rested a hand against his chest, his heart beating fast against her palm. She took a deep breath. "We have too many secrets between us."

CHAPTER FORTY-ONE

Adrian narrowed his eyes. That must have been what Sidony was trying to say earlier. A part of him had known it and hushed her, because he was too greedy and longing for her.

"You're right. We do."

Sidony stroked his cheek. "We're always better when it's the two of us."

Adrian dropped his hands to his sides. "Sidony, there's something I have to tell you."

"Is there a reason you have me naked for this?" she asked.

"No, that just happened. Come here." He helped her down and took her hand, leading her over to the bed. Pulling back the coverlet, he gestured for her to precede him.

She climbed in and sat back against the padded headboard, removing the pins from her hair. "Go ahead." She pulled the covers over her breasts.

Adrian slung on a dressing gown and stood by the side of the bed. He pushed up the sleeves, the cool silk sliding along his arms. Sex had cleared his mind. It was time to tell her everything and then see where she stood.

"I don't know how long we'll be staying. I came back because what I need to find my family is here, and my uncle is gone. I need to get to them before he comes back."

"Right now?"

He frowned. "No, I need a plan first."

He told her about the orb and how Gracchus used it.

"It's here, in Gracchus's apartments." He leaned his fists on the bed. "I have to get it, and then I can see where my mother and sister are."

"Is it dangerous?" Her eyes widened.

He felt terrible saying it, but he'd already held back too much for too long. He could see that now. "Very. That's why I brought you with me."

A frown knit her brow. "I'm safest with you."

"At one time, Gracchus wanted you dead, a sacrifice. He planned to blame it on the rebels. He told me he'd changed his mind, but I couldn't leave you behind because I don't know who to trust." He ran a hand through his hair, disgusted at himself for allowing her to be a part of this. He should have sent her away after Zara disappeared.

Her face drained of color. "He wanted me dead? Why?"

There wasn't a tactful way to tell her.

"He believes certain magics maintain his hold on the kingdom. Some are based on nocturne powers and some are just rituals he uses to try to acquire such power for himself. Some of his rituals involve blood and the use of sacrifices."

Her hands clenched on the sheet. "So my death would help him mystically and politically."

"He believed so. It would ensure that the rebels lost any support they had among the people. I tried to dissuade him. If you only knew how Gracchus is when his mind is set." His words were a weak excuse. Guilt weighed on him. His presence in Sidony and Zara's lives had threatened their safety. "Sidony, I've done this to you."

She drew up her knees. "I've heard stories about him, tales of how he came to be called 'the usurper.' We thought it was because of how beloved the MacKinnons were. That any distant relation taking over the crown would be seen as an interloper." Her hands trembled. "What are we going to do?"

He sat and laid his hands over hers. "I'm keeping you close to me or under the guard of someone I trust. I have a small group of soldiers I can lean on. Then I'm doing everything in my power to get the orb and get out of here."

"My mother doesn't know if she can trust you, but she will grant you sanctuary," she said calmly.

"Thank you. I believe Minah and my mother are still in Embury. They were moved. I missed them by days, but I think they're still here."

"I understand." Her fingers were still beneath his.

Could she? He was glad he'd told her.

"Zara came back while you were gone." Her voice had dropped to barely above a whisper.

"I know."

"She's taken the rebels' side, championing Callum's claim." She met his gaze. "She actually planned to leave with Callum before the wedding."

"She what?" He got up and paced the length of the bed, wondering if it was time to switch his allegiances too. "She pretended it was a kidnapping to convince me?"

"Yes."

"Well, I'm glad you finally told me."

"This doesn't bother you?"

He turned back to her. "No."

She straightened, leaning a bit away from him." Your voice makes it sound like it does bother you."

"When were you going to tell me?" he asked.

"You're hardly in a position to debate honesty."

"True." He sat on the bed, taking her hand. "I have another confession."

"I figured this would be a long night." She pursed her lips.

"The night that Callum took Zara, I had a chance to go after them, to raise the alarm, and I waited."

She stiffened but didn't pull her hand away. "You let her go?"

"I'm not proud of it, but, yes, I let her go. I followed them and watched her in the wagon. Zara had several chances to sound an alarm, but she didn't. I took it as her deciding to go. I could have saved her, although now I know she wouldn't have wanted that. Still, I'm sorry I didn't tell you that part of it."

Sidony stared at him, blinking at all the revelations. "It ended up being the right thing. Zara is quite independent, as you probably understand by now. You were right about Callum. They seem to have something between them. She said he treated her well." She laughed but it was a dry sound.

"You look skeptical," he said.

"Whatever is between them is likely a mess." She took a deep breath. "My mother forbade me from telling you. She's also helping Zara by sending her to Marenburg to aid the rebels."

"Gracchus was heading there because we'd heard one of the rebel leaders was being kept there. We are in great danger if he returns without bringing Callum back with him. I believe he plans to bring him up on charges."

"Would my sister be in danger from the king?"

"She could be. He will go to any lengths to secure his power."

Sidony pulled him closer, her eyes searching his face. "I need to know where your loyalty lies when it comes to your uncle."

There was no question. Adrian didn't hesitate to pledge himself to her. "With you and my family."

"Good." She leaned forward and kissed him sweetly.

Warmth spread through his chest, easing the ache that he carried with him. The glowing gold on the frame behind her head reminded him that they weren't safe yet. "Sidony, as long as Gracchus has my mother and sister, he has a hold over me." He tried to keep the panic out of his voice, but saying it out loud brought home how powerless he truly was against the king.

"Then freeing them is our first priority." Sidony squeezed his hands, anchoring him to her. "Keep me safe, but do what you need to do. Your sister and mother are important to me too. They are my family now as well. You wouldn't be the man I love if you leave them behind." She let go and leaned against the headboard. "Come to bed."

He crossed to the sitting area and brought the small portraits to her, setting them on the bed like they were coals from the grate. One was of him and Minah, another was of his mother.

"Are these accurate likenesses?" Sidony asked.

"Yes. My father had these done right before he died." Adrian swallowed, the ache of longing burning his throat.

"They are quite lovely. You resemble your mother."

Adrian tilted his head to examine the portraits. "That's what my father used to say too."

Guilt ate at him, forcing out the words. "I'm not an honorable man. I gave them up, the life that I had in Sinchon, for this." He flicked his fingers to the side, indicating the room. "And Gracchus hurt them and kept them prisoners."

"You did what you thought was best and fulfilled a promise to your father. You'll get them back." She reached out and ran her thumb over his cheek, her gesture bringing him hope and solace. "We'll find them, Adrian."

CHAPTER FORTY-TWO

*S*idony slept and Adrian stayed awake, pacing their chamber. He waited until the guests and servants had gone to bed, checking the rooms beneath his own with his powers.

He crept down the hallway, his boots silent. Being back at Blackthorne had him remembering all the things he'd done for Gracchus, the secrets he'd discovered for the king. He hadn't had a choice, but he still regretted his actions.

Tonight was new for him. He'd never felt like a thief. He would steal gladly if it meant he could bring his family to safety.

Gracchus's apartments took up an entire floor in a wing all their own. Adrian made it past the main hallway between the royal apartments, most of which were empty, to the king's without seeing anyone. Typically there were royal guards posted at regular stations. Gracchus understood, perhaps better than most kings, he had to be diligent about his safety. There hadn't been any well-orchestrated assassination attempts on him—thanks to Adrian ferreting out the plots before they came to fruition—but the bloody end to the previous Embury monarch and most of his family was warning enough.

Gracchus had taken roughly half of his royal guard to Marenburg. Those left at the palace were distributed around the grounds.

Torwyn's rooms were similarly guarded.

When Adrian reached the door, he swept out his senses and made sure Gracchus's apartments were empty. No one was inside the locked chambers. He stretched his power, unlocking and opening the door from the inside. The hinges creaked loudly.

Damn his black heart.

Adrian remembered too late that he'd needed to oil the hinges. Gracchus preferred being able to detect when his door was opened. Otherwise, there was no excuse for such a sound in a royal residence. He'd have to hurry.

With the drapes closed in the king's absence, the room was completely dark. Adrian used his powers to see around the room. The main pieces of furniture were in their normal locations, and nothing seemed out of place. He located the orb in a locked box inside a cabinet in his uncle's bedchamber. That must have been where Gracchus stored it when he wasn't making regular use of it. After spending years longing for ways to free his family, he'd never dreamed Gracchus would leave the key to their location behind.

He crossed the sitting room and went into the bedchamber. The cabinet stood along the back wall. He opened the doors and pulled out a familiar lacquered box. He tried to open the latch the same way he'd unlocked the door, but his projected finger was too large to fit. He snapped off the lock, slipping the broken pieces into his pocket. He'd wanted to avoid leaving a trail, but he'd be gone before Gracchus returned and discovered the box had been tampered with anyway.

He needed to see his mother and sister. It was quiet, he

could be quick, and, in case he somehow lost the orb, he needed to get a look into it first to have an idea where to find them.

Although he could see the orb with his powers, he was reasonably sure it needed light to work. Reluctantly, he lit a taper from the bedside table and set the box down. He pressed his hands together to still their shaking. He opened the lid and removed a silk bag. The orb rolled out into his palm, as big as an orange, but cloudy gray and heavy. He held it up to the candlelight and tried to remember what he'd seen Gracchus do when he'd used it.

He hadn't seen or heard him do anything other than take it out of the black pouch. The surface had shown a view of his mother and sister immediately.

Did the orb have a lock he couldn't break?

"Show me Minah and T'ae Yoon Mi."

Nothing happened. He pictured them where he'd last seen them, his sister walking the dusty courtyard, his mother vacant-eyed in a rocking chair. The interior of the orb remained opaque.

"Damn."

To come so close. He should have tracked them from the abandoned estate while the king was gone. Had he seized the orb only to have it prove useless?

He used his powers to try to see inside the orb. His vision was quickly repelled, like a poke in the eyes. He rubbed a hand over his face, willing the pain to subside so he could concentrate.

He tried to unlock the orb from the inside, but its surface was impenetrable. None of his powers could pass through it.

It either opened with a key or an incantation. He turned the orb over in his hand and didn't see a lock. Maybe commands were encoded.

Marlowe's words from the letter he'd sent after Adrian's

wedding came back to him: Songbird House, and staying with the king. He hadn't questioned the name of the estate, though the term was poetic, especially given its condition of disrepair. Perhaps Marlowe hadn't merely been giving him directions. He'd given him a key.

"Show me the songbird."

The orb filled with white smoke. Adrian's stomach dropped to his knees. He cradled the globe, angling his hands to keep it in the faint light.

Tendrils of smoke cleared until a vision formed. He saw the room his mother and sister had been in. A pitcher and a large chipped bowl sat on the nightstand between two beds. The room was clean but spartan. It was the room where they'd been kept at Songbird House. Or, how it had looked before he'd destroyed it.

More smoke blew across the scene. When it dissipated, there was another room, this time with round walls, a stone floor, a simple bed, and a trunk. A woman slept on the bed, curled on her side, a hand tucked under her chin. Her hair was streaked with silver, one elegant sweep at her temple. Though she'd aged, he recognized her profile and her hand. Tears ran unchecked down his face at the sight of his mother.

He blinked and strained his eyes, searching for Minah. He clutched the orb tighter, turning it.

"Show me the other songbird."

The view expanded and he saw that the room was at the top of a set of stairs. On the other side, a woman slept on a pallet guarding the oak door.

Minah.

They were both safe and appeared to be unharmed. He didn't know where they were. From the nighttime view, he thought he was seeing them in real time. The problem was the room and the hall were so nondescript they could be anywhere.

"Show me both songbirds."

The view widened again, opening straight down to show his mother and sister.

"Show me more." The view didn't change. He tried again and again, but as long as both could be seen, that's as wide a view as he was given.

Adrian scanned both rooms, searching for a hint as to their location. Finally, he noticed a symbol above the door that belonged to a cloister of holy women. He couldn't see much detail since he was above it, but the shape was simple enough to discern. There were several convents throughout Embury. They bordered the ridge of mountains to the west, the lowlands along the east, and another wasn't far from the capital. Could his mother and Minah be this close? Relief flooded his system. His worry about staying too long in Gracchus's rooms faded in the face of evidence that they were alive and well.

They'd been the king's captives for three years. What he had now was a way to check on them and a narrowed list of places to search. Something about that particular symbol nagged at him. He needed to find a map of the abbeys and get a search party ready to leave by midmorning.

He stood, lost in memories as he tried to cover the evidence that he'd been in the king's apartments. He pictured his sister's face as he'd last seen her when he left Sinchon. She'd clung to him for long moments, weeping against his coat. His mother had hugged him in private the night before. As he'd stood to leave, her chin trembled and her eyes reddened, but her expression was also one of pride. Seeing them through the orb, regret struck him anew. But he pushed it aside, resolved not to spend a moment longer in that emotion now that he knew they were close.

He was tired of the mental games and the constant battle for power and control. He'd abided Gracchus's rules for much of what he could remember of his life. The few moments he remembered spending with his family were, until recently, some of the only happy memories he had.

I will find them.

One of the convents was actually within a day's ride of the castle. Invigorated at seeing them again, and grateful for his abilities, Adrian sent out his powers, hoping his increased speed and distance would allow him to reach well across the countryside. He'd practiced farther distances while they traveled to Embury.

Slam. His senses hit a wall. He'd gone as far as the end of the wing of royal apartments before he'd smashed into a barrier. Quickly, he tried searching for Sidony in their suite. His head snapped around, like he'd been punched in the face. His powers were…fading?

CHAPTER FORTY-THREE

"I knew you wouldn't wait long to get it." Torwyn stood in Gracchus's apartments and leaned back against the door that had noisily announced his entrance. He wore his favorite armor breastplate that he donned for military exercises.

Adrian faced him, slipping the orb into its silk bag. He looped the drawstring over the wrist of his non-sword hand. "Where are they?"

"Who? Your sister? Your mother? Your wife?" Torwyn made a *tsk*ing sound. "Actually, I can't help you with them. Sworn to secrecy." He blinked in mock sympathy.

Tingles of fear made the hairs on the back of Adrian's neck stand up. Sidony being on Torwyn's list was very bad.

"Tell me where they are." Adrian probed with his powers to see if any men waited in the hallway. At least he could use his powers that far. It was still empty.

Torwyn strolled toward him. "I escorted them myself." He stopped and bowed.

Adrian ignored the pulse of adrenaline as Torwyn approached him, keeping his breaths steady.

"My bride. Where is she?" Adrian drew his sword.

Torwyn kept walking, his stride deliberate and slow. His sword rested on his hip.

"Where is she?" Adrian advanced on him, cutting the distance in half. He didn't have time for games. He held back his fear as best he could.

"She's where your liege needs her to be."

No, no, no. A cold sweat broke out over Adrian's body, the hilt of his sword slipping in his hand.

The sacrifice. Torwyn was orchestrating the sacrifice, even without Gracchus. Adrian had not participated in any of his uncle's spiritual practices in years. The last time he had, he'd witnessed: rows of candles, dark robes, a crude altar, and so much blood. He had gone numb, his body wracked with tremors. For days, he'd had nightmares about the ceremony. The physic had offered him laudanum and he'd made himself stop taking it after a week. Gracchus demanded his services but could not make him participate in his full worship and practices.

The tip of his sword hitting the ground shook him out of his memory.

Torwyn had moved closer, but not far enough in range yet.

Adrian raised his sword, running an arm across his eyes to clear them. "Take me to her and I'll spare your life."

Torwyn drew his weapon, shaking his head. "Kill me and you'll never find her."

Adrian held his stance, going on instinct. "Why are you here?"

"Because I'm tired of you getting in the way of all the real work of the kingdom. It's time Gracchus cut you loose."

Adrian repressed a laugh at the absurdity of the statement, but an odd light entered Torwyn's eyes. They circled each other, backing around the sitting room in a slow dance, each sword poised to strike.

"You've come to kill me?" It sounded ludicrous when put into words, but Adrian needed to know who had taken Sidony.

"Gracchus told me he's considered granting the throne to you instead of me."

"And you believed him?" Adrian asked. Gracchus had gone to enormous lengths to legitimize his son. Torwyn, usually in drunken moments, would confess that he feared it would all go away, that ultimately Gracchus would reject him.

"He says it often enough," Torwyn said. "Says I'm a poor excuse for a son."

Torwyn's petulant tone called to mind his customary obsequious manner with the king.

"I suffer no illusions. It serves Gracchus's purpose to have you as his heir."

"Your abilities are what he values. I have served him loyally for my entire life. I've earned my place at his side."

His uncle fostered competition among the men, but Adrian didn't think they vied for his role like Torwyn did. They curried influence with the king.

He flexed his sword arm, momentarily dropping his guard. "You have everything you want."

"I'm his son." Torwyn's voice was raspy. "I was denied that for twenty years."

"He did cross a continent for me." Adrian shrugged.

The words sent Torwyn over the edge as he swung at Adrian.

Adrian blocked and pivoted, stepping out of Torwyn's charge. He had enough power that he could see the distance between himself and Torwyn as if the room were fully lit, but he didn't know how long that would last. Over the past several minutes, he'd felt his powers ebbing. He'd also become so used to using them that he was trying to adjust to what he'd need to do once they disappeared completely.

"Gracchus should have only chosen me. He never needed

you." Torwyn charged again, slashing down with his heavy sword and hitting a chair. The force of the impact snapped the legs like kindling. Adrian retreated to the other side of the room. The taper was now at Torwyn's back, illuminating the field between them.

"He made you legitimate. What more do you want?" Adrian asked. He stayed on the balls of his feet, trying to decide how much he'd be able to learn about Sidony's whereabouts from the unhinging prince.

"I should inherit the kingdom, and not have to share it."

"Where is Sidony?" Adrian couldn't think why he was arguing with Torwyn about this. Talking was getting him nowhere. Adrian charged Torwyn. "Where is she?"

"She's not coming back. And there's nothing your *abilities* can do." Torwyn smirked. "I bound them."

He must have used a spell to contract Adrian's powers. In the minutes they'd been talking, he could barely extend them beyond his own reach. Whatever spell his cousin had used must have accelerated in his presence. Adrian's magic would be useless before he could get to Sidony.

"Cousin, enough." With one last burst of power, he raised his arm across his body and twisted his sword, bringing it down to knock Torwyn across the temple with the pommel.

Torwyn dropped to the floor. Adrian unfastened the captain's breastplate, tied his hands and ankles behind his back, and tossed his cousin over his shoulder.

CHAPTER FORTY-FOUR

*S*idony woke at a sound and stretched, seeking Adrian in their bed. As she felt along the empty sheet, rough hands stuffed a smelly rag in her mouth and gagged her. She screamed and reached up to pull it off, but her hands were yanked behind her. A cord bound them tightly together. Someone threw a sack over her head.

Where was Adrian? Where was her guard?

They pulled her out of bed and carried her. There were two of them. Maybe more? She was jostled and bounced as they carried her, her belly grinding into a bulky shoulder.

Adrian would find her. He would get to her. He could always track her.

After tromping down a long flight of stairs, they hauled her back and sat her on a stool. Then, they pulled off her hood and took out her gag. Her fingers were numb but she flexed them and tried to roll her shoulders to ease the strain. She stood and they pushed her down again, so hard the stool nearly tipped over.

"Who are you? Where have you taken me? Untie me this instant!"

The two men walked down a narrow aisle away from her and seated themselves along the row of benches. They both wore cloaks, their position blocking the way out.

She wanted to squeeze her eyes shut, but she forced herself to look around. Her stool was on a dais. A granite altar was to her left. The ceilings were arched and sooty, with no windows or doors, and no outside sounds. Underground, then. The room was damp and smelled overripe. Sickly sweet. She shivered and tried to breathe through her mouth. Candles blazed along a wall to her left. To her right, the wall was covered with various symbols and numbers in red and black. Her right heel bounced, and she pressed her foot flat, trying not to show it.

Rows of wooden benches faced her. More cloaked figures came down the aisle and filled the seats. Chanting, their vacant eyes stared at her and she fought not to be sick. A single figure stood next to the wall with symbols.

Sidony's thin night rail left her exposed. It had slipped off one shoulder and a gray substance smeared her hem. *Maybe it's ash?*

She attempted her mother's bravado. "There's been a mistake. You need to let me go. I'm your new princess."

They ignored her.

Any minute now, Adrian would come for her.

But as the minutes ticked on, the chanting droned and there was no sign of him.

She counted over a dozen worshippers, the seats nearly filled. Her heel was back to bouncing and she let it.

She wished she'd honed her powers, knew better how to direct them. Here she was, a nocturne in the midst of a group who wanted to create their own nocturnes, and she was essentially powerless.

Two more figures in red cloaks streamed down the aisle toward her and she shrank back. One carried a dagger and the other held a large bowl. Like the others, their faces were painted to resemble skulls. They ascended the short steps and went around to stand behind her.

Desperation streaked across her skin in a shiver. "Release me. You can't do this."

They were still in Embury and she was their princess. Adrian had said the king was the one who had considered her for sacrifice at one time. What they were doing with her now looked like it would be bad…and bloody.

"You have to stop. The king doesn't want this." Her voice broke at the end, but she'd had to try. She couldn't keep the words from spilling out.

Sidony's fear ratcheted, nearing hysteria. Maybe she should stand. That would get their attention better. She made it up on wobbly legs. She took two steps before the chanter with the bowl approached her. He set the bowl down in front of the altar and backhanded her. She fell onto the floor, unable to catch herself since her arms were still bound. Pain pierced her left shoulder and her cheek burned.

The guard along the wall strode over and set her back on the stool. He gave her shoulder a firm nudge, saying in a gruff voice, "Stay where we put you."

She winced at the pain along the right side of her face, tasting blood from where her teeth had cut her cheek.

"Elder Torwyn has been detained it seems, so we will begin without him," Dagger Cloak said from behind her.

Torwyn? Did Adrian know? The muscles in Sidony's legs shook. She pressed her knees together, not wanting to show them she was afraid, but her muscles wouldn't obey her. Her cheek throbbed and swelled. Something had happened to her shoulder when she'd hit the ground. She couldn't move her arm and the searing pain made her dizzy. She tried to adjust her arms, and that sent a bolt of agony through her shoulder and into her upper chest. Chills racked her body.

The guard returned to her side and prodded her shoulder.

She clenched her teeth but couldn't hold back whimpers of pain.

"Young One, what are you doing with her?" Dagger Cloak said. Before Young One could answer, Dagger Cloak spoke to someone she couldn't see. "Up here. We're almost ready for you."

Another red-robed figure joined the group on the dais. She squinted at him. He was huge and carried a giant double-sided axe.

"Something happened to her arm when she fell," Young One said. "Hold her steady, and I can fix it."

Dagger Cloak snorted. "Why would we fix it? She meets with the exalted one soon. She won't need her arm for that."

"For after." There was a long pause, and Sidony struggled to stay conscious. "She cannot look like she was harmed or beaten. At our last meeting, the king said he wanted her beauty preserved."

The hoods all nodded, including those in the audience.

The brute who had struck her yanked on her arm, and Sidony cried out. Her body dampened with sweat.

"We've waited long enough. I'll hold her. Fix it. Dawn is coming." He held her with one hand on her sternum and another along her back, his belly against her ear.

Young One tapped her on her arm once and then jerked hard, snapping her shoulder into a different position. Pain blazed through her socket but quickly dissipated. She could move it again, though it ached.

"Bring her to the stone," Dagger Cloak said.

Young One pulled her up to stand and walked her over to the low stone. He bent her over it, so her head hung off the other side. For a moment, she'd thought he wanted to help her. Having him place her on the altar ruined that theory.

"Ready, Elder Tomas?" Dagger Cloak asked. The one wielding the axe, spit on the ground and grunted.

Sidony knew she was going to die.

CHAPTER FORTY-FIVE

*A*drian debated tying Torwyn up and going after Sidony without him in tow, but he might need his cousin, and there wasn't time to restrain him completely. Adrian gagged Torwyn and lugged him along. With his powers blunted, Adrian took off toward the last place he'd witnessed one of Gracchus's sacrifices.

Along the way, he tried twice more to use his powers, but nothing happened. He got a buzzing sensation, but it fizzled out. Adrian ran across the path that led to the small chapel on the estate and found the cellar entrance in the back. It was closed but thankfully unlocked. Gracchus's worshippers likely hadn't expected any resistance.

He went down the stairs and felt Torwyn startle. He set his cousin on his feet and locked an arm around his neck. Dragging Torwyn at his side, Adrian followed the sound of chanting down a dark hallway and around a corner. The hallway led to both the front and the back of a macabre chapel.

Adrian stopped. Sidony was bent over a stone, crying softly. Self-loathing thudded in his stomach. His love for her had brought her to this. How had he ever thought he could protect her by bringing her to Embury?

Torwyn's head butted his jaw, and he realized regret had loosened his grip on his cousin. He'd been such a fool.

A cloaked man stood behind her with his hand on her back. Another flanked her side. He was massive. Garbed in a red cloak, his hood was off, and he carried a wicked-looking axe. Adrian thought he recognized the man as Tomas, one of the village huntsmen.

The chanting men in the pews got louder.

Adrian had mere moments. His only leverage was the prince.

He pulled out his dagger and held it to Torwyn's throat, gambling that he would be heavily involved with this group and not acting on a personal vendetta against Adrian.

"Stop! I'll kill him." He dragged Torwyn forward with one arm around his chest, and the other hand holding a knife to his throat.

The chanting stopped and heads turned. The only sound was from wax dripping along the row of candles. Sidony lifted her head. One side of her face was puffy and red. Tears wet her cheeks.

"You've brought our Elder Torwyn. Good. He won't want to miss the sacrifice. It was his idea to do it while the king was gone."

The cloaked man behind her seemed familiar, but Adrian couldn't make out his face. Again, he cursed his bound powers.

"Pull her up and untie her hands," Adrian commanded.

The cloaked figures on the dais didn't move.

Adrian drew a thin line across Torwyn's throat, drawing blood.

The same man spoke to him again. "You only please us. Elder Torwyn would be honored by such a sacrifice."

Adrian wasn't so sure. He gripped his knife tighter and

lowered the gag across Torwyn's mouth. "Call them off. Tell them to let her go."

A muscle ticced in Torwyn's cheek. "Never."

The man on the dais spoke again. "Drop your dagger, Prince Adrian. And your sword." A sharp point poked Adrian's side. "Let our future king go."

Adrian didn't know how he would save Sidony, but he had to try. His dagger clanged against the stone floor, followed by the sword at his hip. He released his cousin.

"Let him watch," Torwyn said to the toady who still pointed his sword at Adrian.

The point dropped away, and Torwyn walked backwards down the aisle, a delighted smile on his face. "Not so special now, are you?" Torwyn taunted. "You didn't even know I'd bound your powers. Only I can turn them on and off. You are bound to me, cousin. Who brings true glory to Embury?"

On cue, the worshippers chanted his name. "Elder Torwyn."

"It's time you joined us again to honor your king. I'll give you a choice. You can leave now and try to find your family before the king returns. Or you can stay here and watch your wife die for your sins."

Over his shoulder and down the hallway, he was a step away from escape and going after what he'd wanted for so long. But Torwyn wasn't offering him a real choice.

"You long for them. You don't deserve your title. Go back to where you came from. Embury will thrive without you." Torwyn had reached the altar. He stuck his fingers through Sidony's hair, almost tenderly. "Your bride will be mourned all the more for her beauty. Embury hasn't had a princess in nearly a decade."

Sidony bit her lips to keep her sobs in.

Adrian still had the orb. He'd seen a vision of where his family was being kept. He could find them. But he had to get

Sidony out of here first. With the room full of worshippers, he was outnumbered. He needed his powers.

"Dawn is coming," a red-robed figure said from the dais.

"Let me do the honors." Torwyn held out his hand and a dagger was placed in it.

No, no.

Adrian knew Torwyn held the key. Without any weapons, he couldn't force the other man to reverse the spell. Adrian would be controlled like he always was. He'd gotten the orb, but he'd risked Sidony's life, and she was about to pay the price.

The guard holding Sidony turned and the light caught the side of his face. Wills. He mouthed, "Save her."

Adrian stepped forward, and the orb rolled along his thigh. He reached into the bag and palmed it, crossing his arms behind him to switch hands.

Torwyn's attention was on his audience, reveling in their chants. "Now I will appease my father and spill her blood!"

He'd never get to her in time. Torwyn brought the tip of the knife to her throat. Before it could pierce her skin, Adrian lobbed the orb down the aisle and into the center of the prince's head. Torwyn crashed to the floor, blood pouring down his face. The orb smashed into the stone floor and shattered.

Air left Adrian's lungs and his palms tingled from the surge of returning power.

With Torwyn dead...

His powers came back, stronger than ever.

"Leave him be. Do it now!" the other red-robed man screamed.

The executioner raised his axe. Wills pulled Sidony off the altar, but the executioner slid the axe off his shoulder, preparing to swing it sideways. He brought it around in a slow arc. It stopped inches before it would have hacked into Sidony's torso.

Everyone froze except for Sidony and Wills. Adrian held them all in place with his powers, sweat breaking out over his body.

"Sidony, move away from the axe," Adrian bit out.

Sidony stepped to the side of the altar. She narrowed her eyes, her gaze caught on him with a fresh intensity. She swayed but Wills steadied her before she could hit the floor.

His power strained, Adrian reached with it, snapping the length of cord that bound her hands. She ran to him, and he held out his hand, pulling her into his side. He concentrated on keeping the cloaked men completely still. Something shifted, almost like taking a deep breath, and his senses pulsed outward.

"Is that...working?" Sidony asked. She leaned into him but her body was stiff with strain.

It hit him that she had magnified his powers once again. Save for Wills and a dead Torwyn, he held all of the cloaked men in place simultaneously.

"You've got it just right," Adrian said into her hair.

Sidony pressed her face into his coat. "Adrian, I have to get out of here. I'm going to be sick."

He turned to Wills. "I'll hold them while you tie them up. We'll deliver them to the constable in the morning."

"Yes, Your Highness." Wills bent to secure the guard closest to him, using the worshipper's belt. "What would you like to do with the body?"

Torwyn lay lifeless at the foot of the altar. His uncle would have left Torwyn's body displayed somewhere, a gruesome reminder of his power. Adrian wanted nothing to do with that.

"Let me get her to a safe location, then we'll bury him in an unmarked grave."

He led Sidony out of the room and up the stairs into the clear, outside air. All the while, he froze the men—with Sidony's help—while Wills trussed them up.

CHAPTER FORTY-SIX

*S*idony huddled in Adrian's lap, wrapped in his coat. Pink and orange streaks lit a corner of the sky as dawn broke. His red cloak discarded, Lieutenant Wills approached them as they sat together under a nearby tree.

"Prince Adrian, I can send a rider to alert the constable. He can bring his own wagons."

She couldn't meet the young lieutenant's gaze. Thankfully, he pitched his voice low. Her shaking had diminished as Adrian soothed her, but unexpected sounds started it back up again. Adrian talked her through relaxing her body, focusing her power by concentrating on what she wanted to do with it, instead of tensing her body against any other movement. She pictured her husband holding everyone still down in that pit below the chapel.

She shuddered again. Wills been the one to lift her up off the floor and fix her injured shoulder. He'd come to her defense when one of the priests had tried to strike her again.

Adrian turned his head, his movements controlled. "Send them in our wagons from Blackthorne. I want them off the palace grounds as quickly as possible."

"I have a few soldiers I can trust with that," Wills replied. He took a step then pivoted. "We've taken measures to protect you and the princess, though tonight we failed."

"There were other attempts on my wife's life?" Adrian asked.

"Two. One at Mondelac and one while we traveled."

Sidony flinched, and Adrian tightened his arms around her.

"Are you working for the rebels?" Adrian asked the lieutenant.

"Not precisely. Many in the king's army are more loyal to Embury than to the current king."

"But why help me? Why help my lady?"

Adrian's voice ached with feeling. Had he thought he was alone in the kingdom? That not even Wills would be there for him?

Sidony lifted her head to read the lieutenant's expression. She caught Adrian's hand against her hip and squeezed his fingers.

Dirt streaked Wills's forehead, and dark circles ringed his eyes. He raised his chin. "Because we still have honor, and we do not worship as our king does. Sir, you have earned the loyalty of many, including those who are true to Embury." His tone was solemn.

Adrian swallowed. "Wills, I...thank you. I have to get Sidony to safety, out of Embury. We'll be leaving as soon as possible."

"Wait," Sidony said. "Lieutenant, thank you for what you did down there."

Wills flushed at her praise. "I tried to give the prince time, but—" He shook his head and left them.

"We need to go inside. I have to dress." Sidony huddled closer to Adrian, tiredness seeping into her muscles.

His arms closed around her, holding her gently. He hitched in a breath. "Sidony, I thought I would lose you." His fingers ghosted across her cheek. "And to see what they did to you."

"How bad is it?"

Turning her chin toward him, he scanned her face, his lips in a grim line. "It looks as bad as it could be without being cut. I'm so sorry. I never wanted you to get hurt."

She splayed her hand on his chest, where his heart could beat against her palm. "I know. You thought the threat was over. Torwyn must have told Wills it was time to do the ritual."

Adrian pulled her close and put his nose in her hair. "Yes. He had been spying in their ranks."

"Wills helped me, as much as he could. I think he tried to stall them."

Adrian set her on the ground and stood, holding a hand out to her. "I never should have left your side."

Sidony accepted the hand he offered and stood as well. "Get us out of here."

As they walked across the palace grounds, the sun's rays hit the windows' archways, the gold leaf radiating a reddish glow. Sidony held fast to Adrian's hand, chilled by the sight.

Adrian's gaze followed hers, a harsh line between his brows. "I wanted to have a home to share with you. For a few short hours yesterday, I felt like I did."

"You did, love." Sidony thought of his room, so different from the rest of the cold grandeur of Blackthorne, and where they had finally shared their secrets. She squeezed his hand. "We'll have one again."

ONCE THEY WERE in the carriage and a few miles from the palace, Adrian bent forward, lowered his head, and pressed his temples.

"Darling, what's wrong?" Sidony asked.

He gasped for breath, his heart racing. "I just withdrew my powers from the men who hurt you."

"You've been holding them this entire time?" She gave him an exasperated look. "I wished you'd told me. I let go nearly half an hour ago."

He sat up and leaned back, rubbing a hand across his face. "I'll remember to do that." Finally, more air. "Had to keep you safe. You were extraordinary."

"I'm getting there." Sidony lifted her skirts and moved to sit on his lap. "You must be exhausted." Fatigue from the drain on her powers settled in her limbs and she curled across him.

Adrian closed his eyes. He looped his arms around her, settling her against his chest. "I almost lost you."

"And yet here we are in another carriage," she said softly. She smoothed the hair back from his brow.

His muscles ached. "Torwyn bound my powers. I couldn't sense you."

"So you found me with plebeian skills? No magic this time?" Sidony asked.

He opened his eyes. "Just fear."

"Thank you for saving me." She gave him one of her half smiles.

Adrian cupped her face, careful of her cheek. He couldn't hold it in anymore. "I love you, Sidony." His eyes burned, but he held her gaze. "I wanted to say it earlier. It hit me when I saw you in the chapel. All this time, I thought it was only a matter of time before I'd lose you. It was my fault, for marrying you and pulling you into my world."

Sidony frowned at him. "You should have told me about the sacrifice earlier, and been *specific*."

He nodded.

"You should have taken me with you to get the orb."

Adrian's brows shot up. "Agreed. Torwyn wasn't the only person who tried to kill you to please the king."

Sidony shuddered. "Yes, we know that now." Her hand stole into the back of his hair, twirling and sifting through the strands. "But it's over. We're safe. I believe you. I trust that you'll keep me safe."

"You are my family now, Sidony." Adrian knew he'd relive the moment when he thought he wouldn't be able to get to her. He didn't regret destroying the orb. It had saved her life, and he'd do it again.

"And you're mine." She traced his brows, down his nose, and leaned forward to press a kiss to his lips, sealing her words.

He cleared his throat as emotion swamped his chest. "I saw them. In the orb. They were sleeping." The words came faster. "My mother was on a narrow bed. Minah was on a mat outside her door, but I don't know where."

"Adrian, we'll find them."

"But what if he punishes them, for what I did?"

"You'll get to them first." Her eyes searched his face. "You saw more than that. Look at what you did today. You'll find them."

He released a pent-up breath. "I don't know why you believe that, but I'm glad you do."

"You don't have to do this alone," she said softly, her eyes shining with tears.

He touched a finger to her lips, running it gently along the curve. "When I met you, I wanted to know what it would be like to be with you without all the mess in my life."

"And then?" she asked.

"Though you fascinated me, I was terrified." He looked up at her, still shocked that she was safe. He fingered a loose curl that had fallen over her shoulder. "I still am. But I can't imagine my life without you in it. You make everything brighter." He frowned, feeling it now. "Even the hopeless dark places are better because you're with me."

"I'm here."

CHAPTER FORTY-SEVEN

Mondelac Castle
Kingdom of L'Ortagia
September 1784

"*W*ake me up when you come to bed." Sidony kissed Adrian at the door, lingering in his embrace. When he finally pulled away, they were both slightly out of breath.

"Always. Get some rest. I hope to see you before dawn." He ran a thumb across her cheek, noticing the circles under her eyes. Though she said she slept while he was in the tower room, he doubted she got much rest.

That was part of the reason he pushed himself so much.

"I have a new stack of plays to read. Take your time." Since their return to L'Ortagia and hearing about their ordeal, Isabeau had granted Sidony the permanent title of Grand Patroness of the Arts. It was the queen's way of keeping his wife in the country permanently.

Sidony had taken to her expanded duties with a newfound

sense of determination and joy. She'd also joked that she had a minor role in an upcoming production.

Isabeau had not been amused, but she'd kept her lips closed.

Adrian went up to a quiet room in the west tower in the middle of the night. He sat in a chair from the old library, whose stuffing had been repaired too many times to be kept in the main part of the keep. A map of Embury covered the table beside him. Every convent and abbey was noted: Small coins were placed on those that had already been checked, and bronze figurines marked sites he still needed to investigate.

Adrian had been searching for Minah and his mother for the last four weeks. After using them so extensively the day they escaped, his powers had plummeted the entire duration of their return trip to L'Ortagia. Each day with his wife, they'd gotten stronger. If he focused, his senses could travel vast distances. He was able to arrive at, search each location, and return to the tower room in a single evening. He could go through walls and was able to do it while not being seen. Each "trip" exhausted his abilities completely. So he could only perform a search every three nights. He'd combed through half a dozen sites since he and Sidony had returned to Mondelac.

Despite Sidony's assurances that it was unnecessary, Adrian had insisted on formally requesting asylum from the queen. Isabeau had stared at him in silence for several minutes from her seat in the small throne room. She'd nodded solemnly, hopefully appreciating his acknowledgment of her eminence. Finally, his royal mother-in-law had smiled cannily. He didn't care. He'd beg, grovel at the queen's feet if she wished. "Of course, dear son-in-law. I'm also conferring a dukedom on you and Sidony."

The L'Ortagians were drawing up plans against Embury, considering various options, including supporting the rebels' war. With Adrian on the L'Ortagian side, the queen benefitted politically from the open strife within several corners of the neighboring kingdom.

Adrian and Sidony had petitioned the small council to consider opening the doors to nocturnes living openly and using their magic in L'Ortagia. Instead of stifling their request, the queen agreed to hear it, but only after the immediate plans against Embury were settled. It was something, at least.

Adrian hadn't renounced his ties to Embury, nor his status as an heir to the throne. Gracchus had returned to Blackthorne eventually. He'd sent two communiqués to Adrian at Mondelac, one imploring, the other threatening him to return. Adrian had drafted half a dozen replies, but they sat in a pile on his desk.

What could he say to his uncle? His grief over Torwyn's death wasn't for Gracchus to hear—he'd likely try to twist that into something Adrian owed him. He didn't regret Torwyn's death—it had been his life or Sidony's—but Adrian still mourned his cousin over the last couple of weeks.

His grief would have to wait though. Each day was another opportunity for Gracchus to move his family further out of reach. With the orb destroyed and the kingdom in chaos, Adrian's time to find his family was limited. He doubted his uncle had the forces necessary to move his mother and sister. But he would again, and he would try to strike at Adrian through them.

Tonight Adrian traveled to Thistle Abbey, located in the southwestern edge of Embury. It was a unique place and currently housed not a religious order, but a secular one. The abbey was secluded and old, having been one of the original convents, built hundreds of years prior. Four of the last six convents had met similar criteria of being religious houses for women, though none housed his family.

An hour passed with his body tiring as his senses stretched across the grounds, down corridors, and into dormitories filled with sleeping women. He felt like a specter, some creature of nightmares. He'd tried to search during daytime hours, but there had been so many people and voices and smells that it had exhausted him for days. Also, people tended to stay put when they slept, making identifying the entirety of a convent much easier.

He searched another row of beds, finding a young woman with soft black hair woven into braids. He stepped closer, examining her profile.

"Minah."

She rolled onto her back and opened her eyes. It was her.

Adrian scanned other faces, not spotting his mother in the dormitory. Then he remembered the tower room, so similar to the one his body occupied now. He raced toward the one he'd skipped over, up the stairs and through the door, straining his nocturne powers to reach her. The sleeping woman had winged streaks of white through her hair.

"Mother."

Adrian's body sagged against the chair. At last, he'd found them.

~

"DARLING, HOW DID IT GO?" Sidony pulled Adrian close to her, trying to warm his chilled limbs with her own.

He clutched her to his chest, the staccato of his heart thudding in her ear. It must be good news.

"They're at Thistle Abbey, sleeping peacefully."

Her head came up, and she grabbed his shoulders, leaning down to kiss him. "Adrian, that's wonderful! How far away is it? Did you need another boost to see them?"

"No. I had plenty." His mouth quirked, and she could practically hear his thoughts spinning as he worked out a way to rescue his family. "It's along the southwest corner of the king-dom. A week's ride past Blackthorne."

"Any sign of Gracchus's men?"

"Not that I could tell. They looked to be unharmed."

"We'll get them free. They'll be safe here. You know that."

Adrian rubbed at his forehead. "It's almost unreal." He ran a thumb over her arm. "And to know that I can bring them here. Thank you for that."

"Of course. They're family." She squeezed him close. "I love you, Adrian. We do this together."

He kissed her temple and pulled her along his length. "We do, love."

Sidony lay in Adrian's arms, sighing as his body relaxed against her. These last few weeks had been blissful except for his search. Now that he'd found his mother and sister and could trust they'd soon be safe in L'Ortagia, her eyes slid shut in relief. Hopefully, her sister would someday find a similar contentment.

Sidony knew that in the days and weeks and years to come, she and Adrian would be happy together. That what had started as a playful kiss in the moonlight had become so much more. And while their world would be changing around them, they would have each other.

THE END

ACKNOWLEDGMENTS

Writing a romance novel has been a dream of mine since high school. It was a dream I put away, for many reasons, but never quite let go of. I would not be putting this story out into the world without a lot of help. I am so grateful for the encouragement, critiques, advice, feedback, and hugs I've gotten along the way.

Thank you to Evelyn Berry, my first critique buddy and now friend and RWA roomie. You are always there for me and I am so grateful. Thanks to the Yahoo Romance Critique Group and the Paranormal CPMatch writers group: Chelle, Patche, Colleen, and Sasha. Huge thanks to the Mermaids, the Golden Heart class of '16, for your wonderful friendship and support; for always being there and letting me ask anything. Thank you to my lovely and generous CP Rosalie Redd, and the NaNoWriMo community and friends. *Kissed at Midnight* was my first NaNoWriMo victory in 2013 (under a different title).

Thank you to my editors Miranda and Christa, my proofreader Liz, my sensitivity reader Yvonne, and my cover designer Kim. You've been amazing to work with. Thank you to the 2015 contest judges from the Wisconsin Romance Writers FabFive, the TARA, the Molly, the Emerald City Opener, and the 2016 Golden Heart®. Big hugs to romance twitter for taking me seriously when I tweet that I'm writing or editing or reached some milestone, and RWChat for connecting me with other writers and making the solitary process of writing both bearable and fun. Plus, gifs. Thanks to HBIC Nation for being awesome and empowering.

Thank you to RWA and the FF&P, CRWA, and TGN chapters, as well as my local chapter RAH who replied with a collective "Oh, wow," when I talked about publishing this year and explained what my book was about. To my adopted chapter, Austin RWA: I adore y'all and think you are incredible. Thank you for including me over and over again like it was no big deal. (It totally was!)

Thank you to my beta readers Amber Belldene, Nicole Hohmann, Donna Knoell, and Lainey Marshall. Your ideas and suggestions were so helpful and made the story stronger. I appreciate you and your support.

Thank you to my dear friends Saira John, Sharon Kolbet, and Dave Whitt. When I told you I wanted to write romance novels you all told me to go for it. Your unrestrained belief in me means so much and gave me the confidence to start writing. To my sweet friends Asli and Siri: thanks for being so supportive and excited for my writing and publishing.

A huge thank you to Olivia Dade for encouraging me when I didn't know if I could keep going with this story. I am so blessed to have you as a friend. Your advice keeps me grounded. You have been an anchor in a storm.

Thank you, Ryan, as my first reader and all around wonderful, amazing husband. And, lastly, thanks to my kids for being enthusiastic and patient. Yes, you can now say that mommy's an author. Yes, these are all going to be kissing books. I love you forever.

ABOUT THE AUTHOR

Ainsley Wynter's writing is inspired by a love of fairy tales, social justice, and superheroes. She's been reading romance since junior high and credits the genre with getting her through tough times.

Ainsley is the author of the fantasy romance series *The Lost Royals*. Her debut novel, *Kissed at Midnight* is the first book in the series. She was a 2016 finalist in paranormal romance in the Romance Writers of America's Golden Heart® contest, as well as a 2017 finalist in the unpublished Single Title contemporary romance category of the Maggie Awards.

Ainsley lives in the Midwest with her wonderful husband, three rambunctious, sweet kids, and three (mostly) cuddly cats. When she's not reading, writing, or procrasti-tweeting, she enjoys dancing, baking, Real Housewives, and the occasional excel spreadsheet.

Sign up for Ainsley's newsletter at AinsleyWynter.com to be the first to hear about her new releases and tips for self-care.

Thank you so much for reading this book. If you enjoyed it, please consider leaving a review.

COPYRIGHT

Published in the United States of America.
Ebook ISBN: 978-1-7335898-0-2
Paperback ISBN: 978-0-578-44180-1

Cover design by Atlantis Book Design
Editing by Miranda Dubner
Copy editing by Christa of EditorChrista
Proofreading by Liz Lincoln

Ainsley Wynter Press
PO Box 22041
Lincoln, NE 68542
www.AinsleyWynter.com

❀ Created with Vellum